The Bo

Also by Katharina Marcus

Eleanor McGraw, a pony named Mouse and a boy called Fire

Boys Don't Ride

Katharina Marcus

The Boy
with the
Amber Eyes

For

Fire & Ash
(all of you, you know who you are)

and my sister Barbara without whom my books would remain naked

They appeared from nowhere
On a bridge in thick fog.
I don't think they saw me.
They usually don't.
Unless I'm on fire.

I was on my way home.
If you want to call it that.
Resting my feet.
It's a long walk,
From the beach.

I was trying to spot the traffic below,
Beacons in grey mist.
Watching the sun not rise
On this veiled autumn day.

I heard them before I saw them,
The clip clop of hooves,
Then two shapes emerging
As if stepping through time.

A young man, around my height,
Tawny skin and black hair.
A broken nose, scars on his face.
So much like me,
Yet so totally different.

He walked proudly
By the side of his cowhide companion
And the cowhide companion
Walked proudly
By the side of him

As they passed me by
I caught the scent
Of the air around them.
I drew my coat closer
And wished for a horse.

Chapter 1

It was hot under the duvet.

Despite the October winds battering the four corners of the Watchtower and pushing the cold of autumn through the thick walls into the room, Pike could feel sweat building up on the inside of his thighs. Slowly but surely his whole body was beginning to feel covered in that thin film of clamminess that always came with the battle of insomnia versus exhaustion.

He turned the duvet over to clamp his legs around the cool side for a moment of relief before returning to the book that lay open under the faint spotlight of the bedside lamp. He had to go back four pages to pick up where his attention had waned.

Immediately the words started performing their elusive dance on the page again.

It felt a bit unfair. It wasn't a bad novel and if she had been lying next to him, or even a mile up the road in her own bed, he would have been contentedly engrossed in the writing until his eyes had faltered, probably some hours ago. But as it was, it was 3am and she was too far away to keep the nightmares at bay.

Eight seasons had come and gone since he'd first laid eyes on the fey little girl who was to relentlessly pierce through his despair and bore herself into his heart. Secure in the comfort of her existence he had made progress since, had been weaned off the pills and officially come to an end of therapy, but the darkness of sleep still held terrors he could only face with her in proximity.

It didn't even have to be close proximity.

The same country was normally good enough.

Barcelona, however, was a few hundred miles too far and he missed her. Like crazy. He wondered whether she knew how much his peace still depended on her. How much her nearness still influenced his capacity to sleep, even after all this time.

As if on cue his phone buzzed on the bedside table. He checked the message, a wide smile pulling at the corners of his mouth.

Go to sleep. You're keeping me up.

He felt that familiar rush of being doused in happiness, belonging and arousal all at the same time. So much for wondering whether she knew. Of course she did. She was Eleanor.

Can't.

Try harder. I've got to be back on the road tomorrow.

And I've got to turn out ponies. On my own. The help's run off with a rock star.

The help?!? Landlady, last time I checked. I heard she had pipe cleaners for arms anyway. Fat load of good she was.

Well, I miss my pipe cleaners.

I miss you too.

You still mad at me?

I'm not going to answer that on grounds that I might incriminate myself. Check your mail. And go to sleep.

He got up and made his way across to his desk, carefully navigating the stacks of books that kept the rest of the clutter at bay like custom built paper fortresses, then switched the computer on and waited.

The machine was ancient, beyond obsolete, and took months to boot. He knew it was high time to replace it, but it had been one of the few tangible gifts from his grandmother. She had passed it on to him a decade ago, after a short bout of interest in modern communication had ended in one of her rare temperamental outbursts. As brilliantly patient as Kimimela Hawthorne-Pike had been with horses and people as short fused she had been with anything that had a fuse.

He could see her clearly now, on the day she'd marched into his room. She had huffed that she was too old for these toys and that he could keep the machine, and the modern world with it, before dumping it on his desk.

Little had either of them known that it would be a parting gift, that the modern world would lose the finest British-born trick rider of the 20th century only a year or so later to cancer.

He'd been eight years old.

He still missed her.

Not with the pining pain with which he longed for Eleanor right now or with the near unbearable sharpness with which he had missed his mare Inara after the accident that had killed her and plunged him into the depths of despair, but as a constant dull ache in the background that came with its very own volume dial. Some days it was turned to zero but on occasion it could still reach maximum, with daily servings of any possible nuance in between.

Grief was a funny beast.

He wondered how it was for Aaron, his grandfather, asleep down below on the ground floor in what had once been the drawing room, two strokes from a broken heart later but too well recovered to withdraw from the living entirely. Pike knew the old man still mourned his dead wife, remaining untouchable by

Sarah, his vivacious but chronically broke friend, who had taken up residence on the first floor some time ago. Did Aaron have days when the volume dial was turned to near zero? Moments when maybe he did look at Sarah with the same eyes with which she so clearly looked at him? Occasionally there seemed to be a glimmer of hope for the old man, of the potential for a life continued rather than merely lived out. And if anyone deserved it, Aaron did.

Pike sighed deeply and stepped over a heap of clothing to look out of the window into the pitch black of a starless night.

The world outside was wild but dry. He could hear gusts of wind whistling around the Watchtower, the unique quirk added to the impressive cottage that formed part of the Hawthorne grounds by a capricious architect who had thought a twee turret sticking out from one corner of the otherwise imposingly serious structure would somehow befit it.

He thought of Eleanor again.

Of watching her from up here so many moons ago, a lithe, skinny little sprite dancing semi-naked in the sun around a solitary pony in the paddock, full of carefree joy. A heat wave of passion and desire washed over him and he shuddered blissfully in the cold that was seeping through the rattling window panes.

With Eleanor by his side, Inara's permanent absence, just like his grandma's, had gradually stopped hurting quite so much until only a quietly ambient humming pain had been left. The girl had managed to drag him out of the grey cloud he had walked in since the day he'd lost his mare to find that there was life after death. To find that he could be soothed and healed by the presence of Inara's colt in those very paddocks down there. And also, if he was honest, by riding the beautiful Spanish mare that had moved in alongside Sarah.

A pang of shame for his disloyalty towards Inara stabbed

through his gut but he pushed it aside, leaning forward until his forehead touched the glass.

He knew he was skirting the real issue, was running rings around his own thoughts with more thoughts, but he also knew that a night like this would not let him out of its clutches until he had gone once more where he did not want to tread.

You couldn't keep death away by musing about grief.

With a deep sigh he pushed his face fully up against the window, until his eyeballs almost made contact with the cool surface, and let the night take its toll.

He fell through the darkness in slow motion, allowing time and space for vertigo as his soul was sucked out of his body in the other direction. As the ground came nearer it simultaneously moved further away and he could feel his throat tighten while the black waters of eternity filled his lungs. The desire to gasp for air, to return to physicality, was strong at first but soon gave way to floating resignation.

Peace they call it, what a farce, was his last clear thought before the entity Paytah Hawthorne also known as Peter Pike, Pike, or simply P to his family, dissolved into infinity.

Then there was nothing.

And the knowledge that there was never going to be anything again.

No life. No love. No. Ever. After. Just. No. Thing. No. Body. No. Me. No. Point.

No her, something screamed.

Something. Anything. A noise. Jolts in his chest.

The short whistling tune of a computer's operating system coming to life, somewhere far away.

The rush back.

Doubling over with nausea, vomit stuck halfway up his throat, just below the Adam's apple. Lungs cramped with air all of a sudden.

Then, the desperation.

He could face death.

Death was easy.

What he couldn't face was the loneliness of the never-after.

Still hunched over and disorientated he staggered back to the desk, sat down on top of the clothes that covered the swivel chair's seat and stared at the screen saver.

Slowly his eyes came back into focus.

The picture was new, a photo his aunt Karen had sent only a few days ago.

She was beaming at the camera while cradling a newborn foal in her arms, still slimy and wet with amniotic fluid, another offspring for the new breed she was trying to create with the Scotsman who had lured her away from the South and had mended her splintered soul. Karen's short, silver streaked black hair was standing in all directions, spiked with bits of straw, and her steel grey eyes sparkled on the screen with all the elatedness of a new mother.

He missed her, too. But in an entirely different way.

It didn't hurt.

He missed her counsel and her competence around the horses. Her steadiness, her laugh and her hugs. But there was no pain in there, just a little melancholic wistfulness. After all, she was still alive and somehow it was *right* for her to be where she was and not to be following in Kimi's footsteps any longer. Somehow Karen had managed to carve out another life far away from Hawthorne Cottage and far away from local entrepreneur, amateur equestrian, cheat and altogether arsehole-of-the-highest-order Robert Greaves. Pike felt himself tense with the thought of Greaves and tried to concentrate again on his aunt's face in the picture.

He traced her eyebrows on the screen, along the high cheekbones in the broad, kind face so much like his own yet coloured so differently, so *pale,* down to the outline of her lips.

She looked happy.

It was all that mattered.

He took some strength from that and sat upright.

Time to check his mail.

Chapter 2

He still carried Eleanor's voice under his skin when he woke up early the next morning. The notes followed him as he descended the windy, book lined staircase down to the first floor.

The song she had sent him had been a beautiful piece, full of love and longing.

She had called it *The Boy with the Amber Eyes* and thinking about it fanned the fire in his belly and made him feel humble at the same time. It was an odd, almost shameful, combination and he didn't quite know whether he liked it. So instead he opted for safe emotional ground, wondering for the millionth time since he had first heard her sing how she could withhold this gift of hers from the world without a shred of regret.

Eleanor McGraw, sprite spawn of legendary rock guitarist Jerry McGraw and folk musician Isabel Payne, had quite possibly the most uniquely haunting voice of her generation but steadfastly refused to have it released for public consumption. If there was one thing she was adamant about then it was her refusal to enter the fame game. End of.

Opening the heavy door to the house proper, he told himself to take a long, hard look in the mirror. He wasn't exactly one to talk. He, too, had talents that he wasn't using. He knew that. Once upon a time he had been a hot favourite on the junior dressage circuit, a darling of the crowds with serious Olympic prospects. He snorted derisively at the thought as he crossed the landing. Never again.

The door to Sarah's room stood wide open, meaning she would be in the kitchen to keep Aaron company over the first brew of the day. Catching a whiff of comfrey ointment as he passed, Pike immediately found himself worrying about the progress the healing of her bones was making or, rather, still wasn't making. It had been over two years since his grandparents' old friend had appeared at Hawthorne Barn, the yard side of the grounds, with a broken wrist. The highly strung Andalusian mare she had fallen off from in tow, she had come to ask for help and stayed. It should have been plenty of time to heal even for a seventy-something impatient patient but the wrist carried on troubling her. It bothered Pike, and not for the first time he wondered if he could have done something different in the initial tending to the bones that would have helped the joint in the long run. He sighed deeply, sucked his upper lip through the chip between his top incisors and began chewing on it rhythmically as he made his way down the next set of stairs.

He had instinctively known that the break had been a complicated one when he had first inspected it, had just *felt* the cracks inside upon touching the arm despite there being nothing dramatic to see. Another one of his gifts and one he had never talked about to anyone other than Eleanor. Not that it was much use since it evidently didn't come with the ability to heal. But if his father was ever to pick up even the vaguest inkling of a morsel of interest in said ability he was guaranteed to lay into Pike even more relentlessly than he had in the past. A nice, prestigious degree in medicine to honour the Hawthorne family tradition of a medical professional in every generation would be just what the doctor would order.

'*Preferably obtained somewhere that looks like a cathedral and where they don't pronounce the first 'i' in medicine,*' he heard Eleanor chuckle in his head, her eyes crossed for emphasis.

Which, in the event, would still be infinitely preferable to studying in London and sharing the impersonal flat that John and Alice, the parents he had never lived with long enough to qualify as Mum and Dad, occupied between trips around the globe. He shuddered at the image of their sterile place as his right foot hit the stone tiles that covered the ground floor of the house which had been his home for as long as he could remember.

The hallway lay in darkness bar the light cutting in from the open kitchen door. He heard Aaron and Sarah laugh and stopped for a moment, releasing his lip from the grip of his teeth. The joy emanating from the room that was the heart of the cottage made him smile.

It had never occurred to him that the old man had stopped laughing with the death of his wife until this lady had moved into their lives and brought back out the man his grandfather had used to be. Pike had forgotten how readily Aaron had once whiled away time with banter, how quick to laugh he had been, and how funny. Gradually, since Sarah had arrived, he had turned back into that person. Into the man who threw his small grandson up into the air to catch him in his strong blacksmith's arms and played rough and tumble with the young boy in a way the ever so serious man and prominent research doctor who stood in the generation between them would have never even considered.

Pike walked silently towards the light and hovered in the doorframe for a moment, taking in the scene.

Aaron was standing by the Aga, facing the room and warming his hands behind his back. He'd already been out to tend to the chickens and there was a basket of freshly collected eggs on the table. Sarah was sitting opposite him on the long side of the L-shaped bench that snaked around the big oak table, holding an egg precariously in her bad hand while writing the date on it with the other before transferring it into one of a number of rapidly filling egg boxes. She picked up another egg and smiled at Pike.

"Morning."

"Morning."

"Cuppa?" Aaron asked.

"Please."

While Aaron turned to pour tea from the ancient pot, Pike shuffled up the bench to sit next to Sarah and watch her elegant hands go about their task. The chickens had been her idea and he could see in her smile that she was pleased they were still laying as well as they had all summer. He looked at the stack of already filled cartons. The only problem the hens caused was that there was a finite number of omelettes, soufflés and quiches one could feasibly eat in a week.

"You could take some over to Eleanor's folks, if you like," Sarah said, having read his thoughts. "Take some bantams for Oscar as well. He likes the ickle eggs and they'll stop laying soon. They'll be happy to see you over there. I should think that they miss her, too."

Pike picked up the cup of tea that had appeared in front of him on the table and blew on it before taking a sip. The brew had been on the hob a while, giving it a tangy bitterness even the most generous splash of milk could not take the edge off.

"I was going to walk Inigo," he replied.

"You can do both." Sarah sighed, stopped and took a deep breath before putting the current egg down and fixing him with her midnight blue eyes, a stern expression creeping into them. "It's none of my business, I know, and I wouldn't dream of telling Kimi's grandson of all people what to do with a youngster but you can't just keep walking him and teaching him tricks. He leads perfectly well on the road. He already lunges better than a professional vaulting horse, although personally I do not understand why you won't put side reins on. He long reins like a champion trotter. And if the circus came to town tomorrow they'd welcome you with open arms, no questions asked. What on earth are you waiting for? You've done all you can on the ground. You should back him, Paytah. Now. It's high time. Before the winter comes. If you leave it until spring he'll be full of beans. Now is the perfect time. Don't make it harder on yourself than necessary."

"He's not ready," Pike replied quietly, avoiding eye contact by staring into his mug.

Aaron stepped forward and sat down on the short end of the bench.

"Yes, he is," the old man said softly. "You're not."

Pike could feel anger flare up inside him and hit the back of his eyeballs.

He shot his grandfather a look and without further comment scrambled to his feet, grabbed a couple of egg boxes and left the kitchen.

Both Inigo and Blue whickered gentle greetings through the darkness when he entered the barn. Once the strip lights had spasmed into life, Pike could see the welcoming looks on the horses' faces as they hung their heads over the half doors of their stables. Inigo's, eager to be let out, and Blue's, still curious as to what the day may bring but less intense, less *young*. Casta was nowhere to be seen and Pike guessed that she was still curled up on her soft bed of shavings to ward off the cold that permeated the crisp air. The Spanish mare had never quite acclimatised to the British cold and was the only one of the occupants to wear a night rug.

In the days when all twelve boxes that lined the stable block aisle had always been fully occupied it had never been cold in here, even in the depths of winter. But with only three equine bodies to generate heat it always remained chilly throughout the night now. Eleanor, having saved his life in more than one respect by paying off a bad debt against the yard and thereby becoming the official owner of Hawthorne Barn, had so far put her foot down on any attempts by their respective elders to talk her into taking in liveries. Her stance was that at barely sixteen years of age she did not want the responsibility of being a *real* landlady, no matter how much help was being offered. While the cottage still belonged to Pike's family, this land was Pike's and hers, *their* home, and she didn't want others crashing in on it if she could help it.

Secretly, Pike was relieved.

Until Karen had left he had lived with liveries all his life and mostly they were more of a pain than a gain. Horse people in general all had a screw loose and you could never tell when taking someone in whether their loose screw and your loose screw made a matching pair. And he was neither a Kimi nor a Karen. Of the 'good with horses and people' only the 'good with horses' part had been genetically handed down to him.

He put the egg boxes down on an upturned crate by the wall, rubbed his hands together and blew on them, watching his breath cloud up in a ball. Then he walked past the tri-coloured stallion and Eleanor's little blue roan mare, touching their soft noses gently as he passed, to check on Casta.

The Andalusian was indeed down, her legs tucked under her body, bottom lip hanging as she dozed. She was generally of a nervy disposition and it was rare to see her as relaxed as this, so Pike stood quietly by the box for a few moments, appreciating her peace. With a floppy bottom lip and in her tartan pyjamas, even the most stunning and white of white greys looked quite ordinary and a little silly, which made his heart melt. Looking at her, the last of the sudden flare of anger he had felt in the kitchen dissipated completely.

After a moment, Casta's ears began twitching and he could see the eye that was facing him slowly lose the faraway gaze. Coming out of her dream, the mare retracted the loose lip and for a second she appeared to be smiling before, almost as if consciously remembering her job as resident breathtaking beauty, she took on the serious, grandiose demeanour that characterised her breed and elegantly rose to her feet. She shook herself out gingerly then picked her way over to Pike as if on tiptoes.

He knew that she had liked him from the moment he had first edged himself carefully into her saddle. A proud yet not a brave horse by nature, with him on her back her pride would suddenly take on purpose, all her fears instantly burned away in the fire of his soul and he knew that when they danced together she sometimes felt immortal. Humans in their eternal arrogance usually assumed that they were the only proprietors of self awareness, that only their precious species felt the heavy burden of mortality rest upon its shoulders.

Pike knew different.

He had always suspected as much but after hearing Inara's shrill whinnies as she had struggled against the water taking her, trapped in a trailer sinking in the estuary, any last doubts he may have had had perished along with his horse. Remembering her cries, he could almost feel the water crash in on his lungs again, as it had when he had tried to rescue her. But before the pumping lump of muscle in his chest could remember the electric shocks that had brought his body back to life, he was dragged back into the present by Casta snorting loudly with irritation. He shook off the memory violently.

Once in twenty-four hours was enough.

He realised that he had withdrawn from the box. The mare on the other hand had edged closer to the door, stretching her neck over and pushing her nose out towards him.

'Come back.'

Pike stepped up to her again and she blew gently into his face. He blew back into her nostrils, which elicited a contented, throaty nicker from her. If it had been Blue or Inara, he would have scratched her behind an ear now but she didn't like having her poll touched. There was an ancient, hairless scar there and to this day whatever had happened to her to etch it there made putting a head collar or a bridle on a feat that had to be accomplished slowly, deliberately, and in a particular fashion, involving the ears and neck as little as possible. As Pike took the head collar from a hook by the door and opened the stable, he began murmuring words of reassurance in a low voice. Standing next to the mare he unbuckled the neck strap before holding the nose band under Casta's muzzle.

Then he waited.

She knew what he wanted and after a moment's hesitation lowered her head into the ring. Pike slithered his right arm through the air under her throat and gently placed the neck strap a hand's width behind her poll. He held both strap and buckle end lightly in his left hand to hold the collar up, retracted the other hand and with sure fingers did up the buckle. When he was finished they both stood for a moment and sighed with relief.

It made him smile. It was almost as if the mare herself held her breath whenever the trickier bits of handling her occurred. As if she herself was watching her own reaction, hoping she'd be alright.

Sarah had told him that Casta had not been in the best of shapes when the horse had arrived years ago at the Spanish riding holiday complex where Sarah had been working at the time. The mare had been thrown in free with a bunch of new horses and after it had transpired that she was always going to be entirely unsuitable material for a trekking centre, the owner had turned her out as a broodmare. Half a dozen years later she had still not produced a foal and had been signed off for slaughter. At that point Sarah had stepped in and, at the tender age of sixty-six, had turned a barely broken, skittish, head shy and suspicious horse around to produce a fine if eternally highly strung schoolmistress.

Leading Casta over to the grooming area, Pike reflected on Sarah some more and felt his conscience nag at him. He knew that the woman was fiercely proud of her achievement but also that, somewhere along the line, with the fall that had wrecked her wrist she had lost her nerve. Her loss had been his gain and he had been riding her mare ever since, finding more joy in it than he would admit even to himself sometimes as he slowly fell for the Spanish Lady. Not in that burning hook, line and sinker way with which Inara had owned him but in a gentle, sad way. He knew he was taking someone else's ride, stealing the affections of a horse that weren't his to steal. On the other hand, he was at a loss as to how to help Sarah.

He had seen it before.

When Karen had still managed the barn she had run a lucrative sideline in taking on seasoned riders who had suddenly realised they didn't bounce so well any longer. Amidst his aunt's perpetual struggle to make ends meet with liveries and foster children, while eternally haemorrhaging money by throwing it at the show circuit, these project humans had paid for the hay bill during many winters. Pike had watched her build them back up slowly until they had inevitably rediscovered their own competence and had ridden off into the sunset.

He sighed deeply.

Good with horses *and* people.

He knew he couldn't emulate it no matter how hard he wished he could help Sarah. And even if he could have, she was in a different league from those people at any rate. None of them had once been professional riders or trained actresses or his grandmother's partner in Wild West shows. They had been regular Joes. Sarah was no regular Josephine, which made the state of affairs ever so much sadder.

Lost in these thoughts he had long tied Casta up, taken off her night rug, given her a quick brush, picked out her hooves and was currently in the process of putting a turnout out rug on her, hurried along by Inigo's impatient scratches by the stable door.

The young stallion was getting restless and asking for his turn. Pike called a reassurance in his direction, which was answered by a low nicker, then let his eyes wander over to Blue. She was still resting her head over her stable door, ears half turned back, eyes mostly shut. Dreaming, waiting.

The little mare had grown her native's thick winter coat already, turning her serious summer face into a grey-blue fuzzy felt shape. The softness made her seem contented but Pike could tell she was pining, too.

It had taken twenty-five years on the planet for the famous Blueberry Mouse to find her human amongst all her riders and though she was too old and seasoned to let on, Pike knew the pony wanted Eleanor to come back as much as he did. Pain jabbed his core and before the longing got unbearable again, he turned his attention back to Casta.

She was waiting patiently for him to finish the job and do up the rug's belly straps. Before he did, he let his hand run lightly along her underside until he found her navel. She let out a long happy snort as he began circling his fingers against her belly. A second later her whole body visibly melted into the sensation.

Just then the barn door opened and Sarah entered. She stood rooted to the spot for a moment and Pike could feel her hurt more than he could see it in the expression on her face. He left off Casta's massage and busied himself with fastening the straps, ducking down next to her, so the horse was between him and the woman. The Andalusian bent her long neck around and started nuzzling his hair disappointedly.

"What can I do for you?"

He hadn't intended for it to sound unfriendly but it did.

He fastened one strap while he watched Sarah's legs come closer. They stopped on the other side of the mare. Pike kept fishing for the second strap until Sarah crouched down stiffly, handing it to him across the belly.

"I've come to ask whether you could pick up a Friday Ad on the way. Might find myself a horse."

Pike took the strap, hooked it in and stood up slowly.

It wasn't an unusual request. Sarah religiously window shopped for horses in the free paper every week by way of entertainment but there had been an edge to her voice just now.

"You have a horse."

Sarah's face met him across the mare's back. There was a faint sarcastic smile around her lips when it appeared in view.

"Have I?"

Pike swallowed, composing himself.

"You reckon you could turn her out? I still have those two to do."

He pointed vaguely in the direction of the other two stable occupants, both of whom were now following the action in the aisle with interest.

Sarah's smile broadened and she winked at him before she unravelled the lead rope from the ring it was tied to.

"Don't worry, just teasing. Wouldn't be the first time a Hawthorne takes my ride, you know…"

Her voice trailed off with a husky undertone. She turned her attention back from untying the knot to Pike and laughed at the shock in his face.

"Not like that. Youth! You have a filthy mind, young man. No, your grandfather has only ever loved one woman. I may have introduced them but, for the record, I hardly knew him beforehand myself. No, I was talking about a horse. Of course. We had this beautiful Arab stallion in the show. Wild Spirit they called him. And he was, I tell you. Most stunning horse I have ever laid eyes on. He was supposed to be my ride but I had trouble with him, I admit. I went off one afternoon and when I came back Kimi had got him all sorted. Following her like a dog, lying down on request, the whole number. Did you know that the Sioux of all people don't actually have a word for horse? They call them Big Dog. Interesting, isn't it? Ever thought about what that means for those great Indian Chiefs that have Horse in their name? Changes the perspective, doesn't it?"

Pike could feel his hackles go up for the second time that morning. He was tired, his eyes were burning and the last thing he was interested in was having a debate about Siouan semantics. But as ever he couldn't help but rise to the bait.

"It's stupid, is what it is. One's predator, the other's prey. The Sioux are obviously idiots if they can't tell the difference between one and the other."

Sarah deflected the venom with grace and a warm smile.

"Hm," she added wryly as she began leading Casta away, "You know, you might want to consider cutting your hair short again." She glanced back at him over her shoulder. "You are starting to look an awful lot like something you despise."

Chapter 3

As soon as he picked up the lead rope to walk Inigo out of the yard, Pike felt at ease with the world and himself in it.

It was as simple as that.

There were no issues here, no rummaging for trust, no uneasy questions about loyalty, just amicable companionship. The rope was slack between them, the only moment of hesitation on the stallion's part occurring when they passed the mares, *his* mares, which he was being asked to leave behind.

"We're coming back." Pike's voice was barely above a whisper but Inigo had heard him nonetheless and briefly rubbed his cheek against the young man's shoulder before willingly continuing to cross the paddocks.

Hawthorne bred, Pike thought, not without pride, *there is a reason it used to mean something.*

The weight of that meaning, he knew, lay only fractionally in the blood.

'Hawthorne horses are mongrels like us,' Kimi had always used to laugh. 'One part mustang, three parts native, two parts Arab, one part whatever else is running around the yard at the time and a pinch of donkey for good luck.'

The secret lay in the handling.

Hawthorne horses had the reputation of being trusting and trustworthy, being able to turn their hoof to anything and of giving their all for an owner who treated them right. Mostly because more often than not their owner had remained a Hawthorne from cradle to grave. Neither his Lakota great-great-grandmother, who'd come to Britain as a performer with Buffalo Bill and had started with one lame mare stolen from the show, nor Kimi nor Karen had ever been good at selling their foals. For a long time the horse side of the family business had consisted firmly of breeding and training stunt and trick horses but in the end, after demand for both had fallen to subzero in the British Isles, they had continued the line for the sheer love of it.

And now he was walking the last of that line.

The thought made Pike feel laden with heritage and he breathed out a heavy sigh as they stepped through the large metal gate onto the twitten that ran between Hawthorne Cottage's flint stone garden wall and the fenced in hedgerow that enclosed the paddocks. Inigo echoed him lightly with a long snort declaring his joyful expectancy at the adventure to come. It immediately lifted Pike's mood again.

A sudden sharp gust of wind made its way up the path as horse and human started walking down towards the road. It twirled up the leaves that had gathered in heaps at the base of the chestnut trees lining the wall and blew them around their feet. There was iciness in the air. It made Pike shudder and he rested the lead rope over Inigo's withers, freeing his hands to do up the buttons of his thick navy coat. He turned the collar up in preparation for the wind to turn around and come back down the narrow channel. The garment's sturdy, military felt chafed against his neck and he stuffed his hair between the rough fabric and his skin.

Sarah was right, it was getting long.

He hadn't cut it since he'd met Eleanor. She loved running her fingers through the black brown mass, forever fascinated by how something that thick could feel so smooth and soft at the same time. He didn't care one way or another for hair as a fashion statement but he did care for her caresses, so he'd left it to grow.

Inigo, left to walk unguided, had put his nose to the ground and was sniffing and snorting at the leaves on the path, looking slightly startled and more like a foal than an impressive young stallion when one of them began moving in the air stream coming from his nostrils. Curiosity followed straight in the footsteps of surprise and he began blowing on it on purpose, spooking himself with delight every time it hopped along. Pike caught the lead rope as it slid off the horse's shoulder, not wanting to disturb Inigo in his newly invented game. The stallion looked, felt, *was* so much like his mother just then it brought tears to Pike's eyes. He lightly touched the large bay patch that stretched along Inigo's entire left side, the outline of which was identical to Inara's. The horse raised and turned his head to nudge at one of Pike's promisingly deep filled coat pockets in response.

"Careful, boy." Pike pushed him away gently, ruffling the black and white streaked forelock. "There are eggs in there."

They had reached the road and Pike strengthened his grip on the lead, prompting the stallion to straighten up, prick his ears and look purposefully at the traffic. As they approached the kerb, Pike took a deep breath and exhaled slowly.

The horse halted on cue.

They had completed about half their round when that part of Pike's brain that denied him the possibility of deceiving himself for any substantial length of time told him to concede defeat and admit that Sarah and Aaron had a point.

Inigo had behaved impeccably throughout the walk.

During their first pit stop at the newsagent, where they had picked up the paper Sarah had requested, a bus had pulled up to the stop outside and the young stallion had not batted an eyelid as the passengers had spilled out onto the wide pavement around them.

On the next leg of their journey they had been overtaken by a group of riders from a nearby yard and even when the last in line, a mare in season, had playfully lifted her tail and squeaked a high pitched chase-me-squeal as she had trotted away, Inigo had merely given a small grunt. He had curled his upper lip to check out the mare's odour more intensely and his neck had remained arched while he had pranced rather than walked for most of the remainder of that trail. Still, at no point had he tested Pike's hold on the lead or stopped tracking straight on the road.

By the time they had turned into Eleanor's street to deliver the eggs to her house, he had calmed down completely again, plodding along next to Pike like an old cart horse and making the young man wonder what exactly Kimi's 'whatever else was running around the yard' had included over the years.

While Pike had pushed the door bell, the knowledge that Eleanor wasn't there making him feel like a complete stranger in front of this house in which he had spent so many nights, Inigo had started munching the front lawn, unperturbed by the ogling peroxide blonde neighbour or the vacuum cleaner that she was wielding over her car in the driveway.

Finally, when Eleanor's stepfather Kjell had opened the door with her little half brother Oscar on his hip, even the toddler's delighted, ear piercing shrieks of 'Ike', 'Eeego' and 'Eggies' had done little to rouse the stallion's temper.

They had indeed been happy to see him, Oscar's enthusiastic hug making Pike feel both a little awkward and grateful at the same time. It had dawned on him then, how little human touch there was in his life when Eleanor wasn't around.

Contemplating that realisation now, he slung an arm over Inigo's shoulder and felt the warmth of the animal by his side as they waited to cross a main road.

On the other side was a well trodden path through a farmed field, stubbly and burnt in large patches to fertilising ash. The shortcut led to a footbridge over a dual carriageway that carved the ancient hills stretching into the horizon noisily in half.

The bridge was scary territory for any horse, with the roaring monsters rolling underneath and the crosswinds whistling in your ears, but even this test of courage was one Inigo had passed with flying colours the last few times they had done this round.

Today though, there would be little whistling. The atmosphere was quiet beneath predatory, threatening skies lying in wait, slate grey and fierce. There was an ominous stillness to the air. It was the perfect, looming calm telling Pike that the winds of the last night had just been a teaser. The real storms were yet to come.

They crossed during a gap in the traffic and began filtering through the field, Inigo's nostrils working overtime as they took in the smell of burnt straw.

Walking up the arching footbridge the stallion suddenly became agitated, dropped his head and began snaking around his human protectively. With his neck stretched out in a long thin line and ears pinned back he made sweeping motions in the air around them, showing an invisible enemy his teeth.

It was an ugly look that Pike had never seen on the horse before and he was a little taken aback by how fierce it made soft, loving, well-behaved Inigo appear. He tugged on the lead sharply to bring the stallion's head back up.

"Pack it in," he demanded in a low voice. "There is nothing here."

That's when he heard it.

It wasn't loud but it was unmistakable.

Grunts, punches being thrown, somebody being kicked.

The metal railing rattled and chimed from impact.

Someone was whimpering to stop.

A 'fucking scum' from an aggressor as a boot found its target once again.

Pike and Inigo became one in an instant, jogging in step towards the noise. As they reached the top of the bridge Pike could see the attackers on the downward slope, startled in mid-motion by the sound of Inigo's hooves reverberating on the asphalt.

There were three of them.

Why was it always three?

Boys, a few years younger than Pike. Two lardy, one scrawny. Two in grey sportswear, one weasel in black.

Standard issue.

There was a man on the ground, curled in a foetal position, naked soot-black arms shielding his face from the onslaught, his equally grubby hands pressed protectively against his close shaven skull. A tattered, half opened rucksack was propped up against the railings, being ransacked by the weedy kid.

The element of surprise gone, Pike could see the boys unfreeze and shift their attention to him and Inigo. He breathed to the horse to stop as the pug faced leader of the pack stepped towards them.

"Fuck off pony-boy, there's nothing to see here."

"Yeah, fuck off, you," the weasel added lamely as he rose from his crouched position to sidle up to his friend. He was trying his hardest to look menacing by putting his hands in his pockets, while jerking his head like a clucking chicken. If the situation hadn't been so serious, Pike would have laughed, but the third one was still hovering over the man on the ground, looking feverishly back and forth between his prey and the intruder, obviously waiting for Pike to vanish from the scene so he could finish what he'd started. His huge, doughy face, which sat atop an equally humongous body, was so densely layered in fat that his eyes had all but disappeared into their sockets.

"I beg to differ," Pike stated evenly.

He tapped a finger lightly on the lead rope a couple of times, praying that Inigo had paid attention during the last few sessions and would do as asked if need be, even though they were side by side rather than facing each other as in practice. He couldn't risk taking his eyes off the boys but sensed the stallion's shoulder rise as he made himself stand tall next to Pike.

Pugface frowned. Pike could see his brain cells rubbing together in the infinite void behind the dark circles that framed lustreless button eyes. Pug gave a short whistle through clenched teeth and with a disappointed sigh and a last weak kick at the head, Doughball let go of the fallen man and joined his companions.

They advanced on Pike and Inigo slowly, blatantly unsure how to add the presence of the animal into the equation. That was, if they could add at all. Pike stood his ground, waiting with a smile on his face. He could feel his eyes firing furiously behind the mask of studied calm, his pulse beating in his stomach. He still had no idea of the stallion's exact stance but was almost certain that Inigo was threatening them with his best fearsome face.

Behind the three gringos their victim slowly unfolded and rolled onto his front. Pike willed him to stay down. He could control this as long as the guy kept a low profile. He caught his eye. There was a bolt of understanding and the other stopped moving but stayed on his elbows, hands spread like a sprinter in the starting block. He kept his head up, watching intently through narrowed eyes. There was something sleek and poised about him, like a puma waiting to spring into action. Pike steered his attention back to the boys.

"At this point in the proceedings," he addressed them, "I would strongly advise you to just walk on by, gentlemen."

"Or what?" Pugface jerked his chin for punctuation.

"Or this," Pike responded tonelessly before he opened his hands around the lead rope and raised his arms, "And up!"

The stallion reared.

His front hooves swam in the air, striking out far enough away from the boys not to cause any harm but close enough for their faces to turn white.

It was over before Inigo hit the ground again, ducked low and began sweeping the space around Pike with his ears pinned back once more, this time not just baring his teeth but biting the air between them and their audience.

There is a lot to be said for a horse that can improvise, Pike thought dryly as he watched the boys scramble over to the railings on the other side and make as wide a berth around them as possible in their sudden exit.

"Thanks."

Pike turned back in the direction of the voice. He'd clocked the other jump up in the background, pick up his bag and some of the possessions strewn around it when Inigo had been mid-air. He hadn't seen him produce the stick he was carrying now though, approaching hesitantly. As he came closer Pike realised that it was a juggling utensil, a fire baton with burned out ends.

Inigo who'd dropped the dragon act with the disappearance of the three boys, curled his lip up for the second time that day as the smell of paraffin and bonfires oozed in their direction. The young man stopped some distance away, frowning. Pike could see that he was a lot younger than he'd assumed, somewhere around his own age. He was wearing faded black jeans ripped at the knees and frayed at the bottom and an equally washed out t-shirt. His left boot was wrapped in duct tape and the lace on the right was tied half way up for lack of length. The thing that gripped Pike most about the other's appearance though was that, at first glance, it was curiously like looking into a mirror that had only had half a mind on its job. Not only did they share height and stature but the guy's nose, like his own, had obviously been broken in the past, although from the way it was crushed flat, it was clear this had been achieved through full frontal punches rather than by hitting a dashboard too hard. His face, like Pike's, was full of scars but the craters bore witness to teenage years spent in acne hell rather than to getting a gob full of windscreen glass.

That was where the similarities ended though. The other's face was narrow and rectangular, his complexion pale under a fine film of soot, the stubble on his head ash blonde and his irises the lightest of silver grey.

"What's he doing now? Laughing?" he asked, staring at Inigo in awe.

He had a hoarse voice with a London twang, yet not the overstated one of those who fancied themselves cockney hard men from an era gone by.

Pike glanced back at the stallion.

"No, smelling."

"Hm." The guy moved closer towards the horse. "Sorry, I don't smell so good, mate," he said quietly, reaching out. Inigo unfurled his lip and brought his head down sharply to look at the proffered hand with interest. The guy took a step back. "I don't taste so good either," he added nervously.

Pike laughed.

"Don't worry he doesn't bite. He's looking for a treat. He thinks he's done well."

He could see tears shoot into the other's eyes as he stepped up to the animal fully, laid his hand on Inigo's cheek and whispered, "I'd agree there. – Thank you, mate."

The guy was shivering violently and Pike wondered for a moment whether he was about to go into shock.

"Haven't you got a jacket or something? It's freezing."

. The other turned his head towards the railings.

"The little bastards threw it over."

It was then that Pike recognised his profile. He'd seen him before.

"Weren't you here a few days ago? That morning in the fog?"

The guy looked back at him, stunned.

"You saw me?"

"I'm not fu—" Pike corrected himself swiftly, "Flipping blind."

"Fu-flipping?" the other mocked him with the smallest of grins. "Nice. Watching your tongue, are ya? Got a small one indoors?"

"What? No! Do I look like an idiot to you? I got a deal going with my grandpa, I stop swearing, he stops smoking."

With a short snort, the other smiled approvingly.

"Nice."

Chapter 4

The jacket was toast.

It had landed in the outside lane and had been run over a dozen times or more by lorries and cars alike.

Contemplating it from the top of the bank that led down to the hard shoulder, the young man next to Pike winced each time another set of wheels rolled across it. Tears were streaming down his face. On a bush in the central reservation fluttered another piece of his clothing but his eyes were stuck firmly on the ruined jacket. Inigo, who had begun ripping at the knee high grass around them with unashamed devotion, blew out his nose happily a few times, his joy a complete contrast to the despair happening to Pike's left.

"Got anything valuable in there?" Pike finally asked, just to say something.

"Like what?" The words were slung rather than spoken.

Pike sighed.

"I don't know. Wallet. Driving Licence. Phone."

The guy turned to him angrily.

"Do I look like I can afford a driving licence, mate?"

Pike tugged at Inigo's lead rope.

"Come on boy, time to walk on."

Reluctantly Inigo lifted his head out of the banquet and followed Pike back to the track.

They had almost reached the outbuildings of a farm, the only dwelling this side of the dual carriageway for miles, when Pike heard the voice behind them.

"Hey, wait up, Chief!"

He shut his eyes and waited for the ball of fury to form in his stomach. It didn't happen.

Curious.

He turned, Inigo seamlessly moving with him.

The guy was jogging towards them, rucksack flapping on his back. He slowed to a walk when he realised Pike had stopped. When he came to a halt in front of them Pike could tell that he wasn't remotely out of breath yet was deliberately making a show of leaning forward to put his hands on his thighs and breathe heavily, looking up at him.

"I'm sorry. I — I — haven't — even — thanked you." He held out his right hand, still bent over. "Name's Ashley. Ashley Parker. Ash."

Pike frowned. The submissive pose didn't suit the other at all. Whatever he was, he wasn't the meek type. He was undernourished in a sinewy, tough way that made the veins stand out and reminded Pike of underfed ex-racehorses awaiting their fate at auction. At second and third glance he really looked like someone you didn't want to face in a fight and Pike found himself wondering how those kids had got one over on him in the first place. Lost in his evaluation, he didn't realise that he had looked at the strange hand a split second too long. He saw the disappointment in Ash's eyes as he began to retract it. It stung.

Pike snatched him by the wrist before it was too late and folded his fingers around the other's arm. Surprised, Ash mimicked the action, sliding his hand up into the sleeve of Pike's coat.

It was if somebody had slipped an ice cube inside. His palm felt deadly cold against Pike's skin, and Pike wondered whether there could be any feeling left in those frozen fingers at all.

Ash shuddered, obviously caught in the sudden temperature difference between his body parts. He slowly straightened up to his full height and Pike felt himself grow taller with him. Then they stood, eye to eye, their pulses tripping against one another before falling into a mutual rhythm until Pike could feel his whole being expand and contract in his body with the beat, generating heat to warm the subzero foreign object clinging to his arm. Ever so slowly Ash stopped shivering.

They remained in this position for a long time, both unsure how to dissolve it.

In the end it was the stallion who broke the spell.

Having waited patiently next to them, he suddenly whipped his head up, pointed his nose in the direction of home and trumpeted a loud whinny. Ash let go with a start, jumped back and immediately began hugging himself as he swung around.

"What's he doing now?"

Pike shrugged.

"Calling to his ladies. Something's probably upset them. Or they think he's been gone too long."

Ash began scanning the surroundings as if he was expecting a herd of wild mustangs to come across the great rolling plains of Southern England.

"I can't see any horses."

Pike smiled.

"They're a couple of miles down that way." He tilted his head towards home. "As the crow flies. See that track past the farm there?" He indicated the way ahead. "That's where we're headed. It loops around to an underpass, where the dual carriageway goes through the hill. We're on the other side. There are some woods and after that we're the first house on the right. That's where his ladies are."

He patted Inigo's neck reassuringly. Half way through the penultimate sentence he'd begun asking himself why on earth he was giving this stranger, this stray, directions to Hawthorne Cottage. For all he knew, the guy could be a psychotic nutcase.

Visually, he definitely fitted the bill.

But Ash didn't seem to have heard any of it. He was still staring across the fields, rubbing his arms.

"Wow," he said in disbelief, "And he can hear them that far away? That's impossible."

"It isn't hearing so much, it's more like he can feel them."

"Hm. Imagine that kind of belonging," Ash stated hollowly then turned back to Pike. "Let's mosey, huh? We're kinda going the same way. Gotta keep moving. I'll peel off after the underpass, don't worry." He shivered. "I'm fucking freezing. Little shits."

Pike shrugged himself out of his coat and held it out.

"Here. I'm warm enough."

"Nah, I can't take your coat, mate. It's fine. I'm fine. I got more clothes where…where I'm staying. Never put all your eggs in one basket and all that. Let's just get going, huh?"

"Take the fu –, take the coat, Ash."

Ash flinched but didn't protest further and let his rucksack fall off his shoulders to accept the offering.

"Cheers," he mumbled as he put it on, his eyes on the buttons. "What's *your* name, mate?"

"That depends on who you talk to." Pike laughed quietly. "I have a few. But most people call me Pike."

Ash, having finished buttoning up the coat and shouldering his rucksack again, looked infinitely happier than before. He grinned widely.

"Would that be most people you like or most people you don't like?"

Pike weighed it up.

"A good mix. – My therapist did."

Ash frowned, scrutinising him.

"What were you in for?"

"PTSD."

"Good therapist?"

"Yeah."

"Well," Ash said, beginning to walk ahead, "Then Pike is good enough for me. — Come on, Pike-of-many-names, let's get us home before you get cold."

They walked the rest of the way in companionable silence, to the tune of Inigo's clip-clopping hooves. After they had passed through the underpass, Ash stopped where the woods began.

"That'll be me, then. I'll cut through here," he said, beginning to take his luggage off in preparation for returning the coat.

Pike held up his hands.

"Keep it."

"What?" Ash stopped mid-movement. "You can't just give me your coat. That's silly. I told you, I'm alright."

"Yeah, well, I don't want it. It's a pain in the neck."

Ash looked at him astonished.

"It's a good, warm coat, this. You can't just give that away."

"I just have," Pike stated, matter-of-factly.

Their eyes locked.

Suddenly Ash's expression became serious.

"Okay. If you really don't want it, I'll have it." He patted himself down, extracted the rolled up paper from the inside pocket and handed it to Pike. "Here, yours I believe. But you're gonna have to let me give you something for it. I'm not taking your fucking charity, alright? You two helped me with those trolls, that's me plenty indebted to you already. Here—" He extracted a battered wallet from his jeans pocket, opened it and took out a folded piece of paper, grubby along the creases. "It's all I got. It's crap, I ain't no poet, but it's yours. Consider it an IOU. Don't look at it until I'm gone though. I get embarrassed." He shoved it in Pike's hand and extended his arm to touch Inigo's nose. "And give him a carrot or something from me tonight, yeah?"

He turned abruptly on his heels and disappeared among the

trees.

With Inigo pulling impatiently towards home, Pike slipped the piece of paper in his pocket and wandered on.

They were alone once more.

Chapter 5

The skies remained dark and the days gloomy but the storms wouldn't make their move. Eventually the air became stagnant with anticipation, and time, which seemed to pass more and more slowly in Eleanor's absence, came almost to a standstill. Yet the more slowly the hands went around the clock, the more restless Pike found himself.

Expecting the weather to turn at any moment, he didn't dare take the stallion for another walk and he'd already stopped hacking Casta out with Eleanor's departure, knowing full well that without anyone else riding by her side venturing out was nothing but a prolonged, stressful ordeal to the Andalusian. So they stayed confined to the schooling area behind the barn. He rode dressage tests with Casta above and beyond any level Inara and he had ever attained, lunged and worked at liberty with Inigo, or played ball with him and Blue when not roaming the streets on his own, looking for something he couldn't name.

Everything always seemed hollow, boring and pointless in this perpetual twilight but underneath he could feel a yearning that had nothing to do with the atmosphere or the empty space in his bed. He found his thoughts wandering back time and again to the scene on the bridge, to the smoothness of the action, the beauty of the victory. He could see it as if on screen. The three gringos, the outlaw with the heart of gold and the Chief with his spirit horse — the instant bond of two strangers thrown together by fate, the triumph of righteousness over scum.

He grinned to himself now, as he crossed the road, heading back home after another pointless circuit, hands deep in his pockets.

It was funny how Ash had managed to cast him so effectively in a role he had fought so hard against for most of his life. How the stray had cut through his defences so smoothly despite addressing him with that most evocative of words. He pondered how much of it lay in the magic of the grubby piece of paper that was pinned to his wall now, below the photograph of Inara with Inigo as a foal at foot and right next to the picture of Eleanor sitting on his bed strumming the guitar.

The poem had surprised him but what had truly stunned Pike was the illustration next to it, a rough sketch in pencil of a young Indian warrior — braids, feathers and all — and his horse, stepping through a tear in time. Pike had gone round and round in his head, asking himself why neither Ash's 'Chief!' nor the drawing had brought the familiar taste of bile to his mouth that automatically got induced whenever people tried to make some kind of big deal of his Sioux heritage, and that never stood in any proportion to how minute that heritage really was. Innocence, he had concluded, was non-bile-inducing. Ash had drawn the vision he'd seen that morning in the fog. No more, no less. And he'd called him 'Chief' for sheer lack of knowing his name, the same way Pike had christened Doughball, Weasel and Pugface.

Well, maybe not quite the same. There had been no jibe in what Ash had said. Neither had there been any search for some ridiculous blood mysticism of the kind Aaron was so fond of, nor any of the ruthless money-making-from-skin-tone ambitions Kimi, the professional squaw, had developed as soon as she'd held him, the little throwback, in her arms.

And that's what you are. A throwback, he thought to himself. *Deal with it. It's about time.*

Self-analysis over for the day, he wondered for an instant where Ash was right now, a recurring thought since the moment he had watched him disappear among the trees.

He only hoped the other was keeping warm somewhere.

Arriving at the wrought-iron gate that led to the front garden of

Hawthorne Cottage he debated briefly whether to go through and into the house or whether to carry on and walk up the twitten to spend some more time with the horses.

The house held little of interest other than tea, sudokus, books or early studying for his exams next April. The idea of all of these made him feel heavy in his boots again. Although the thought of school work nagged at him a little, it seemed like such a futile exercise. He still had no idea what he was actually taking his A levels for, or what on earth he was going to do next with his life.

He turned towards the entrance to the path.

He saw her outline from afar, sitting in the dirt with her back to a water trough, forehead resting against drawn up knees, arms slung around the legs. She could have been a boulder but for the shudders that were rippling through the arrangement of limbs at regular intervals and the burnt copper on top that shone brightly even in the sunless grey of this day.

Blue was grazing in close proximity to the girl and even though Pike couldn't actually hear it from this distance he could see in her vibrating nostrils that the pony was giving off little regular snorts of warning to her field companions, telling them to stay away. Neither Inigo nor Casta seemed overly interested in the visitor though, grazing nose to nose next to each other on the other side of the paddock, only the occasional curious glance across betraying their outward nonchalance.

It made Pike smile.

For all Inigo's prowess and for all Casta's grandeur, at the end of the day there was no doubt as to who ran this herd — and it was neither of the horses. Sensing him approach, Blue lifted her head and whickered at him before moving over to the child and gently nibbling at her short-cut auburn hair. The girl lifted her head and a hand came up to stroke the pony's cheek gratefully.

As Pike approached further he could see Blue blow warm air into her face and a smile creeping through the tears. She didn't look at him when he plonked himself down next to her under the benevolent eyes of the pony, who promptly moved off with an approving grunt in her throat.

"Hey, Wendy."

"Hey." She snuffled, still avoiding his gaze by resting her eyes on the horses. "Inigo is beautiful. So big. I remember him being born. First foal I've ever seen born. He was so cute. Are you riding him yet?"

Pike stopped looking at her to watch the stallion, too.

"No."

In the periphery of his vision he could see the girl drag a sleeve across her round face.

"Why not?"

Pike shrugged.

"What are you doing here, Wendy?"

She mimicked the shrug and looked at him, fresh tears rolling down her cheeks. When he met her soft brown eyes, it was like being stabbed right through the core. There was a pain in there that shouldn't have been allowed to exist.

"Come here." He put an arm around her sturdy frame and drew her into his chest. His chin resting on the crown of her head, he held her as cascade after cascade of unhappiness poured out of her. When the tremors had subsided somewhat, Pike lifted his head and gave her shoulder a little squeeze.

"Whatever it is, it's gonna be alright," he whispered.

It sounded hollow even to him.

Wendy shook her head violently, loudly snorting snot back up her nose as she turned out of his hug back to the horses, wrapping her arms around her legs once more.

"No. No, it's not," she stated matter-of-factly. "So why aren't you?" she added after a pause, indicating Inigo with her chin.

Pike took his arm away, copied her posture and shrugged again. He contemplated the stallion. It took a while but once the words had formed it was so simple it could have made him laugh.

"Because I've never done it before. Not on my own. I've helped Karen but it's never been on my head. And it's...*Inigo*, you know."

"I miss Karen."

"Yeah," he sighed, "Me, too. – I really need her for this, I need someone else on the ground."

"She used to give me cuddles. And Charly. I really miss Charly, too. She used to make me laugh. It's never been the same without them around."

Pike knew what she meant. The departure from the southern equestrian circuit of his aunt had been bad enough. The exit of Charlene Gunner, the last, most enduring and most loved of all his foster siblings, had left a humourless void in its wake that was even bigger than Charly's legendarily ginormous stature, which fit on nothing less than a seventeen hand working hunter.

"Can't believe she got to be groom at Karen's new place. Some people have all the luck." Wendy continued her lament before returning her attention to Inigo. "Can't Aaron help you?"

Pike chuckled dismissively.

"How long have you known this family, Wendy?"

"Forever?"

"And how often in forever have you seen my grandpa ride?"

A faint smile appeared around the girl's eyes.

"What about Sarah?"

Pike shook his head gently.

"Sarah is good but she's got...issues and she is, you know, *really* old school. It's all total obedience and spurs and shit." He dug his right heel into the dirt. "It's not my style. Not anymore. It's not what I want for him. It's not what I want for any horse."

"Properly old school is not that bad. Better than rollkur," Wendy offered with all the confidence of a knowledgeable twelve-year-old. "And Karen used to say 'they might make you wear the spurs but it doesn't say anywhere in the rules that you have to use them'."

"Hm. Yeah, no, Sarah is…" He paused to rub the thumb and middle finger of his left hand inwards along his brows then pinched the skin in between hard, trying to squeeze the thought into shape. "Just not the right person for the job. I need Karen or Charly or…"

"…or another one of you."

Wendy elbowed him with a grin.

It made him laugh.

"Yeah, another one of me would be perfect."

"Good luck with that. What about Eleanor?"

"Don't be daft. She's only been riding for a couple of years. She's gonna be great one day but she's not helping me back a stallion any time soon."

"Shame. I like her. She's nice. She waves to me at school. Tink never does." She paused on a heavy breath. "But I haven't seen her for a while. Where is she? Is she ill?"

"No, special leave. Work experience. She's helping out on her father's tour."

"Really? Is it true then? Is he famous? Tink says he's dead famous."

"He was pretty famous, yeah. – How come *you're* not at school?"

Wendy didn't answer but Pike wasn't listening at any rate, lost in thoughts of Eleanor. The idea that she would make a point of waving to a girl who she hardly knew and who was four years her junior made him feel warm inside. Suddenly he could hear

Wendy giggle next to him.

"Huh?"

He turned to her.

She cocked her head, smiling widely.

"You got it bad, boy."

It sounded like a line from a movie.

He screwed his eyes up at her.

"You, little Miss Jones shouldn't even know what 'having it bad' means yet."

"Hah," she retorted, raising her eyebrows, "Just 'cause I haven't experienced it doesn't mean I can't see it."

"Touché. How is it going at The Black Horse? How's Tinkerbelle's wonder horse?" Pike finally asked, while both of them looked ahead again.

"Hm."

Pike couldn't really have cared less how his onetime pas-de-deux riding partner on the show circuit was doing these days but he knew full well that asking about her sister would be the quickest way to the root of Wendy's unhappiness. It always was. Yet there was such an encyclopaedia of opinions in that one little 'hm' sound that he suddenly found his interest genuinely piqued.

He elbowed her gently.

"Go on."

"Not good." She took a deep breath and blew out her cheeks before she continued. "They've done terribly this summer. Properly badly. Rob's dead angry 'cause he's spent, like, a gazillion pounds buying Walt and another gazillion on trainers. They're on number five now. And Walt really is amazing. But it's just not working. Most of the time, they don't even get placed."

She'd said it without any glee, just with immense sadness.

"How come?"

"What do I know?"

"More than them. Go on, what's the problem?"

A big smile stretched across her face then, illuminating her eyes as she looked at him.

"You really, truly think so?"

"Uh-huh."

"Wow." She took a deep breath. "Ok, I tell you what the problem is. No fun, that's the problem. You know how Karen wouldn't ever let you ride a test the last couple of days before a show? How she would always either take you out on a hack or play ball with the horses or like that time she took us all to that beach where you are allowed to ride into the water? And we swam with them?"

Pike shuddered at the memory.

"Yeah I remember. It was flipping freezing."

"Maybe," Wendy carried on enthusiastically, "Whatever. But it was *fun*, don't you see? For them and for us. I've figured out why she did it. *Because it was fun.* Get it?" She was gesticulating wildly now, cheeks burning.

"I hear the word fun a lot," Pike said dryly.

"Yeah. And that's what's missing." She sighed. "It's all work, work, work. Last year, Tink was still taking him out on hacks in between. It wasn't all serious. But she won't anymore now. She won't admit it but he bolted with her and it scared her. So now it's passages and piaffes and pirouettes all day every day. It's *booooring*. They are bored. Both of them. You can see it. There is no...I don't know."

"Fun?" Pike offered.

"Yes! Exactly! No fun!"

Wendy blew out her cheeks again, this time with a short breath that made her sound like a pony pleased with itself.

"Hm, I see." Pike started getting up. "Come on, my bum's getting cold. Let's go in the house. Isabel brought cake around yesterday."

Wendy hesitated.

"I'll come in the house," she finally said, "But I won't have cake. Rob says I'm too fat. He won't let me ride Straw anymore." The tremor instantly back in her voice, she swallowed hard. "Who's Isabel?"

The question drew Pike away from his rising anger over the image of Robert Greaves telling this beautiful, thoughtful, passionate little girl that she was fat.

How could she possibly not know that Isabel was Eleanor's mum? Little Wendy, who'd been part of his life since her arrival on the planet. He saw a myriad of pictures floating past his mind's eye.

A ginger, gurgling baby with big round eyes lying in a pram next to the schooling paddock while her big sister was having her first lead rein lessons under the watchful eye of Karen, with Wendy's and Tinkerbelle's mother Jenny, Karen's best friend since school days, looking on critically. Bigger Wendy, herself old enough to sit on ponies now, a technical klutz compared to her sibling but oh so much more tuned in to the animal underneath her than Tinkerbelle would ever be. Another, yet older and increasingly plumper version, a day before her first off the lead rein show, standing in the stable block of The Black Horse Equestrian Centre, brimming with excitement, grooming Blue, who was to be her ride, for hours on end until the little blue roan mare had glimmered silver.

And that's where the slide show ended abruptly.

The next day had been the blackest of his life and after that nothing had ever been the same again. When he'd come out of hospital weeks after the accident that had killed his mare everything around him had already changed beyond recognition. Robert Greaves had ceased to be his aunt's fiancé and had moved out of Hawthorne Cottage to set up home with Jenny in a poxy holiday let near The Black Horse, the big yard Greaves ran as a hobby alongside his flourishing business in care homes for the affluent elderly. Tinkerbelle and Wendy, who had been fixtures at Hawthorne Barn for as long as Pike could remember had, of course, gone with their mother to live with Greaves. Blue who had been over at The Black Horse for the summer had been returned. Her long-term partner-in-crime and field mate, Tinkerbelle's red roan pony gelding, known to the show circuit as Strawberry Mouse, had not. The devastation had been complete when Karen had started dissolving the business at Hawthorne Barn, telling the liveries to find another home and looking for jobs outside, as far away from the disaster zone as possible.

Nevertheless, there were people that you always carried under your skin no matter what and the broad, gentle girl sitting next to Pike now, still looking up at him inquisitively through those round brown eyes, was one of them. And somehow one assumed that the people you carried with you knew where you were at and who was who in your life, regardless of how many quasi-divorces had exploded between you. So he had never thought about how much in all of this little Wendy had got left behind. In short, it would never have occurred to him that she wouldn't know who Isabel was.

"Rob's an idiot. But we know that." He watched her eyes light up, then continued, "Isabel is Eleanor's mum. And she makes the best cakes. You'd be stupid not to try some. Come." He got up and offered her a hand. She let him hoist her to her feet and he winked at her. "Straw can carry a lot more than that, I tell you."

Wendy blushed and grabbed the sports bag she'd been keeping by her side.

"Here, allow me." Pike took it off her and shouldered it, surprised by the weight. "Jeez, what have you got in there?"

The girl smiled but didn't answer as she slowly followed him out of the paddock while dusting off her bottom, only to succeed in rubbing the damp mud deeper into her jeans. He grinned, put his free arm around her shoulder and pulled her along. "Come on, you."

After a few steps she peeled herself out of the embrace again, turning her body back towards Blue and the horses to look across the land.

"P?" she asked quietly into the distance.

"Yeah?"

"Straw and I," she paused, "Do you think we'll ever be allowed to come home?"

It broke his heart.

Chapter 6

The house was ostentatious and vulgar, a bold statement in extraordinarily ghastly taste.

It's erection had eradicated a chunk of the South Downs the size of a football pitch, not counting the generous grounds that had been included around it behind the glass shard topped garden walls. Yonder lay something that was part bred Spanish finca and part bred Colosseum crossed with a mock 14th century English castle, complete with corner towers. The Doric pillars holding a modernistic electric gate in place, on which ordinary bad taste would perhaps have placed a couple of lions, were the supports for two rearing gold-painted horse statues with fake ruby eyes.

It was simply horrendous and Pike and Sarah gaped at it through the windscreen of Sarah's beaten up Polo for some time before Sarah finally found her voice.

"I guess that is what they call a crib these days, isn't it?"

"When did he stamp this out of the ground?" Pike asked incredulously.

They were parked up on the verge, next to the large sign that announced the entrance to The Black Horse Equestrian Centre. To the left of the long drive that led up to the yard, which until recently had been flanked by immaculately kept paddocks, this ode to revolutionised planning law had been vomited. On the opposite side there was something still under construction that looked suspiciously as if it was going to be a tennis court. Something in the way the heavy machinery had been abandoned, and in the way a bank to the side of it had collapsed told Pike that the enterprise was not going well. It looked like the hills were fighting back their hardest against being levelled.

It made him want to throw himself on the ground and hug the earth.

"We moved in a couple of months ago," Wendy said quietly from the back, where she was cowering in her seat. "Most of it is finished. The swimming pool isn't tiled yet."

"Swimming pool?"

It came out in one voice as Pike and Sarah spun around simultaneously to look at the girl. She nodded resignedly, her eyes wandering between Pike's and Sarah's with no joy. She grabbed her bag from the seat next to her, a hand on the door handle. "Thank you." She locked eyes with Pike. "See you around."

She turned to the door.

"Wendy."

His arm darted between the seats to grab her other hand. She looked at him with a shrug and a forced little smile, let go of the bag straps for a moment and slipped her hand into his, gently returning the pressure. Her palm felt clammy. Then she abruptly let go and scrambled out of the car, leaving him with a lump in his throat.

They watched her press the entry system buttons, speak into the intercom with shoulders slumped and head bowed and walk through the slowly opening gates.

Sarah turned the key in the ignition with a sigh.

"She's going to try again, you know. I know the look. I just hope she is smarter than that."

"Try what?"

"Running."

"What? Running away?"

"For someone who is so intuitive with horses you can be astonishingly blind where people are concerned. Yes, running away. What did you think was in the bag? Robert Greaves' body?"

"There's always hoping," he replied feebly as Sarah pulled

away, turned the little car around and steered homewards.

They missed them by a hair's breadth.

If Sarah hadn't already slowed down just before the bend in order to pass a woman walking her dog, they would have hit them for certain. As it was, the bonnet of the Polo stopped inches away from the pony's flank. It was edging backwards, diagonally across the road, its hind tucked under and the jaw pushed into its chest in a futile attempt to evade the pressure of the bit, on which hung the entire weight of the child on its back. The little red roan's rider was leaning forward, leg behind the girth, pulling on the reins with one hand, while raising her crop in sheer panic with the other. She hit the pony with full force while simultaneously kicking it hard in the ribs and Pike heard himself shout out in protest behind the windscreen.

Fuelled by adrenaline and anger, he was out of his seat belt and outside the car in a split second. He got to Straw's side just as the crop was about to come down on the frightened little gelding once more, grabbed the reins under the bit to pull them out of the girl's hands, nearly unseating her in the process, and snatched the fibreglass stick midair.

He flung it into the bushes.

"You stupid little cow, what do you think you're doing?"

Although seething inside he was trying to breathe calm into himself and the pony at the same time and it came out more menacing than furious.

"Easy boy, it's alright," he whispered and slipped a hand under the bridle's brow band to place it flat against the pony's forehead and rub the whorl lightly with his palm. As he watched the white in the gelding's eye slowly disappear back into the socket, there was an odd moment of alien disorientation beyond the panic that Pike couldn't quite fathom. He tried to harness the sensation but the girl kept muttering something and then it was gone.

She had let go of the reins completely and was shaking with fear, searching Pike's face with rabbit-caught-in-headlight eyes. He only had half an eye for her, still trying to bring Straw back from the brink of complete mental meltdown. After what seemed like minutes the gelding finally pushed his nostrils into the crook of his arm and Pike knew that he had the pony's attention — and trust.

"Walk on," he commanded and the pony followed him obediently as he brought them out of the road onto the verge. Pike changed sides to stand between traffic and pony and signalled for Sarah to drive around them into a lay-by, some fifty yards down the road. The girl was sitting limply astride Straw now, having surrendered all control.

"I can't do it," she kept repeating vacantly.

"No, you can't," Pike stated wryly. "Do you know why he went backwards?"

She shook her head.

"Because you were asking him to. You had your legs behind the girth, leaning forward and pulling on the reins – those are the aids to go back. But you were whipping and kicking him at the same time, telling him to go forward, and he didn't know what to do, so he got confused and started backing into the traffic. You're really lucky we didn't hit you. A lesser pony would probably have reared with you. If you ask to go backwards and forwards at the same time, most horses will go the only way that's left — up. Strawberry here is better than that. And—" He looked at her sternly, clenching his teeth. "You do not hit a horse like that. Ever. Do you understand?"

He could see that only half the lecture was going in despite her head bobbing up and down wildly in agreement. Her face was oddly devoid of emotion and it struck him that she was scared out of her wits, agreeing purely to ensure he would not desert her. He took a deep breath and the first real look at her.

She was only about nine or ten, of slight built with black hair coming out in a single long pleat from underneath her skull cap. The satin cover of her hat shone bright purple and bore diamante stars, complimenting the rest of her country glamour get up. There was something vaguely Asian about her face and the dark, straight-lidded eyes. All in all, she looked like she would have been more at home doing a floor routine at a gymnastics championship or twirling pirouettes at a ballet class than riding a pony along a badly lit country road in the grey of an overcast late autumn day.

"You shouldn't be out on your own, anyway. How come there is no one with you?"

"My mum's walking just behind," she replied in a toneless voice.

Pike looked around, frowning. There was nobody in the vicinity and other than the dog walker he couldn't recall seeing anyone.

"Does she have a collie with her?"

"Yes."

"Hm. She should be coming around the bend any minute then. What's your name?"

"Lilly. With two ls."

"Hi, Lilly with two ls." He searched her dull dark eyes under the peak for a reaction but her face remained expressionless. "I'm Pike. I tell you what, I'll walk you to the lay-by and we wait for your mum there, okay? I don't fancy standing on a blind corner much longer."

The girl nodded compliantly. Pike got the impression he could have told her he was just going to park her in hell for a moment and she would have agreed. He let go of the reins, so she could take hold of them again but she just sat there, lifeless.

"Lilly? You need to pick up the reins now. I'll walk with you but you need to be in control up there, you hear me?"

She looked down at the strips of leather under her hands as if they were some unidentified foreign object that had just dropped out of the sky. Then, suddenly, she took them and shortened them up sharply and with expertise, straightening her back in the process and pushing her heels down neatly in the stirrups. Like someone had flicked a switch onto position 'rider'. The change was so abrupt and the picture of her seat in the saddle so exemplary, Pike found himself doing a double take before he started walking. Straw didn't move and he stopped in his tracks again, looking at rider and pony over his shoulder.

"Come on, then." He could hear impatience creeping into his voice now. This girl was driving him spare. "Ask him to move."

Finally, an expression other than blank fell over Lilly's face. It was a frown.

"How? *You* threw my stick away." The sudden accusatory whine cutting through the monotone of her voice pushed him over the edge completely and he could feel himself lose his composure.

"WHAT?" He turned back and faced her, rekindled anger burning in his veins.

Breathe. Just breathe. She is just a stupid little girl. She doesn't know any better. But doesn't she? Don't you have to want to hit an animal to hit an animal? And don't you have to want to hurt it to hit it that hard? She shouldn't be anywhere near a horse, let alone Strawberry. Why is she riding him anyway? Why would Rob let her out on a pony if she doesn't even know the aids? Why on this pony? — Because the idiot saw how pretty she sits and assumed she knew what she was doing. That's Rob all over for you: obsessed with how it looks. Idiot.

He had a bad feeling that that wasn't all there was to the story though. He took his own advice and inhaled deeply before he carried on talking. Somewhere far, far away he could hear his voice. Not the one that carried on ranting in his head without missing a beat but the one belonging to the up and coming equestrian star who had lead reined a million and one beginners. Stupid and bright ones, athletic and clumsy ones, gentle and ham-fisted ones, empathic and, now, apathetic ones.

It was cool, matter-of-fact, clear.

"Make your wrists soft, brace your back and give him a light squeeze with your legs — there you go."

She had followed his instruction to the letter and Strawberry had started moving. Her eyebrows shot up briefly in surprise before her face settled into its default expressionless mask again. He let the pony level with him and side by side they began their march to the lay-by.

"So, Lilly, how long have you been riding?"

"I don't know," she replied flatly.

"How can you not— "

He was cut short by somebody yelling from behind.

"Excuse me! Where do you think you are going with my daughter? Stop there immediately! Immediately, I said!"

Here comes Mummy.

He didn't turn around but carried on walking, raising an arm above his head to point ahead at the lay-by.

He despised these mothers.

At Hawthorne Barn they had always been mythical creatures at best, any urchins that had been adopted by Kimi or Karen as junior riders having come motherless, fatherless and carerless as standard, even when they had not been official foster children placed with them by social services. But during the time that Rob and Karen had been an item, Pike had spent his time split between home and The Black Horse, helping with lessons at the big, prestigious yard.

There, mothers had been in abundant, annoying supply.

Tinkerbelle, when she had still had a sense of humour and hadn't yet turned into a carbon copy of her two-faced mother, had often joked that they came in one of three kite marked issues: Mummy Dippy (flip flops in the yard, always in the way but usually nice), Mummy Dearest (devoted servant to her little princess, buys pony before daughter is ready, before long throws pony away to humour next fad) and Mummy Darling (bossy, lives through offspring, does everything to further darling's future career in equestrianism). This one sounded like it was mostly the latter, although there was an authoritarian undertone which made him wonder whether Tink had missed a trick back then: Mummy Draconian.

He glanced sideways at Lilly to gauge her reaction. There was none. She sat statue-like in the saddle, eyes glazed over while staring ahead.

Weird child.

Ahead of them, Sarah had stepped out of the car and was leaning against the boot of the Polo, facing them with a concerned look on her face. She was staring past Lilly, Straw and Pike and lightly shaking her head at the woman behind them who appeared to be gaining ground. Pike could hear Lilly's mother come closer, panting and muttering under her breath. They arrived at the lay-by at the same time. Sarah instantly began fussing over the girl on Straw's back.

"Are you alright child? That must have given you a terrible fright."

She touched Lilly's arm lightly and a second later it was as if the girl had been magically defrosted. She began shaking and sniffling with tears.

Pike rolled his eyes and turned towards the woman behind him just as she began talking in a clipped voice.

"Who are you people? How dare you walk off with my daughter like that?"

"Who are *we*? Who are *you* lady?" he spat back.

He knew he was towering over her relatively petite frame and that he was frightening her thoroughly but he didn't care.

"And how dare *you* let an inexperienced little girl go off on a pony on her own *on the road*. We nearly ran them over."

"Nonsense."

Nonsense??? What the—

The thought was aborted by the woman carrying on in a defensive staccato.

"Lilly is an excellent rider. Very talented. This animal is a HOYS winner. Do you people know what that is? Very experienced pony. Perfect for my daughter. Excellent match. Now, excuse us."

It was rare for Pike to be lost for words and it felt strange. But since her last sentence was not accompanied by any action to follow it through, he had time to gather his thoughts around his astonishment. The speaker, who was like an older, shorter-haired and positively more Asian version of her daughter, was obviously waiting for Sarah and Pike to take the initiative and clear off. Instead, Pike cleared his throat.

"Firstly, 'this animal' is called Strawberry Mouse. Secondly, I know perfectly well that Straw is a Horse of the Year Show winner. I happened to be there at the time, riding alongside him. Thirdly, your daughter doesn't know the first thing. She looks good in the saddle, that's it. Lastly, he is a *dressage* pony. That doesn't make him safe to be plodding around on country roads on his own with a child on board who, I repeat, does *not* know what she is doing. He's always been skittish out and *hates* hacking on his own. He'll do it because he is a good pony but he needs a *competent* rider he can trust. At any rate, even if your daughter was remotely competent, she would still be too young to be out here alone. So, if you are walking with them, you stay by their side, lady, do you hear me?"

He stopped and drew back, suddenly realising that there was something missing from the picture. Sarah who had been plying Lilly with tissues while comforting Straw with a scratch of the neck looked up at the same time, scrutinising the scenery.

"He is absolutely right, you know," she said in an almost incidental tone. "Where is your dog?"

Lilly's mother raised her eyebrows in undisguised disdain, looking Sarah up and down.

"And you are?"

Pike had to suppress a grin as he watched Sarah's fine features under the short cropped silver cap of hair take on an air of royal breeding and unquestionable aristocracy. She stepped around pony and child and extended a hand.

"Quite so, how very rude of us. Lady Sarah Osbourne, Olympic Equestrian Team 1956 and 1960, how do you do?"

She took Lilly's mother's limp hand and shook it deftly. Pike could see that the woman had already faltered at the mentioning of the word 'Lady', the Olympian credits proving entirely unnecessary to impress. One day, Pike would have to ask Sarah how much of it was actually true and how much of it the performance of a RADA trained actress. He felt a bit thrown when she decided to drag him into the act by introducing him in an equally formal manner.

"And this," she said, elbowing him to extend his paw, "is my dear friend, Paytah Hawthorne. A knowledgeable lady like you will certainly have heard of the famous Hawthorne horses."

Pike thought she was laying it on a bit thick but Lilly's mother was lapping it up, her eyes resting on Sarah in awe, while she absentmindedly shook his hand. A shudder went through him.

"Now, where is that beautiful dog of yours?" Sarah continued, all smiles and fairy glamour.

The woman, who had introduced herself as Odelia Smith, made an abrupt dismissive gesture.

"Not mine. My sister-in-law's. He runs off. He'll turn up at her house later."

Pike could feel anger flare up in him again. In the periphery of his vision, he could see a shadow fall over Sarah's face, too. Despite her old school philosophies where horse training methods were concerned, she was still an animal person through and through and was as taken aback by the lack of concern for the collie's welfare as he was.

Just then, right above them, thunder growled and the first spatter of rain fell on their heads. Straw, who had been nuzzling Sarah's back pocket during the round of introductions, whipped his head up and gave off a series of hectic snorts. Lilly shrieked and was promptly scolded by her mother.

"Don't be stupid, child."

Sarah had automatically grabbed the gelding's reins under the jaw to bring his head back down and was looking at Pike with a question in her eyes. He scanned the sky as a second roll of thunder shook the air.

"Right. That's enough of the chitchat, ladies," he decided sharply. "We have about two minutes before the heavens open. You —" he said, indicating Lilly with his chin, "Get off the pony. Sarah will drive both of you back to the stables. I'll walk Strawberry home."

I'll walk Strawberry home.

The words kept going round and round in his head as he was wading through sheets of rain with the little red roan's cheek pressed firmly against his side, seeking guidance and comfort.

I'll walk Strawberry home.

And every fibre of his existence screamed in tune with the lightning bolts scratching the sky, shouting that they were going in entirely the wrong direction.

I'll walk Strawberry home.

When they arrived at The Black Horse, it was as good as deserted, Lilly and her mother evidently having already left for cosier surroundings.

Only Sarah and a lonely groom were waiting for them under the projecting roof of the brand new purpose-built American barn stable block which had sprung up to the left of the original brick stables. The groom, a wiry girl Pike had never seen before with the swagger of those who'd paid their dues at racing stables, met them half way across the yard and unceremoniously took Strawberry from him. She thanked him curtly for his assistance and left him standing in the big, empty yard. Drenched to the bone, he watched the pony's behind disappear through the rain and into the light of the stable block. He knew full well that for all his faults, Robert Greaves ran a ship of the highest standards. Straw would get rubbed down and wrapped in a cooling rug, put into a clean and comfortable big box, fed and watered.

Still, for the second time that day Pike felt like a traitor.

Chapter 7

The storm raged all night. Although the thunder and lightning didn't last, as darkness wore on the gales gathered such speed that Aaron deemed being anywhere in the house other than the ground floor was unsafe.

Thus the three residents of Hawthorne Cottage and the irregular visitor known as Nameless, a ginger tom with one ear missing, were gathered together in the sitting room by an open fire. Each of them, aside from Nameless who had opted for sprawling on the rug, was occupying one of the various period style sofas that furnished this room. After dinner, they had dragged three of them closer together to form a semicircle in front of the fireplace, chatting about this and that, laughing, and being companionable — yet all the time Pike had felt absent and hollow.

He'd been unfairly terse with Sarah on the way back in the car, chewing his lip until it was raw but still getting nowhere near a solution for the knotted ball of wool that constituted his thoughts. Now he was staring into the flames, still no closer to an answer but mesmerised enough by their dance not to feel quite so scrunched up inside.

Sarah and Aaron were engrossed in their own pursuits, seated on separate settees, left and right of Pike's, which fronted the burning logs. Aaron was reading the biography of some world famous British actor of the 1970s that Pike had never heard of. Sarah, refusing to be defeated by her wrist, was awkwardly trying to mend a tear in one of Casta's turnout rugs. Despite having been cleaned the rug gave off a strong, mareish odour.

It has changed, Pike noted to himself absentmindedly, staring into the embers, *she used to smell way less extreme.*

"Pardon?"

Sarah was looking up from her task in his direction. Apparently he had spoken whatever the thought had been out aloud but having wandered on in his brain already, he could only vaguely remember what it had been.

"Casta's smell," he answered, retrieving it by the skin of his teeth before it could sink back into the oblivion of the subconscious. "It has become lots more intense from how it was when she first arrived."

"Oh," Sarah said apologetically, "I'm sorry. It's rather pungent isn't it? Is it bothering you? Should I be doing this somewhere else? Ouch."

She had pricked her finger.

"Nonsense, woman." Aaron put the book aside and made his way over to her. "Here, let me help you with that. Between us we might make a functioning human being."

Nonsense.

The word reverberated around the room and threw Pike right back into the thick of it.

The staccato voiced woman. The puppet like girl. The crop coming down. Strawberry pushing his nose into the crook of his arm. Wendy crying. Home. How?

How? How? How?

In the periphery of his vision he became vaguely aware of the tableaux Sarah and Aaron were forming now, sitting almost primly next to one another, the horse rug thrown over their knees. Sarah had begun holding the fabric so that the two flaps of the tear lined up and Aaron was busy with the needle. His right hand had remained unaffected by either of his strokes and he worked swiftly and accurately with the precision of a good farrier.

Sarah giggled.

"If I'd known you were such a good seamstress, I would not have attempted the job in the first place."

The old man grunted in response and mumbled something

about the stitches needing sealant.

Eleanor, Pike thought, *I need to talk to her.*

He checked his phone for the time. She'd still be at whichever gig they were playing tonight. It would be at least another three hours before she'd be back in a hotel somewhere. He willed his eyes away from the flames and got up.

"Where are you going?" Aaron asked, a mild tone of panic underneath the gruff exterior.

Pike smiled.

"Kitchen. I'm going to make some tea. Anyone want one?"

Aaron and Sarah both murmured appreciatively and Pike left them to it, navigating the dark hall by the illumination of his phone's screen as he typed.

Ring me.

The noise of the storm seemed infinitely amplified in the kitchen, the wind and rain rattling relentlessly on the back door and drumming against the windows.

As he put the kettle on, Pike worried about the horses in the stable.

He leant against the polished granite worktop, closed his eyes and stretched out his being until he could grasp Inigo around the edges of his consciousness. In front of his mind's eye, the stallion was pacing the box restlessly but didn't seem overly frightened. He could feel the mares, too, both infinitely calmer than the youngster. He let out his breath and opened his eyes again. The light in the kitchen appeared unreal and colder than before, the little specs of silver in the stone beneath his hands seemingly hovering an inch above the surface. He straightened up and busied himself with washing out the teapot that had been a resident of the cottage for longer than any of its present inhabitants, while waiting for his vision to return to normal. He opened the tin of Assam and placed a generous pinch of the long leaves in the pot's strainer then poured in the boiling water. Watching it cascade from the spout of the kettle, he found that his perception of light had readjusted and he looked around for something to entertain himself with until the brew was ready. The kitchen, as always, was cluttered to the hilt with cooking utensils, stacks of National Geographics, paperbacks, scrap books, photo albums and sundries.

After Aaron's second stroke, the occupational therapist at the hospital had suggested taking up a hobby that involved hand-eye coordination and fine motor skills for both hands but wasn't time dependent. The old man had taken the advice, much to Pike's and Karen's astonished delight, and after a failed attempt at knitting had set about sticking the newspaper clippings that his wife had shoe-boxed over the years into scrap books. Once the documentation of Kimi's extraordinary life had been completed, he had gone on to put the photographs that had previously been scattered in drawers all around the house into albums. While he had filed Kimi's career in strict chronological order, the photo albums were themed volumes he would still work on from time to time, even now. One of them was lying on top of the fridge, a small number of pictures scattered on top, waiting to be inserted.

Pike tilted his head to decipher the writing on the spine.

Children, it stated simply.

Pike shuffled the loose photos and the envelope they were resting on, which bore his aunt's sober, almost technical hand writing. They were printouts of the same bunch Karen had mailed him, of the foal and her. Pike took a quick look at them, smiled, stacked them neatly and picked up the album. He transferred it to the worktop and began flicking through it back to front. The last completed page was a collage of pictures that Pike's father had sent from various research trips to Africa.

His parents in their natural habitat. In a number of shots they stood smiling awkwardly into the camera, shaking hands with foreign dignitaries or eminent fellow researchers, the two of them always hip to hip, shoulder to shoulder. An indestructible team forged by a common goal in life, which absorbed everything else that could possibly matter in the furnace of its importance. In others, they were squatting among some of the poorest people on the planet, looking almost human.

In one particular shot that caught Pike's attention, his mother was crouching with a circle of children and a little black girl was shyly touching Alice's white blonde, candy floss hair. One couldn't see much of her pale blue eyes but Pike hoped for the girl that they had had some form of benevolence in them at the time rather than the cold, calculating scientist's stare that had earned her the nickname Titanium Lady in medical circles. He shuddered and let his eyes wander to his father in the shot, leaning tall, serious and competent against a tree, talking to what appeared to be a village chief yet with his eyes stuck firmly on his wife. There was a hawk-like look to Dr John Hawthorne's features at the best of times with a classic hook nose sitting in the otherwise broad facial structure he shared with his son and sister, and that bird of prey quality was thrown into stark silhouette by the colour contrast in the picture and echoed in the way he had cast his attention on the woman in his life.

In the picture beneath it the roles were reversed.

John stood at a podium, giving a lecture with his wife sitting at the far end of a panel behind him, her hair swept back and secured fastidiously with combs behind her ears, accentuating her sharp, pointy-nosed profile as her eyes hung on John with proprietorial criticism.

Possession, Pike thought, *they possess each other. To the exclusion of all others.*

The thought was not a new one but it still choked him and he turned the page.

Karen and horses. At shows, at home. A couple with Robert Greaves in them even, looking like a cheap Redford in his forties — without the endearing laughter lines.

The rest of the album was what it said on the tin.

Pages alternated between Karen with horses and John plus Alice with either important or dying people. It quickly became repetitive and he started opening up earlier pages at random.

John long before Alice, always with a book in his hand or in conversation with another serious looking person. At school receiving an award. At university being handed another, with his lab partner, future spouse and mother of offspring, hovering in the background now, as yet unnoticed but already staking her claim.

Karen as a toddler sitting on a piebald, led by Kimi. As an older girl, doing a handstand on a broad backed bay pony, grinning into the camera. At eleven, riding Blue's mother, the famous Bracken, with Blue as a foal at foot, accompanied by her best friend Jenny on a black Fell pony, as sturdy as its rider, just behind her.

And so on.

He stopped to take the strainer out of the teapot and poured himself a cup.

He didn't really want to go back to the sitting room yet and disturb the two almost cuddling people he'd left behind there. The realisation he'd had some days ago about how little human touch there was in his life when Eleanor wasn't around had lingered and he'd looked at his grandfather in a different light since. Ten years without physical closeness, ten years with only the occasional hug from a daughter, a friend or a grandson but no lasting warmth from another person was a very long time.

He returned to the album, sipping his tea. More horses and Karen, more people and John – most notably one of the latter holding a baby into the camera.

Me, Pike thought in a detached way, *that's me.*

He didn't like to look. Didn't like to have to concede how much love was in John's eyes looking at the baby. It was a look that went with another memory, equally unwelcome. The last time he'd seen his father alone, without his mother ring fencing every ounce of John's attention and without a lecture of some sort or another. When he'd woken in hospital after trying to save Inara had nearly killed him, John had sat by his bedside, crying. It was the only time Pike had ever seen his father shed a tear. He fled the image and started to flick through the pages again, backwards but much faster now and almost without paying attention.

So he went past it at first, without taking it in, before the realisation hit him. There had been something odd. He went back a few pages and there it was.

John on a horse, against the background of the barn. Pike couldn't help but evaluate his father's posture. He sat well. Straight in the core but at ease, knees forward, heels casually down and toes pointing at the horse's nose despite riding bareback, which always tended to put the rider in a more casual position. Behind him sat a young woman, pushed up tightly against him, arms slung around his waist, leaning her cheek against his shoulder and looking into the camera. Pike could hardly make out her features under the riding hat or properly see her body as it had almost melted into John's back but he could still tell that she was beautiful. She must have been relatively tall to reach as high up against his father as she did, and what one could see of her tanned legs sticking out from cut off shorts was the proverbial long and shapely. Most of her face was obscured by hat, straps and strands of straight, black hair that had been cut into a bob to frame a sharply chiselled yet still somehow feminine chin below full, wide lips. The eyes were overshadowed by the peak of the hat and hard to make out, but nevertheless seemed to glow with intensity at the observer on the other side of the lens, the other side of the photograph. Pike found himself taking a step back from the counter as he felt his skin prickle.

Whoa, what the –

He shook himself.

Just then Aaron entered the kitchen, startling him even more.

"Are you alright, boy? You look like you've seen a ghost," Aaron chuckled, opening the door to the fridge and sticking his head inside. "Now, where would it be? There is a ghost, you know. The ghost of Hawthorne Cottage." He was addressing the contents of the vegetable drawer but his voice had taken on the Irish lilt of his childhood, as it usually did when he was warming up to spinning a yarn. "Ah, here we are, with the tomato purée, as should be, as should be." He emerged with a blue tube of rug sealant. "Where was I? Ah, yes. The ghost, the ghost of Hawthorne Cottage. Have I not told you about it before?"

Pike shook his head.

"Hm. I probably thought you were too young still. Not easy to think one could be related to a murderer."

Pike had never quite managed the art of arching an eyebrow but he felt his forehead muscles attempting to have a go.

"You see," Aaron continued, unperturbed, "They say your great-great-grandfather, the original Dr John Hawthorne if you will, murdered his first wife after he found your great-great-grandmother hiding in the woods. They say he was bewitched by the pretty Sioux woman and that she made him poison the nice English lady who he was married to at the time."

"Who are *they*?" Pike asked dryly.

"People."

"So not the law then. And? Did he?"

"Don't be daft, boy. She died of tuberculosis like every self-respecting middle class doctor's wife at the turn of the last century. Now, what happened to that tea you promised us?"

"In the pot," Pike answered, turning back to the picture of Dr John Hawthorne, the unoriginal, and his mystery riding companion. "I didn't even know my father could ride."

Aaron who'd begun taking mugs out of the cupboard looked at him over his shoulder.

"Where did that come from now? Of course John can ride. Can you imagine a child of Kimi's not riding? He was quite good at it, too. Not as good as Karen or you but few people in the world ever are. What have you got there?"

He'd sidled up to his grandson, mugs in hand, and was staring with him at the picture now.

"Ah."

The sound was short. The old man turned away abruptly, preparing to pour the tea.

"Who's the girl?" Pike asked, running a finger tip lightly over her outline.

Aaron watched the red-gold stream of liquid flow into his mug, then Sarah's.

"That," he sighed at last, his voice having lost all but the faintest trace of Irish, "is the real ghost of Hawthorne Cottage." He turned to face Pike's frowning profile. "And not my story to tell. It's a conversation you should have with your father one day. Might make you understand him a bit better."

He went back to the fridge for the milk but stopped half way to contemplate the album again. With shaking fingers he carefully separated the picture from the page and held it out to Pike.

"Here, you should take it. Ask John about it next time you see him. But best do it when your mother is not around, if you catch my meaning."

"Sure." Pike took the offering with a sarcastic grin. "Thanks. Next time hell freezes over and the Siamese twins get separated, I'll give it a go."

He was about to ask whether the ghost had a name, when a strange, sudden stillness cut through the air outside. Later, when he would try and explain it to Eleanor, he would find himself somewhat lost for words, stuttering helplessly about a sound wave of such magnitude that it pushed aside the howling winds in its path. But in reality there was nothing to hear. It was an ominous absence of sound, which he felt as pressure on his ears and compression in his heart. It only lasted a few seconds and then a series of tremors went through the earth, reaching the soles of his feet through the kitchen floor while the noise of the storm became audible again, as if someone had released the pause button on it.

He stared at Aaron, speechless, heart racing with fear.

Sarah appeared in the door half a minute later, white as a sheet. "What was that?"

"I think we may just have lost a tree," Aaron stated heavily.

Chapter 8

He woke in Blue's stable at dawn, having made himself a nest in the far corner of her box. He was still clutching his phone to his chest and a soft breeze of warm air was flowing over his face. The pony's long muzzle hairs tickled his cheeks then wandered along his left arm as she let her lips gently glide over him. His hand found her nose blindly and he ran a finger along the edge of a nostril. Blue whickered quietly.

'Time to get up.'

He pushed off the fleece rug he'd been using as a blanket and sat up, bleary eyed, the expectant eyes of the pony following his every move.

"Morning," he greeted her.

She snorted lightly in return and inspected the phone in his hand. He shrugged and touched the animal's cheek.

"She hasn't rung yet."

Just then he saw some bars appear on the screen and a second later the case began vibrating in his palm.

Ah.

He picked up the call.

"P? What's wrong? Are you alright?"

He could hear badly hidden panic in her tone and realised with a jolt that she had been fretting all night, while he'd been fast asleep in one of the many receptionless pockets of the barn. Her always slightly throaty voice, which could reach the most amazing high notes when singing and which seemed so utterly misplaced in such a tiny person, sounded coarser than usual, worn.

He felt guilty.

When they'd first met he'd been suicidal. Properly suicidal. Not in a flirting with the memory of death while making himself fall through the darkness way, but in a having picked the time of day, date, method and things-to-finish-up-first sense. And even though she never said anything he knew she still worried about his stability. One day, somehow, he would need to make her see that he would never, ever get to that point again. But not today, today there were more pressing matters.

"Yes. Sorry. I've been in the stable all night. You know what reception in here is like."

"Why? What? Are the horses alright? I tried the landline but that's dead, too. Is Blue okay?"

In that moment the little mare came closer and blew loudly into Pike's face and the receiver.

"Yes, all good." He laughed. "That's her saying hello. — We lost a tree."

"Come again?"

"There was a hurricane last night and we lost the tree at the entrance to the twitten. Completely slayed. Must have taken the phone out, too. You should see the roots, Eleanor. They are massive. It's taken the entire corner of the garden wall out."

"Whoa," she said slowly, "So it hit the house? Is everyone alright?"

"No, no. The *roots* took the wall out. It went the other way, across and into the corner paddock. I think. It was hard to tell last night in the pitch black. To be honest, I was more concerned with checking on this lot here. They were a bit spooked but that's it. Everyone's fine. But that's not..." He stopped himself. She had sounded so tired and deflated. "How are *you*?"

"Tired. I want to come home now. I'm done here."

"Don't be daft. You're on tour with a legendary rock star. You don't want to come home yet. Nobody in that position wants to go back to boring same old that quickly."

"This *is* my boring same old. Oh, and that rock star is old enough to be my father, oh no, hang on a sec, he *is* my father. Phew. That could have been creepy otherwise."

Despite her attempt at fluffy sarcasm there was real prickliness seeping through the connection that Pike couldn't ignore.

"Uh-huh. What's really bothering you?"

She grunted.

"He keeps pestering me to record a duet and it's starting to really annoy me. He wants to rekindle his career so he has a pension one day, fine. But not off the back of sacrificing *my* privacy. I want to come home and horse around with ponies now, gaze into your stupid yellow eyes, play with your stupid hair and snog you senseless. I've had enough. I miss you."

The edge had given way to a soft undertone that made his heart instantly beat faster. While he floated in the amazement of having her in his life, he heard her collect herself on the other end. When she spoke again, the characteristic lightness, which told the world that there was very little in it she took seriously, was back in her voice. "Go on, so why *did* you ask me to ring? It won't be because of the tree. Have you seen the guy on the bridge again?"

This was Eleanor through and through.

In the last call he'd only mentioned Ash in passing, putting the emphasis on how proud he'd been of his stallion that day, but perceptive as she was, she had somehow registered that it had mattered on a completely different scale. A scale Pike himself still hadn't worked out. He smiled and got to his feet, sliding his back up against the stable wall. Blue had lost interest a while back, and had wandered off to hang her head over the half door for a conference with Inigo in the adjacent box. Pike stepped up to her side and leant across her back.

"No," he finally answered Eleanor's question, stroking the barrel of the pony's body. "No, I haven't. I tell you who I have seen though. Straw. And Wendy. Separately. There's something funny going on up there. I don't like it."

"Shame. He'll turn up again, I'm sure."

"What makes you say that?"

"Hunch."

"I like your hunches."

"I know. — Carry on."

Pike took a deep breath.

"I think Rob is trying to sell Straw to this awful woman and her daughter. They were *hitting* him, Eleanor. Hard." He could feel tears pricking his eyes but swallowed them down, squaring his jaw before he continued. "Would make sense in a Robert Greaves kind of way. Pony's past serious competition age, they don't do the pony club thing over there, Wendy's outgrown him. So he's just a liability now. I'm sure Rob's looking to shift him. I want him home, Eleanor. He's not safe there anymore."

"I've got to go, we're loading the bus. Look, why don't *we* just buy him then?"

Pike slipped a hand into the back pocket of his denims and extracted a handful of loose change, provoking a sharp turn from Blue's head away from the stable block aisle to investigate his backside. She started nibbling the corners of the pocket while he looked at the coins in his hand.

"I have one pound fifty four," he stated dryly.

"The record company gives me pocket money," Eleanor responded, "I haven't really spent it though, Dad keeps paying." She sighed, a deep exasperated sound. "I'm starting to understand how someone can have sold that many records and still be penniless. He's just a child, P. My dad is a complete and utter child. Anyway, so provided I stick out the entire tour and I don't blow it by telling him where to stick his duet and come home early, I'll have about two grand. Would that be enough?"

Pike heard himself take in a sharp breath despite the muscles in his face wanting to break into a smile.

"Don't you maybe have to talk to your mum about that first?"

"No," she said resolutely, "It's my money. To do with as I please."

He knew Isabel well enough to believe her but it still left an unpleasant taste in his mouth. It felt like she was bailing him out. Again.

At long last, she broke his silence with a quiet chuckle.

"Don't you worry, one day I'll ask for a kidney or something."

The smile that had been playing tug-of-war with his discomfort finally won.

"I thought you said you didn't want any more horses here."

"No, I said I didn't want any more *other* people's horses there. I never said *we* couldn't have any more."

"You serious?"

"Deadly."

"You can't keep buying me land and ponies, Eleanor."

"I'm not. I'm doing it for Blue. He's Blue's friend, right? You always say, they used to be inseparable, so let's un-separate them. Answer the question. Is it going to be enough?"

"Should be," he replied hesitantly. "But it's Rob. He'll milk it for all he can. If he can get more from that woman he will. The man has no soul."

"Well, try him," she stated. "And P?"

"Yeah?"

"*Try* not to piss the man off before the pony is ours."

With that, she rang off.

Chapter 9

"I told them that tree wasn't sound last time they came to cut the branches. Told them, when the gas people dug up the pavement on the corner they did something those roots didn't like. But nobody ever listens." Aaron shrugged dejectedly, leant heavily on his walking stick and scratched his head. "The Council are going to have to deal with it. Shame it fell across the path and not the road, really. Otherwise it would be gone by tomorrow. But like this? It might take months before they get around to it. Still, mustn't grumble. Could easily have gone into the house."

Aaron, Pike and Sarah were standing outside the garden gate in the middle of the twitten, looking down the path at the massive tree trunk that now completely sealed off the entrance at the bottom end. In the sober, grey light of day the destruction the chestnut had wreaked with its fall presented itself as far vaster than Pike had been able to gauge the night before in the diffused beam of his torch.

As soon as he'd stepped out of the barn to turn the horses out he'd seen it from across the paddocks, the crown reaching deeply into the far corner enclosure and changing the entire landscape with its sudden presence. On closer inspection it became clear that the trunk had flattened everything in its way, fence and hedgerow alike. Chalk rubble and earth were still trickling from the upturned roots that had dug up a sizable section of the flint stone wall which enclosed the garden of Hawthorne cottage, lending the scene of devastation an eerie special effect.

Pike felt immense sadness washing over him.

Four hundred years old. And gone in seconds. Dead.

"We're going to have to tidy this up as best we can," Aaron carried on lamenting. "Can't repair the wall till they've shifted the lot. We'll have to board up the gap in the meantime somehow. If we don't, we'll have all sorts wandering in soon. And I guess we will need to open the main gates to the yard. Otherwise hay delivery is going to pose a bit of a problem."

Sarah frowned.

"What main gates?"

"*The* main gates," Pike explained absent-mindedly, still inwardly eulogising over the demise of the ancient giant in front of him. "If you go along the fence by the road, about half way, where the dropped kerb is, it's actually a gate and not just fence panels. We'll need to cut the hedge on the other side though. It's been shut since Karen left."

"Do you need some help?" a rough voice with a London twang asked from behind.

While Aaron and Sarah spun around, Pike remained firmly in place in an attempt to hide the broad smile that had suddenly cut through his grief and conquered his face. He inhaled deeply, catching a whiff of paraffin, smoke and damp camping.

"Ash, meet Sarah and my grandpa. Sarah, Aaron, meet Ashley," he said loudly into space in front of him then listened as behind him introductions were made.

Ash stepped up to his side.

"Hey."

"Hey. Help would be grand."

"Good. I still owe you."

Pike looked down at the other's feet. The boots were more duct tape than leather or sole by now and were squelching with mud. Ash had obtained a piece of baling twine from somewhere to fashion a new set of laces. Pike stared at the orange string, so familiar to him yet so alien on this guy's boots.

"You'll owe me even more once I've found you some decent footwear," he stated soberly.

He heard Ash exhale slowly, a smithereen of pride in every

molecule of carbon dioxide leaving his lungs. Finally, Pike could feel a wave of reluctant concession emanating from the young man next to him.

"Go on," he added with a grin. "Treat yourself. I'll even throw in a pair of dry socks."

They worked until early noon, all four straining their capacities in near silence, punctuated only by the occasional appreciative grunt from Ash about the luxury of dry feet and ever more frequent curses from Sarah condemning her malfunctioning wrist.

After they had tidied the debris of the wall to one side and cut back the roots, Pike and Ash went to fetch fence panels from the barn and patch up the hole.

They took a tea break and, bringing their mugs with them, went back out into the twitten. They climbed up onto the chestnut's trunk to examine their handiwork, while Aaron and Sarah went inside.

Presently, Pike was watching the other over the rim of his mug. Ash was sitting opposite him on the tree, entirely preoccupied with stroking Aaron's old blacksmith's boots, caressing the steel toe caps that were shining through in small patches where many a horse's hoof had rested during a pedicure.

"Sorry they're a bit worn," Pike said apologetically.

"Are you kidding me, mate? Look." Ash stretched a leg out in front of him and rotated his foot. "No holes. And they fit. I can't tell you how grateful I am," he added, wiping the ball of his right hand across each eye in turn.

Just then, Sarah stepped through the garden gate balancing two plates, on which towered a pair of doorstep sandwiches, and carefully made her way down the path. Pike placed his mug in a knot in the trunk, jumped off and met her half way. When he returned he saw Ash's eyes fix on the food in a way that reminded him of a half starved wild pony, freshly arrived from the forest or moor, eyeing up a bucket of proffered pellets.

"Hungry?"

"Starving."

Ash took a plate and started wolfing down his sandwich.

Puma, Pony, Wolf.

Pike suddenly had to laugh as he put his own plate on the trunk. Ash frowned at him quizzically over the crust of the bread.

"You induce feral similes, amigo," Pike answered while he jumped back up onto the tree.

"Ya what?" Ash tried to ask around a sizable chunk of food in his mouth.

A second later he was choking.

"Whoa, whoa, whoa." Pike slapped the other's back. "Careful with that. Believe me, death is an entirely overrated experience."

Ash regurgitated the lump that had gone down his windpipe and carried on coughing for a while. When he'd finally cleared his throat and mouth sufficiently and had taken a sip of his tea, the air between them had changed in a way Pike didn't understand. Ash was looking at him sideways, taxing him through narrowed eyes, a hand on the trunk, poised as if he was about to jump and run.

"How do you know?" he asked under his breath.

Pike was confused.

"Know what?"

"How do you know?" Ash repeated, jerking his chin at him. "That death is overrated?"

"Oh, right."

Pike breathed a sigh of relief. For a moment he'd wondered whether he had somehow offended the other. He shouldn't have cared but he did. He shrugged, picking up his food.

"Cause I've been dead. For about twenty minutes. And it wasn't all it's cracked up to be."

He bit into his sandwich and watched Ash watching him. What little colour the other's complexion had borne had drained from his face. Ash looked at the rest of the food on his own plate and pushed it gently to the side. The next question came in a whisper.

"What was it like?"

"Death?"

"Uh-huh."

"Crap." Pike took another bite, chewed and swallowed. "Infinite. Lonely. Joyless."

He raised the sandwich to eye level and examined the deep delicious filling between the two slices of bread, losing himself in the detail.

"There is no food, nothing. It's...void. Hard to explain. — But somehow oddly addictive."

He grinned sarcastically at his snack, before sinking his teeth into it again. His gaze went back to Ash who was staring at him intensely.

"But you remember it, right? You're still *you*, right? When you're dead. You don't just stop?" he asked after a pause.

Pike shook his head, savouring the taste in his mouth.

"No, not really. I mean, yes you do. Stop, I mean. Cease to exist. It's like...this is hard." He rubbed his forehead violently. "I've never even spoken to Eleanor about this...I don't know...there is no real you, at first there is this fuzzy kind of memory of having been a something and then there is just...void."

As he spoke he could feel the fear reaching out for him and a violent shudder ripple through his soul. His heart racing ahead, he suddenly felt like running. Running until he ran out of ground. He hated this. The fear of death. It could make you want to kill yourself just to stop fearing it.

He wished for a horse, for the warm body of Casta underneath him, Inigo's shoulder by his side or Blue's forehead leaning against his chest, earthing him. Instead, he tried to anchor himself in Ash's eyes but what he met there was something in even more need of a life jacket, something raw and ashamed and utterly unspeakable. Unflinching, he held the other's gaze until Ash's eyes darted away.

"You want to come say hello to my horses before we crack on with finding the gate?"

It got him a faint smile.

They were standing amidst the little herd and though still a little wary of them, Ash appeared a lot less nervous than he had been of Inigo during their first encounter. The sun had finally broken through the remnants of the storm and here, in the middle of the paddock, it was now quite warm. Ash had slung his coat over his shoulders and all three equine muzzles were pushing towards him, inspecting the visitor's scent.

The stallion retracted his nose first then stepped back to rub his cheek against Pike's shoulder. Casta carried on sniffing the air around Ash, her nostrils crinkling up and down in little waves, her tail high in the air behind her. Blue stepped closer to gently investigate the newcomer's hands and bare arms with closed lips. A little shiver of pleasure played over Ash and Pike could see goose bumps appearing on the other's skin.

Ash smiled, a small smile accompanied by a frown, appraising the sensation.

"That's kinda ticklish — but nice."

Inigo grunted quietly into Pike's ear then moved off, Casta following hard on his heels. Pike could tell that despite the sudden turn in the weather they still carried the storm in their bones, a subdued restlessness lingering under the exterior of calm. Only Blue remained with the two young men, finishing her inspection of Ash leisurely and then resting her forehead against his midriff.

She likes him.

Pike realised he'd been holding his breath.

Ash looked at him enquiringly.

"She wants you to scratch her behind the ears."

Ash tentatively began circling his fingers around the indicated spot. Blue pulled a face.

"Harder," Pike added, "Proper scratch."

"They like that?"

"Some do. Some don't. They have different preferences. Just like people. *She* does."

Ash had obviously changed the pressure to Blue's satisfaction and her disapproval was rapidly giving way to unadulterated bliss.

"That's the ticket." Pike smiled. "Now she's happy."

"Hm." Ash looked around at the two horses. "You ride any of them?"

"I used to ride her." Pike nodded in the direction of the little roan. "She was my pony but she belongs to Eleanor now. Now I ride her." He pointed at Casta.

"What about him?" Ash asked.

His fingers slowed in their action as his eyes sought Inigo. Blue promptly nudged him, a gentle reminder of the job at hand. Ash laughed and looked back down at her.

"Demanding little thing, aren't ya?"

"He still needs breaking. He's young," Pike answered the question.

"I always thought horses were a girl thing," Ash said quietly. "Stupid really. I mean, thinking that. I mean, look at you. Cowboys and Indians, you know. Men, horses. Goes together, doesn't it? I never thought about it until I saw you on the bridge that day. The first time, you know." He ran a finger along the edge of Blue's left ear. "These are nice. Can I ask you a question?"

"Uh-huh."

"No offence but that's not your real grandfather, right? You're like adopted or something, right?"

Pike could feel his core tighten. Here it was again, the old irony that of all the kids passing through Hawthorne Cottage, he, the one who truly belonged, looked so utterly different.

"No, that's my real grandfather alright."

"But you look..." Ash's voice trailed off.

"What?"

Pike could hear the aggression in his own voice clearly but couldn't rein it in. Blue lifted her head and shot him an annoyed glance. The little mare hated discord.

"Well, not really like you're from around these parts, you know," Ash finished his sentence.

Pike squared his shoulders.

"I'm as British as anybody on this stupid island alright? Born and bred."

The pony gave a couple of short snorts before raising her head to gently blow some air into Ash's face then moved off to join Casta and Inigo.

"Keep your hair on, Chief." Ash turned his full attention on Pike. "I'm no racist or some shit like that. You can't afford to be racist where I come from. Well, actually, you can. If you're black."

"You keep calling me Chief," Pike stated soberly, staring at the other's quicksilver irises. "To a Native North American that's incredibly racist."

Ash's face broke into a broad, mocking smile as he stepped up to him.

"Well, I'm fucking lucky you're British then, aren't I? – I didn't know that," he added more seriously then grinned again. "Don't meet that many of them over here." He leant into Pike's face a little. "In *Britain*."

The sparkle in his eyes was too infectious for Pike to remain artificially offended for any length of time and he found himself grinning back at the other.

"So, what's the story then?" Ash kept digging, retreating a little. "You're at least half cast, right? I mean your middle name must be Crazy Horse or some shit like that, right?"

Pike sighed.

"Your terminology is getting worse. And no, I'm not. And no, it isn't."

Ash's forehead pleated itself into a deep, disbelieving frown. Pike rolled his eyes before he continued.

"I'm one sixteenth Sioux, if you must know. For the rest you tick 'British white' on the ethnic origin question, okay? Happy?"

"No way, mate," Ash stated categorically. "I draw people. Badly. But I draw them. I draw what I see and I know what I saw."

"Do you know what a throwback is?"

Ash shook his head.

"It's what it's called in horse breeding when a different breed mixed in generations ago suddenly shows in a foal. Like, for example, when a sturdy mountain pony gives birth to a fine limbed, dished nosed foal that raises its tail when galloping along and basically looks just like its Arabian great-great-great-great-grandsire. And that's what I am."

"What? You lost me, mate. You're an Arab now?"

Ash looked at him with a dead pan expression but before Pike could answer, the other grinned again and air punched his arm.

"Ha, gotya. Just yanking your chain, mate. I got no idea what you're talking about with the horse breeds but I get it. Can I ask you another question?"

"If you must."

"What does it mean, when a horse stamps its feet all the time? Yours don't do that."

That's when Pike twigged. He cocked his head and laughed quietly.

"You've found yourself a friend in a field somewhere, haven't you?"

Ash looked at his feet and nodded. It was a little boy's mannerism in a hard man's guise and for a moment Pike could see the child Ash had been. Before scars and sinew.

"Hm. You want to be careful with that," Pike said thoughtfully. "Horse owners are a funny lot. They usually don't like sharing their horse's affection."

"I don't think they get much affection from anyone else," Ash mumbled, still staring at his feet.

"Is it a feathered horse?" Pike asked. He got a blank look back. "Does it have really long hair on the legs?"

"Yes!" Ash exclaimed in amazement.

"Could be anything. Feather mites. Mud fever. Eczema. Or all of the above. Probably wants clipping, treating and growing from scratch. Nothing you can do about it. None of your business. Owner's job."

Ash who had started staring at the ground again kicked the mud despondently then raised his head sharply to look at Pike again.

"Let's go see to this gate of yours."

At first they couldn't find the gate from the paddock side at all.

With nature's typical stoicism the hedgerow had closed the gap up convincingly in the three years since Karen had shut it to the world. In the end, Pike took Ash around to stand in front of it by the road then wandered along the hedgerow within the paddocks, shears in hand, until he heard the other's voice on the other side.

"Got it!" he shouted back and clipped the first branch. As it fell to the ground, a shiver of excitement danced along his spine.

Ash returned to his side a few minutes later and under the watchful eyes of the horses, they worked silently once more — cutting and clipping and digging up roots until their fingers bled.

Literally.

"Fuck!" Pike exclaimed as yet another thorn embedded itself in his flesh.

"Wear the gloves," Ash grunted at him while trying to pull a particularly tenacious set of roots out of the ground.

"I can't stand the things," Pike replied, extracting the intruder from the back of his hand with pinched fingernails. "I was disqualified from a dressage competition once because I forgot to wear the stupid gloves. Rode a perfect ten, too."

The root gave way and Ash stumbled backwards a couple of paces. When he'd caught himself and flung it on the heap of terminated shrubbery behind them he turned to Pike, laughing.

"Dressage? Isn't that —" He made a few dainty little dance steps. "Tiddly tiddly on horses? You?" He laughed harder. "That's priceless."

Pike felt around for some anger but couldn't find it. He'd heard it all before. So many times. It was old. It was boring. He didn't even look at the other when he picked up the shears again to attack the next section of hedge.

Ash stopped laughing and his tone took on an earnest note.

"Hey, do you reckon, I could watch you some time?"

Pike smiled to himself as he answered, "Sure."

"Tomorrow?"

"Tomorrow," Pike agreed absent-mindedly, distracted by his phone vibrating in his pocket. He took it out, examined the unknown number and decided to pick up.

"Hello?"

"Peter?"

Robert Greaves sounded short already. Pike hadn't really expected a call back from him when he'd left a message with a stable hand at The Black Horse that morning. He'd been fully prepared to have to hound Greaves down until the opportune moment arose. The sudden confrontation threw him and he took a moment to answer.

"Yeah?"

"You called the yard," Rob stated impatiently.

"Yes, I— "

"Keep it short. I'm about to go into a board meeting. Is it urgent?"

"No. Yes. I wanted to come and talk to you."

"Horses?"

"Yes."

"It can bloody well wait then. I— "

Pike cut through the sentence, frustration tightening his throat.

"No it can't, really. It's about Strawberry. We'd like to buy him off you. I have— "

"Like I said," Rob interrupted, "it can wait. I have real business to see to. I'm in London all week. Two o'clock next Friday. Come to the yard."

The line went dead, leaving Pike shaking with fury.

It was odd to think how quickly Rob could drag out of him what only a moment ago he'd looked for to no avail. Ash stepped up and gently took the shears away from him.

"Here, I think I'll have those for now, mate. Who on earth was that?"

"Ex-almost-uncle," Pike pushed out through gritted teeth.

He took a deep breath and shut his eyes, trying to soothe the fire behind them.

"You ever feel like you're a pawn on someone else's chess board and try as you might you can't get out of their game?" he asked into the darkness.

"Not anymore," Ash answered. "Used to though."

Pike opened his eyes in time to see a sarcastic grin spread across the other's face.

"But then I made an illegal move and jumped right off the board. Changes the view. – But *you*," Ash added in a low voice, turning away and starting to snip at the hedge, "You're not a pawn anyway. You're a knight."

It was getting dark by the time they finished.

Neither Aaron nor Pike could remember the combination for the padlock on the gate, so Aaron brought out the bolt cutters. Sarah, too, had come out to watch and they looked on solemnly as Pike snapped the chain. When the deed was done, they tried the stiff hinges, opening the gate wide to look out onto the road.

Standing between the posts, they watched the evening traffic go by for a while.

Finally Aaron inhaled deeply, a contented smile playing at the corners of his mouth.

"Open it and they'll come," he stated ominously. "We had better triple up on that hay order."

Chapter 10

It was a glorious day — crisp, clear and peaceful with no distractions.

There had been some frost overnight which had sucked most of the moisture into the earth, making the ground in the schooling paddock just the right side of hard for Casta's liking and to all intents and purposes the mare should have been in her element with the routine Pike had picked. But despite all this she was struggling today. Normally a horse with great natural cadence she'd lost her rhythm twice already in the first few minutes after warm up.

Pike frowned and briefly shut his eyes during the trot.

Pelvis, he thought, *she's still tight over the croup. You didn't give her enough time. You're impatient because he's watching and you want him to have something to see.*

He slowed the horse back to a walk and let her chew the reins out of his hands to start from scratch.

He shot Ash, who was leaning against the outside of the fence, an apologetic glance.

"Sorry, this is probably quite boring for you but she needs more warm up. She's tight in the rump."

Ash grinned.

"That'll be the arse end, right? Whatever you say. I haven't got a clue what I'm looking at anyway. But you look great, mate."

After that Pike let the world blur away to concentrate on the horse beneath him — weaving and bending and making her step under, followed by reams of lateral work in walk and trot, stretching and collecting over and over, until at long last he could feel the mare's suppleness return. By the time he felt she was finally ready for some more accomplished moves she seemed tired though, too exhausted for a full test.

He took her into a collected canter and down the centre line for a series of two stride flying changes, which she performed correctly but with minimum propulsion and no panache.

Then he gave up.

Her heart just wasn't in it today, the mind link tenuous at best. Her brain had gone into far away, almost dreamy recesses he couldn't touch. Her body was obeying his orders but there was no joy, no elasticity in the dance. He leant over her neck and patted it, drawing a thumb along her crest to the withers. She came back to him then and answered with a long drawn out snort, happy to still be loved even if she wasn't on top form.

When Pike looked over to where Ash had been standing, he realised that the other was no longer alone. Neither was he watching Pike now.

While the young man was bent over a sketch book, drawing ferociously, a square shouldered girl with copper red hair was looking over onto the paper from her perch on the fence next to him, pointing and evidently commenting on bits of the art work. Pike felt a jab of jealousy then shook it off like a fly one couldn't swat at.

He rode over to them.

"Hi Wendy."

She beamed up at him.

"Hi." She scrunched up her nose. "What's up with her? She's moving like an overweight pony rather than an Andalusian schoolmistress."

Trust little Miss Jones to hit the nail on the head.

He shrugged, scratching Casta around the withers.

"I guess she's just not feeling it today."

The horse sighed deeply as if in confirmation and sank into her shoulders.

Pike jumped off and began unsaddling.

"What are you doing here, Wendy? Shouldn't you be at school?"

"Insect day," she answered defensively. "Holidays next week, so obviously teachers need an extra day to do their *planning*. Like they ever plan anything. I'm supposed to be in town with Tink buying a costume for Halloween but she gave me a twenty and told me to get lost. She's meeting her *boyfriend*. Rob's in London all week and Mum's in the Maldives or somewhere else starting with M."

Pike wasn't looking at her but could hear the rolling eyes in her voice each time she emphasized a word.

"I can leave if you don't want me here," she added sullenly.

He looked at her across Casta's back, her assumption of rejection cutting deep inside and resonating in a part of him he preferred to ignore.

"Don't be ridiculous," he heard himself spit out contemptuously and watched her flinch. "Like I'd ever not want you here."

Ash, whose pencil scratches on the pad had become more dawdling over the course of the exchange, stopped drawing and looked up at Wendy.

"Man, he's a charming git, isn't he?"

"Ha!" Wendy responded. "You ain't seen nothing yet. That's why we all love him so much. You want to meet him when he's got *real* issues."

Pike examined the comedy duo in front of him with a mixture of rekindled jealousy and suspicion.

"Ash meet Wendy, Wendy meet— "

"Yeah, we've met," they informed him in unison.

Pike frowned.

"Well, since you are here you might as well make yourself useful and take this to the tack room for me."

He'd slipped the saddle off Casta's back, had stepped around the front of the horse and was holding it out to Wendy now. The girl jumped down and reached for it over the fence with a wide smile.

He waited for her to disappear out of ear shot before he vaulted back onto Casta's bare back. He looked down at the top of Ash's head, boring his eyes into the skull below him.

"I take it you know each other."

"Before the storms she came to the beach every night to watch me. Sometimes she goes around collecting money for me," Ash stated quietly, busying himself with his sketches again. "I thought she had trouble at home."

"You're not far off. You been looking out for her?"

Ash nodded at the paper.

"Thank you, my friend," Pike sighed.

The other looked up at him sharply.

"You shouldn't call me that." His eyes darted away before he added more softly, "You don't know who I am. Or what I'm capable of."

His gaze returned to Pike and Pike held it, a violent shudder moving down his spine.

The horse underneath him picked it up, carried it and shook herself then suddenly rose in her frame to stand alert and proud, ready to respond to the smallest of aids.

Pike only vaguely registered the change in her, probing the opaque mercury of Ash's eyes. And there it was again, the terrible thing he'd seen the day before, the unspeakable shame floating in quicksilver.

Pike squinted, swallowed and set his jaw.

"Every one of us is capable of everything," he stated matter-of-factly. "The question is, would you harm *her*?"

The surprise which came back was as genuine and as serious as could be, robbing the other of any last shred of pretence.

"What? Wendy? Never! No. I don't...I...no!"

"Protect her?"

"Of course."

"With your life?"

"Absolutely."

"Kill for her?"

Ash stared at him wide-eyed for a moment, cocked his head as if about to ask something but in the end broke eye contact instead to look back at his sketch pad. He almost imperceptibly shook his head.

"You really have a sense for the melodramatic, haven't ya?" he whispered hoarsely.

Pike laughed.

"Well, two out of three is good enough for me — *my friend.*"

On that note he rode off to warm down a horse that all of a sudden seemed as alive and connected as one could possibly wish for.

Chapter 11

The night was alive with glow worms and fire dragons, blazing horses and gigantic burning flowers. The air at his back was icy from the cold sea breeze but facing Ash's display and with Wendy sitting between his drawn up knees, Pike's face and front were toasty warm with fire and wonder.

He had seen a fair few fire jugglers in his life, some of them professionals from Kimi's vast circle of circus friends, some amateurs courtesy of a childhood by the sea where the poor man's busking skills alternated between bongos, didgeridoos and setting the beach alight. But never had he seen someone do what Ash was doing.

The other was drawing pictures into the dark with his batons, telling whole stories in throws, catches, drags and twirls at eye watering speed. Beyond the hiss and swish of the flames, the October ocean washed noisily against the pebbles, waves crashing against the groynes like little claps of thunder and giving the show a deservingly magnificent soundtrack.

Pike looked away briefly at the girl's head in front of him, at the fire reflecting in the shiny red of her hair and pondered how someone could be missing from your life for as long as she had, then slip back in so naturally. As if nothing had ever happened. As if she had been sitting between his knees the entire time.

She must have felt his eyes on him because she turned just then to grin at him over her shoulder, her whole face gleaming with pride and happiness.

"He is good, isn't he?" she whispered and as if to verify her words in the same instant the crowd around them started applauding enthusiastically.

When they had first come down to the sea that evening it had been practically a private performance since Ash had insisted on setting up a mile from the main drag. He'd wanted a deserted stretch, too far out for the coppers to bother making their way over and moving him on. Pike had doubted he'd find much of an audience along here but as he looked around now he realised that he'd been wrong. Many Friday night revellers had been lured away from the fairground lights of the promenade to walk the distance and by now a fair number of them were sitting around them. They were huddled together in little clusters — icy butts on the cold autumn beach, eating chips and doughnuts and taking swigs from bottles, cheering the firefly.

In the distance, Pike could see more small groups of people approaching through the dark. Among them moved a clutch of teenagers, playfully shoving and pushing each other, their raucous laughter floating above the noise of the sea, the murmur of the crowd and the swish of the flames. At the edge of their little enclave the silhouette of a well endowed girl in a skin tight dress staggered along on unsure feet, not drunk but clearly unaccomplished at handling her choice of footwear.

He couldn't help but smile.

Despite all the carefully honed emulation of her high maintenance mother, Tinkerbelle Jones simply could not hide the fact that for most of her upbringing, and still for the larger part of her days, she walked around in jodhpur boots. There was something endearing about it, regardless of the bad blood between them, and also something heart warming in the fact that he would still recognise her shadow from so far away. Just like the girl in front him, her elder sister was woven into the fabric of his existence, a Hawthorne child not by genetics but by history. He remembered a conversation he'd had with Eleanor just days before she'd left, while she'd made him watch some of the old clips of Tink and him riding their perfect pas de deux routines on those two famous roan ponies, Blueberry and Strawberry Mouse, the little darlings of the British show circuit from half a decade ago.

They had been good together.

They had sparkled.

Then.

"You were brilliant, the four of you", Eleanor had stated, shoving a handful of popcorn in her face to unsuccessfully try and hide a wobble of jealousy in her voice. *"So why do you hate her so much now?"*

He'd shrugged.

"Because Tink knew her mum and Rob were cheating on Karen long before we found out but she didn't say a word, just carried on as if it was all hunky dory. Convincingly. So I don't trust her as far as I can throw her. She's a two-faced cow."

Eleanor had simply arched an eyebrow in response, in that sprite way of hers that meant 'we'll pick this up another time' and had said nothing more.

Now he wished she had.

Wished she'd left him some advice on how to deal with his hatred.

Eleanor was good with people, good with *him*.

And right now he could have done with some of her wisdom.

Right now, looking at 'the cow' he didn't know what to do with the knotted ball of loathing that had taken up residence somewhere around his diaphragm so long ago. Because what he saw was not the callous, calculating fiend who'd silently stood by as her mother broke up his home. What he saw, *truly*, was a two-year-old filly on the edge of a new herd, trying to fight her place in from the edge. Long-legged and awkward, bitey and kicky but really just scared of not being accepted into the fold. He sighed as he watched her exchange words with some lanky boy and break away from the group.

"Right," he heard Ash call across the crowd, taking his attention away from Tink for a moment.

"For the next part I need a volunteer," Ash continued with a grin. "She must be small, well-balanced and have hair that goes with the colour of fire."

"Uh, that's me."

Wendy who'd remained blissfully unaware of her sister's approach jumped to her feet and flashed a smile back at Pike before making her way towards the juggling area. He watched her weave through the crowd, agile and light on her feet despite her heavy frame, until she reached Ash. While Ash was explaining something to Wendy, Pike took his eyes off them again to scan the horizon for Tinkerbelle. She'd come a lot closer than he had anticipated, making a bee line for him.

She arrived in front of him and tipped her head in a curt greeting then stepped to the side to look around at her sister who was presently clambering onto Ash's shoulders.

"What on earth is she doing?" she asked loudly into the air.

Pike found it was a lot easier to hold on to the hatred once she had opened her mouth and sounded exactly like her two-timing mother.

"Having fun," Pike stated dryly. "Why are you here Tink?"

"To get my sister and go home?"

The condescending question mark along with the little snaking move of the head was plucked straight from a TV-teen-drama. It should have served perfectly in making the warm feelings that he had felt towards this caricature of a person just moments ago evaporate further but he felt too peaceful tonight to play this game.

"Look," he pleaded, "She's happy. Let her have this. You can take her in a bit."

Tink precariously lowered herself onto her haunches next to

him, wobbling on her platform shoes. He stretched his arm up to support her elbow on the way down. She frowned at it but leant on his hand all the same before shaking it off gently once she had steadied herself.

"What's it to you, P? What is it you want?" she snarled.

"Me?" Pike laughed quietly, watching Ash and Wendy on his shoulders juggle lit batons between them. "Battles and brimstone, fire and ash, fight evil and win, die a hero and return, marry the sprite princess, raise little Eleanors, bring up foals and…" He leant into her a little then. "I don't flipping know – to somehow *matter*, I guess."

Tinkerbelle shook her head and silently watched the show for a while.

He should have known it would be lost on her.

"They said your brain suffered a prolonged lack of oxygen when you tried to save Inara," Tinkerbelle finally said with the hint of a smile breaking a crack into her foundation.

And within that little fissure, for the briefest of moments, he could see her again, underneath the polyfilla and the cloud of artificial floral scent — the girl from long ago: sharp and funny in her own way and willing to hook into his brainwaves, despite not understanding the half of it. He cast his mind back to when they'd been in the show ring riding their silly little twelve hand ponies to a perfection that had stunned even international dressage judges.

It took two to tango and four to ride a decent pas de deux.

He looked at her and sighed, wondering how they'd got from there to here.

"What do *you* want?" he asked amicably.

She made a sarcastic little noise.

"Get to the Games and get a medal, then slap it around Mum's face and get out of this place. Be someone in my own right, not depend on some bloke as a meal ticket." She faced him fully then.

"Not to end up a whore like my mother."

She turned away again and put a hand flat on the pebbles to push herself off then scanned the surroundings. Her eyes lingered for a moment on her sister, basking in the applause that had erupted around them once more. She waved to her friends who were loitering at the edge of the crowd now and finally turned back to Pike, raising her voice to make herself heard above the clapping hands while looking down at him with an almost pained expression.

"Look, piece of advice, get yourself a horse, P. A real one. Not a Hawthorne pony that happens to be tall enough. You wouldn't have got anywhere with Inara anyway. You must know that. So get over it and get back on track. Remember what that judge at our last Hickstead show said? You have more talent in your little finger than the whole British squad put together. You'll find a ride easily. People would be chucking horses at you left, right and centre if you put yourself out there. Don't waste it. If you carry on like this you're just taking the piss out of the rest of us."

Her eyes followed his movement as he rose to his feet.

"You know," she added more quietly when he was upright, "I used to want to be you." Her face broke into an honest, self deprecating grin and for the briefest of moments she really was the girl he always tried so hard not to remember. "Have the house, the horses, the history, the *background*. Not be from a crappy council estate, always hanging around for handouts and freebies. And when you gave up, well, I *liked* it." She took a deep breath and broke eye contact with him, already poised to walk off. "But the truth is, I'd rather get a silver, second to your gold, than a gold knowing you're out there letting all that talent go to waste."

She nodded a goodbye as sharply as she had nodded her hello and walked off.

Chapter 12

It had been well into the small hours before he had returned to the Cottage.

It was a long trek from the beach but Ash had insisted on walking him home nevertheless, cheerfully chinking a bag full of change every so often before leaving him on the door step to disappear into the night.

The lateness of the hour and the solace of company en route had helped to neatly circumvent the nightly battle with insomnia and he had fallen asleep quickly and soundly as soon as his head had hit the pillow.

As ever, the miracle of a good night's sleep made rousing the next morning somewhat of a struggle. For the longest time Pike remained cosily trapped between dream world and reality, the outer fringes of his consciousness vaguely aware of the smell of paraffin in his hair and salt on his skin and of the fact that daylight was already shining through the window, while his inner core remained firmly asleep, clinging to Morpheus' gift.

In his dream he was riding a flaming horse through a magnificent forest full of ancient trees and mythical beasts. They were cantering three abreast; Eleanor and Blue to his left, Ash on a huge feathered draught horse to his right. He could feel an army of other riders behind them, following their lead, searching. Pike was desperately trying to hold off wakefulness proper until he found out for *what.*

He didn't want this adventure to end yet the harder he tried to stay in there, the more forcefully the day tugged at his presence. He'd already pretty much conceded defeat when his phone began vibrating on the mattress next to him.

He picked it up without opening his eyes.

"Hello?"

"You still asleep?" Eleanor asked gently.

"Uh-huh."

"Shall I ring back later?"

Her voice went straight through him, pulsating in every cell and making his body hum with pleasure. The picture in his mind changed: they'd come to a halt, Eleanor had ridden ahead to turn Blue around and ride up close to his side, facing him. He leant in and grabbed her by the waist, lifting her off the pony to lower her onto his lap.

"Uh-uh. Keep talking," he mumbled. "Tell me a wake up story."

His dream self hugged her close and ran his fingers through her hair. In the fantasy it was still long and honey brown, as it had been when he'd met her. He'd liked it like that but these days the colour changed on an almost weekly basis and it kept getting shorter and shorter. He wondered briefly which hair incarnation was on the phone right now but the thought threatened to drag him out of the forest. He wasn't ready to leave it behind just yet.

Not before he'd stolen at least one kiss.

He tilted her chin up and moved in. As their lips met, a sense of incomparable wellbeing washed over him.

He groaned softly.

The real Eleanor laughed at the other end of the line.

"I'm not sure I can come up with the kind of wake up story *you* mean, but well, a story I can do. Let's see. Once upon a time there were two little ponies that were always together because they were best friends. Then one day a big tragedy happened and one of the little ponies got sent off to live somewhere else. The remaining little pony was very sad until eventually she met a girl. She told the girl her woes and then the girl went and spoke to her mother and said 'Mum, I need some cash to go and buy my pony her friend back, I'll repay you once I've finished traipsing around Europe with the oldest boy-child on earth.' And the mother was so delighted with the fact that her daughter had recognised the oldest boy-child on earth for what he was that she responded, 'Sure, hon, no problem, just find yourself a knight in shining armour who will collect the dosh from my house and who goes and fetches you that pony from the bad man who holds it prisoner.' That's it. To be continued. I'm looking for that knight now. Have you spoken to Greaves yet?"

Pike sat bolt upright in bed.

This girl!

His girl.

The real one.

She was incredible.

"Run that by me again? Yes I have. Well, kind of. He's…I'm meeting him next Friday. "

"Fab. Basically, Mum's going to lend us the cash till I get back. — Oh no!" Eleanor exclaimed, sounding suddenly hectic. "Oh no, no, no, no, no. I've got to go. Love you, miss you, write to me, you owe me a mail, go get Strawberry. Bye-eee."

The line went dead.

Pike took the phone away from his ear and stared at the display.

The clock screamed 11.28am at him in no uncertain terms.

He scrambled out of bed.

When he scooted into the kitchen five minutes later, to grab some food and run, Aaron's slow motion calm which greeted him there felt almost physically jarring in its total contrast to his own haste.

The old man was sitting at the table, evidently in the middle of opening the post.

Aaron frowned at the letter in front of him, then wiped the corner of his right eye before looking up at his grandson with a sad smile.

"Morning. Good night? Cuppa?"

"Brilliant." Pike grinned. "Thanks but no. I had better go sort those horses out before they climb up the stable walls, poor sods."

"No need, Sarah and I have done it already. We're old, you know, not imbeciles. Like I said the other day, together that woman and I, we make a functioning human being. You can ask us to do it any time. You're young. You *should* have nights out and party until dawn. Just take it easy on the booze. You're part Irish, part English, part Sioux. That's cirrhosis of the liver pre-programmed from three sides. And beware that alcohol is a depressant. Young people don't realise because it makes you merry but in the long term it messes with the chemicals in your brain, makes you depressed. And that's the last thing *you* need."

Pike squinted at his grandfather.

Aaron's National Geographic readers' twist on the classic lecture on boozing and partying should really have made him smile but there was something odd about the old man this morning, something sad.

"I don't drink, Grandpa."

"That's good," Aaron replied, massaging his forehead with the ball of his hand. "Make us both a cup of tea, will you? And come sit for a bit."

Pike did as he was bid.

While he busied himself with the brewing operation, Aaron changed the subject.

"That stallion of yours? I have to say that's a job well done, boy. You did well to ignore us. You back him when *you* think he's ready. What a well behaved gentleman of a horse. And at such a frisky age. Kimi would be proud of you."

The tenderness with which the old man mentioned his dead wife's name caused a sharp pain to bore through Pike's heart. He kept his back to Aaron a little longer than necessary as tears shot into his eyes. He pressed his lips together and dabbed at them surreptitiously before finishing the concoction of Assam, milk, sugar and nutmeg that passed for a decent cuppa in Aaron's world.

By the time they were both sitting down opposite one another with the steaming mugs in front of them they were both wearing neutral expressions again, regardless of the palpable sense of gravitas in the air.

Eventually Aaron touched the letter in front of him and breathed out heavily.

"Another funeral to go to. I'm of that age now." He picked up his mug and took a tentative sip of his tea. "They're dropping like flies. Seems like I hardly have time to get my suit cleaned in between."

There was a long pause but Pike knew his grandfather well enough to know that he was still skirting the real issue, so he kept his mouth shut and waited patiently.

After an age the old man finally squared his shoulders.

"Makes me think about what if I'm next," he stated soberly.

Pike took a sharp breath but Aaron warded any potential interruption off with a raised hand.

"It could well happen tomorrow, boy. I could have a third stroke, in which case I pray to all that is or isn't out there that I *do not* survive. Or my heart could just stop. Heaven knows I haven't exactly looked after it with all the smoking and drinking I used to do. I don't think giving up at the twelfth hour made a blind bit of difference other than that it shut up all of you pestering meddlers. So what if I keel over tomorrow? You'll be fine, I know you will. You're not a boy anymore, you're strong and you've had more than your fair share of grief in your life already. Hell, you've had more bereavement than most people three times your age. You started on that one as a mere babe and it's the same with this as it is with all things in life. The more you practise, the more accomplished you get. And John won't ever sell this house, so you'll always have a roof over your head. I don't think Karen would come back. I think she is happier where she is now than she has ever been. But Eleanor's folks would look out for you, I'm sure. They are good people. And you're starting to make friends again. That's good. Friends are important. No man is an island. Point is I'm not really worried about you. But what about Sarah? Where is she going to go when I'm dead? I'm not sure your father would let her stay on rent free once I'm gone, unless *you* put your foot down. And she hasn't got the means."

The words had gushed out of Aaron at such a tremendous speed that it took Pike by surprise when the flow was stemmed abruptly as the old man's hands reached across the table to sandwich Pike's right between them.

His grandfather's palms were rough, calloused and cool, the squeeze strong with urgency.

"Promise me you'll put your foot down? Promise me she'll have a place here for as long as you have a say in the matter?"

Pike swallowed hard to clear the lump in his throat.

"I promise," he replied solemnly then let his mouth widen to a grin. "Should you kick the bucket, I'd need her here at any rate. I'm not cleaning out those stinking chickens."

Aaron let go of his hand and sighed audibly with relief.

"Good."

In the same moment, the door bell chimed. It was followed immediately by an impatient knock on the door. They frowned at each other shaking their heads. Neither was expecting anyone.

Pike got up and made his way out of the kitchen, stopping briefly in the doorframe to turn back and smirk at his grandfather.

"Alternatively you could just marry her, you know. Make her an official part of the family." He watched Aaron's eyes grow wide with astonishment before he allowed himself to continue with a chuckle. "But these days it's customary to kiss the bride *first.*"

Then he left to see who was outside.

Ash was frantically pacing up and down by the steps that led up to the front door. He seemed entirely out of sorts, the pallor of his skin honouring his name.

"Whoa — you alright, mate?" Pike asked as he descended towards the other.

Ash stopped mid-motion and stared at him. He was still wearing the same clothes he'd worn the night before and looked like he'd slept in them, though not much. He clearly hadn't had a wash yet either. His face was still blackened with soot and his whole presence exuded the smell of burned out fires and paraffin. Within an already intense morning Pike noted another strange sensation. For it was in that exact moment that he realised that for the rest of his life, *this* smell would forever be associated with the person standing in front of him, that even at ninety years old it would always mean Ash.

"No, I'm not alright," Ash responded, running a hand over the stubble on his head. "I know you said she is none of my business but she needs our help, man. Now!"

Pike was confused. He couldn't remember any part of last night's conversation where he might have stated that Wendy's troubles were of no concern to Ash.

The other had started to-ing and fro-ing again and Pike jumped the last step in time to land in front of him, grabbing onto his arms. He kept holding him in a gentle vice, just below the shoulders, half expecting the other to shake him off but Ash just stood there, looking at Pike through inflated pupils. His eyes were shiny as if he had been crying but there were no tear streaks in the dirt on his face.

"Stop," Pike said gently. "Start from the top. What's going on? Who are you talking about?"

"Missy," Ash answered. A quiver went through his bottom lip.

"Who's Missy?"

"My friend. The horse with the whatyamacallits. Don't really know what her name is but that's what I call her. Normally she comes over, soon as she hears me, but not today. She just ain't moving. I don't know. She's not okay, Pike. Really ain't. You can see her bones. I mean *really* see her bones. She's not dead, she's on her feet, but she's, like, swaying, ya know. And she doesn't seem to know I'm there. As if she's gone inside her head. I don't know how long it's been like that. I didn't go up there for a couple of days. But I went this morning. Made quite a bit of money last night, so I bought her a carrot." He shrugged defensively. "I know you're not supposed to 'feed the horses' and all that but she's my *friend*. Normally I just sit on the fence and talk to them. That's the other thing, the little pony she was with, it's gone. I thought maybe they'd taken it out for a ride but I waited three hours for someone to come back. Nothing. Come take a look at her? Please? Even if she's none of my business?"

Pike snorted decisively and let go of Ash.

"Give me a sec, I'll get my boots on."

Chapter 13

It took Pike all of ten seconds to assess the situation.

The Clydesdale had been left to die.

It was as simple as that.

Before he'd even killed the engine of his vintage 50cc Yamaha, which had struggled valiantly along the dirt path with two up, he had already clocked all the markers of desertion.

There was no padlock on the gate, no battery or fence energizer to charge the electric wire, no temporary plastic posts to section off an area of grazing for the coming winter, no wheel barrows, troughs or buckets, no rug hanging in the back of the rickety field shelter or on the skeletal giant of a horse swaying in the field for that matter. Just a small paddock covered ankle deep in manure and the lonely figure of the frail animal, her head hanging low as she balanced herself against the light wind as if it was a gale.

Pike knew this piece of land, had ridden past it on countless occasions in the past.

It was one of the many little pockets of pasture the council owned but couldn't build on for a variety of reasons, so let out to private horse owners instead. This one was around the back of some houses, adjacent to a bridleway that led out onto the Downs. Historically, the equine inhabitants changed at regular intervals. Most horse owners preferred for their charges to be kept at yards with at least some amenities and here, if Pike remembered correctly, there was not even any running water. It had to be brought in from outside.

Water.

He scanned the field for a receptacle of any description. Nothing.

The fucking bastards.

Bile rose in his throat as he switched off the engine and waited for Ash to dismount. He parked up the bike and hopped off himself, swearing loudly as he took his lid off.

Ash followed his lead and looked with disdain into the ancient crash helmet Pike had found for him.

"Man, that's big. Whose is that? My skull feels like it's been stone-washed."

"It was my grandma's. It was her bike," Pike answered absent-mindedly, already making his way towards the gate, his eyes resting firmly on the Clydesdale.

Ash jogged to keep up.

"Big-headed woman, was she? — So what do you think?"

They had reached the gate. Pike opened it without losing a single stride and stepped through.

He shrugged and turned to Ash who was hesitating.

"Are you coming or what? I can't take a look at her from over here."

It was a lie.

He could, and he had.

He already knew the horse was on its last legs. Literally. She probably didn't have long before they would give way under her. Her metaphysical presence in the world was already negligible, only the rake of a body remaining. A statue in accusation of humanity's heartlessness. Once she was down, it would be game over. She would never get up again.

When they arrived at her side it didn't need much checking for Pike to see that he'd been right about the dehydration. The big mare was taking shallow, rapid breaths only. Her coat, which would have been bright bay in better days, was dull and bristly, her skin as inelastic as a worn out rubber band. She kept her eyes half shut while he felt for her pulse on the jugular vein and counted a heart rate in the sixties, well above normal. He moved around to face her full frontal and gently lifted her kind, heavy head up to peel back the lips and press a finger onto her pale gums. After he released the pressure, the capillaries stayed white for what seemed like an eternity.

Pike remained as detached as his raging heart would allow throughout the entire process, which the mare endured without any participation on her part, good or bad. Even when he reassuringly rubbed her broad, perfectly straight blaze, ruffled her greasy forelock and let his fingers trace a little crescent shaped bay patch amidst the white there was not the slightest bit of acknowledgment on her part. It was like handling an over-sized ragdoll.

In a way, Pike was grateful. It made staying clinical so much easier.

He found that he couldn't hold her head up much longer and let it sink back to its default position, a metre above the ground.

His eyes found Ash who had been standing silently by the animal's shoulder, propping it up with his own, all the while stroking her neck. He looked back at Pike, his face one big question mark, begging for hope.

The kindest thing would be the bullet. And I mean the bullet. I'm not a fan of putting them to sleep. Takes too long. Nicer for the human, horrific for the animal.

But he didn't say it out loud. One of the many things he had learned from being with Eleanor was to occasionally keep his big gob shut.

Instead, he let his eyes flit away to search the back of the houses.

It was Saturday lunchtime. The chances of someone being in and able to help them out with a few buckets of water were not terrible. He looked back at Ash and then down at himself, briefly picturing the two of them going up to one of the front doors with the somewhat absurd request of water for their horse. Two scar-faced, broken nosed, unkempt teenage ugly boys, of differing

ethnic origin with holes in their jeans, close up one of whom —
there were no two ways about it — reeked of homelessness.

They'd need to bring the evidence.

"You could do with a bath, man," Pike said while unbuckling
his belt.

"No kidding," Ash responded acidly. "What are you doing?"

"Taking my belt off."

"I can see that. What for?"

"To try and lead her out of here."

He had freed the belt and slung it around the horse's neck.

"We're stealing her?" Ash asked in a voice trapped between
disbelief and gratitude.

Holding both ends of the leather strap in a clenched fist just
below the mare's throat Pike tugged gently.

"Can't steal what's been thrown away. — Walk on, beautiful
lady," he commanded the horse.

For the briefest of moments the animal lifted her head an inch
and breathed one long, proper breath. Then she sank back.

"Come on," Pike encouraged her. "There'll be food and water
and warmth and a bed and others of your kind. – Walk on!"

He'd tugged harder and raised his voice sufficiently to make
even the most recalcitrant donkey-pony move but the Clydesdale
had given up.

Not even a twitch went through her body.

Pike shot Ash a glance and softly shook his head. He unwound
the belt from her neck, stepped around to face her again and leant
forward to put his forehead against hers, holding her cheek bones
between his flat hands.

I'm sorry.

He let go, turned and began walking back towards the gate,
tears brimming behind his eyes. He needed Aaron. He had no
idea what the protocol was for shooting a horse that had been

abandoned.

"Wait, where are you going?" Ash's voice drew nearer as he spoke.

The other fell into step next to him.

Pike shook his head violently.

"Forget it, man. She's done. Best we can do for her is to find her a man with a gun."

"What? No!"

Like lightning Ash had moved to block his way and punched Pike's shoulder. Hard.

It stung.

"Give me that belt," Ash demanded roughly.

Pike handed it over with a sigh then swerved around him to continue towards the exit. He understood only too well. What was driving Ash was what had driven him to jump into the estuary while Inara's trailer had been sinking into the water.

And he knew the outcome for Ash would be the same.

Try and fail.

He couldn't watch.

So he waited by the gate with his back to them, images of Inara swirling in his mind. And of other horses. Dead and injured animals of all colours, breeds and sizes. Horses he'd seen shot, horses he'd seen go down in accidents at events, horses with gashing wounds and frail, old ones waiting for the man to put them out of their misery.

He would be here when Ash would give up, too, and he would sit with him until he didn't need anyone to sit with him any longer.

But he couldn't watch.

A quarter of an hour had gone by before he finally heard Ash call from behind.

"Oi, open the gate, will you?"

Pike felt her movement in his back even before he heard her hooves clip clop hollowly on the ground.

A rush went through his veins as he turned around to watch them move slowly towards him. The Clydesdale stumbled on every step she took and Ash was half leading her, half pushing her up with a hand on her shoulder — but they were in motion.

Pike swiftly opened the gate lest the big lady lose her momentum if asked to stand again. Excitement pumped through him and also awe as her body passed him by. He caught Ash's eye on the way and saw the other smile almost shyly before he returned all his concentration to keeping the horse on the move.

As Pike closed the gate after them, he saw a trail of tiny white objects appear on the ground wherever she walked. He squinted at them and finally bent down to see what they were. They were wriggling.

With every step the mare took, more maggots fell out of her feathers.

They had struck it lucky on the eighth house.

After some deserted driveways and some rustling behind curtains but no opening of doors it had been the most unlikely property where they'd finally found help.

After five minutes of announcing from within the beige-brown bungalow that she was on her way, the occupant had eventually appeared in the doorway, leaning heavily on a wheeled walker. An ancient lady with snow white hair and a face like a shrivelled apple, out of which two lively green eyes peeked into the world, had assessed Pike thoroughly before asking him his business with stern politeness. The implication, Pike had thought, was that there was a blade hidden in the rollator's frame and that she was not afraid to use it.

He had hastily explained their situation, pointing at Ash and the mare who were parked by a lamp post a couple of houses down. As soon as she had assessed the animal from afar, clearly weighing up Pike's story against the picture that presented itself, the woman's stance had changed abruptly. Within seconds she had organised him through the garden gate to unravel the hose towards the street, ordered him to empty one of the recycling boxes for use as a bucket and was shouting instructions across to Ash to bring the horse nearer.

The energy of bustling activity coming off the old woman's perfectly immobile body in the doorframe, coupled with her still powerful voice travelling along the street, had soon coaxed a fair few of the curtain twitchers out of their homes.

Presently Ash, Pike and the dying Clydesdale found themselves surrounded by a number of people watching the mare refuse to drink from the offered liquid.

Her head still hanging low, just inches above the water, she had exhausted the last of her reserves to come here and had withdrawn again.

Shivers that signalled the end of the line rippled through her body at regular intervals now.

A murmur of disappointment went through the small crowd. A couple of them quickly turned away to go back into their houses.

Pike breathed a quiet good riddance to them, while he watched Ash crouch down and hold up water in his cupped palm to the mare's mouth to no avail. Just as the old lady who'd started her approach some time ago, steadfastly refusing any help from anyone, finally shuffled up to meet them, the remaining rubberneckers also gave up. As quickly as they had appeared they vanished with a friendly and, Pike noticed with a certain sense of reassurance, slightly intimidated nod to Gladys, which is how they addressed the old woman.

Gladys frowned deeply at Ash's attempts to rouse the mare's

interest in drinking, making her face look more like something from a shrunken head collection than a dried out fruit.

She shook her head at Pike.

"Well, there goes. As they say, you can lead a horse to water but you can't make it drink. – I don't know much about animals, boys, but when people are so dehydrated they won't take on liquid anymore, you start by daubing their lips and tongue. A drip helps, too. You, Hawthorne— " she said sharply then paused dramatically to watch Pike flinch before a wicked smile made her crinkled lips disappear into her mouth entirely, "Should know that. I'm right, aren't I? You must be of the latest Hawthorne generation. It is interesting how you all look the same in some way or another. I worked under Tama Hawthorne. Greatest midwife there ever was around here. She had the touch, I tell you. People put it down to the Sioux blood but you know what her real secret was? Dedication and knowledge. She must have been what to you?"

"Great-grandmother," Pike replied politely, "but she died when I was a week old, so I don't remember her."

Pike was used to people, *horse* people, recognising him from the show circuit or simply because he was the grandchild of the famous Kimimela, a character who had been known to all and sundry around these parts, and he always took it in his stride. Yet this kind of recognition, the one tied to the other side of his family, to that dynasty of doctors, nurses and midwives, which had imprinted its presence on this small seaside town for over two-hundred years, delivering babies, saving lives and soothing deaths, always made him feel small and insignificant. Every time it happened it was like his father was watching over his shoulder saying: *'See?'*

"Shame. She was a formidable practitioner, your great-grandmother, and a great mentor. What about you? Which side do you fall on, medical or horse?" Gladys continued merrily as if she could see straight into his head before glancing at Ash and the mare and sighing deeply. "I suppose it's the latter. Pity. I remember how disappointed Tama was when that daughter of hers decided not to follow in her footsteps and ran away with the circus. But you can't suppress what's in the genes, you know. She was delighted when her grandson took up the baton though. Your father, is it?"

Pike stared at her numbly, an affirmative sound leaving his throat. The last thing he had expected at this juncture on this peculiar day was a casual lecture by a complete stranger on the conundrum of his life. In the corner of his eye he saw Ash stripping his upper body to take off the t-shirt underneath his many layers of clothing. Soaking it in water and pushing his hand into the mare's mouth, he proceeded to wet the horse's lips and tongue as Gladys had suggested. Pike couldn't shake the feeling that he should be helping somehow, that he should be doing anything but having the conversation he was having. Plucking any remaining maggots from the mare's legs and finding their putrid source immediately sprang to mind.

But Gladys hadn't finished yet.

"Good doctor, fine young physician he was. Completed his internship at our hospital," she carried on undeterred. "A little awkward with the patients perhaps but very intuitive. Shame he was lured into research. So how about your brother? Is he going to be next in the family line of doctors?"

Pike frowned. This was getting increasingly more surreal.

"I don't have a brother, I'm afraid," he responded politely.

Gladys cocked her head.

"My mistake, your cousin then?"

"I don't have a cousin either. Ash here is just a friend," he explained patiently.

"Well that's obvious," she cut him down. "He looks nothing like a Hawthorne. Well, how curious," she added. "I clearly remember Tama coming for a visit with a small boy in tow, same funny yellow eyes as you. But that boy was a toddler, not a newborn. How very odd."

She lightly shook her head.

How very odd, indeed, Pike agreed silently. His heart had quickened and he could feel a gooey mass of unidentified suspicion bore itself under his skin. But there was no time to pursue it, even if he had wanted to, because just then Ash rose to his feet clearing his throat.

He gently touched Pike's shoulder where he'd punched him earlier.

"Look," he whispered.

Pike turned his attention away from the old woman and glanced at the hopeless case.

The mare had shut her eyes and was holding the fabric of Ash's t-shirt between her teeth, slowly suckling the water up through it as if it was a straw.

Pike breath caught in his throat.

Sweat! Salt! Of course! I'm an idiot.

"Gladys?" Pike faced the old woman with new found purpose. "Is it alright if I call you Gladys? Would you happen to have some regular table salt in the house and maybe even some LoSalt and possibly some apple juice or cordial and an old blanket or duvet or something?"

The old lady beamed back at him with satisfaction, letting go of her walker for second to clap her hands together.

"Now, *that* is a Hawthorne question."

"I'm not loading that," the Black Horse groom stated categorically and spat onto the pavement. "You'll pay me for the call out but I am not loading that. Look at it. I'd need to disinfect the whole box after. Boss would go ballistic if he knew I'd let that mangy elephant onto his truck. I should have known this was a waste of time when the klutz got involved."

She indicated Wendy, who'd come along in the shiny silver horsebox they had called out from Greaves' yard, with a jerk of the head and a sneer.

The little girl was standing out of earshot with Ash, fussing over the Clydesdale, while Pike, Gladys and the groom who hadn't introduced herself or wasted any time on common courtesies were gathered by the horsebox's side.

It had taken an hour but eventually the mare had drunk most of the isotonic concoction Pike had mixed for her. She had perked up a little since but still looked more dead than alive in the old peach coloured quilt Gladys had found to wrap her in, her hip bones pushing the throw towards the sky in two triangular pyramids. Ash and Wendy were taking turns in ripping handfuls of grass from Gladys' front garden and offering them to her. Though she still wasn't eating them, Pike could see a little will to fight now in the way her lips were stirring the grass blades in the humans' hands. But he wasn't fooled. They were still on a time scale. They needed to get her wrapped up indoors on a soft bed and hopefully some warm, molasses-laced bran mash into her as soon as possible if they wanted to stand the slightest chance of saving her, or at the very least of easing her death. And he was damned if he was going to let them fail because of one heartless, jobsworth bitch. He shut his eyes for a moment to gather his strength but before he could come down on her like a ton of bricks, Gladys had already stepped in.

"First of all, young lady, spitting is disgusting behaviour. Like coughs and sneezes it spreads diseases, so I will kindly ask you to refrain. Secondly, see that green bungalow across the road? That just so happens to be the home of the editor in chief of the Evening View. I am sure it would be very bad publicity for your boss if the local paper ran a story on how one of his employees refused to transport an animal in need."

The groom shrugged.

"Yeah right, lady."

"Besides," Wendy growled having suddenly appeared at Pike's elbow, "if you don't help us, I'll tell Rob that you're the one who's had her hand in the till."

Pike did a double take sideways at the youngest Jones.

She was standing with her arms crossed in front of her chest, her feet hip-width apart, one leg shaking in anger and glowering at the groom in an uncanny impersonation of her mother.

The groom examined the little devil in front of her with undisguised dislike.

"That's a lie," she stated unsurely.

"I know," Wendy responded coolly. "But you know what one of the perks of never lying is?" The girl's face broke into a smug grin. "When you do, people believe you."

It was pitch black outside by the time Pike finally got to dress the last leg.

He shifted a bit to get out of his own shadow under the strip lights. His back was numb from crouching too long but he didn't dare rest on his knees for fear of the Clydesdale collapsing on top of him. Instead, he remained poised for getting out of the way in an instant, should Ash or Wendy call out a warning from their position at the horse's head. He was working as quickly and methodically as he could, while the large body of the animal heaved and wobbled above him. He carefully dabbed a clean muslin towel at the freshly shaven and washed fetlock in front of him. Once he had clipped them, it had become obvious that the sores on the mare's legs were a chronic condition, with many scars and patches of proud flesh telling the story of an ongoing battle. The currently active wounds had been putrid and puss-filled but thankfully not too deep and Pike had removed the remaining maggots with a certain amount of regret. He knew the little wrigglers would have helped to keep the infection at bay, feeding on necrotic tissue while leaving live flesh well alone, and it felt somewhat traitorous to discard them so unceremoniously.

"And? How is she doing at the front?" he called out as he smeared some ointment onto the dressing pad.

"Still not eating," Wendy replied.

The girl and the other had been trying to ply the horse with bran mash all evening but the mare's reaction to the nourishing goo had been the same as it had been to the fresh grass offered earlier in the day. She would nuzzle it politely but not take it on board. She had drunk more though, which was something at least.

After Greaves' head girl had dumped the mare with Wendy by the front gate to Hawthorne Barn, and had driven off without waiting for Pike and Ash to arrive on the bike, the girl had done a sterling job in rousing Aaron's and Sarah's attention and together they had managed to manoeuvre the shaky animal into the Barn.

When the two young men had arrived, they had found all hands on deck already.

Aaron had roped off a section of the aisle between the empty loose boxes, just past the occupied stables, and had made a deep bed of straw on some rubber matting. Sarah had found an extension cable to drag the small electric heater out of the tack room and into the aisle. Together they had filled a water bucket, mixed up some food and secured Gladys' old quilt to the horse with a lunging roller. Once Pike had started seeing to the mare's legs, Aaron and Sarah had left to prepare dinner.

The three other horses had looked on as the humans had finished preparing the makeshift infirmary. Their reaction to the dying newcomer was more telling than Pike had hoped for. Both Inigo and Casta had shown merely a feeble interest in the inert Clydesdale swaying in the aisle awaiting her fate and in all the strange activity surrounding her. Only Blue seemed to have recognised the horse for what it was and hadn't taken her eyes off the giantess all afternoon, whickering softly to her at regular intervals.

Pike could hear the pony now, above the scratchy noise of the vetwrap bandage as he finished up his task. He rose stiffly to his feet, patted the bony rump of the bay underneath the quilt, glanced at Ash and Wendy and dived under the rope to go over to Blue. As soon as he reached her half door, she pushed her head over further, pressing her nose into his chest and snorting against his shirt. A warm shower of familiarity vibrated through him. He reached out to give her a scratch but to his astonishment she snaked away from his hand and kicked the door instead.

In the same moment there was a shriek behind him and he spun around in time to see the big mare buckle and go down. There was hollow thud as her body hit the straw.

Wendy's hand had flown to her mouth. Ash looked on aghast, a series of 'no-s' tumbling from his lips in a desperate plea but the horse was already down, flopped flat onto her side.

Pike shut his eyes.

Shit. Shit. Shit. Shit.

There was a hoof's impact on Blue's stable door for every *'shit'* in his head, like an accompanying drum beat. The noise roused Inigo and Casta who immediately started circling their boxes, the stallion trumpeting out a single alarm whinny.

Pike opened his eyes again in time for the little roan to snort at him impatiently. There was annoyance in her tone and also urgency.

He watched his hand find the bar on her door to pull it back. He stepped aside and Blue pushed the door open to step out, walking straight towards the rope. She pawed the ground while she waited for Pike to catch up and let her through. He did as he was bid and observed the pony pick her way around to stand by the horse's head. On the opposite side of the temporary enclosure, Ash respectfully shuffled back, his eyes still large with shock. Wendy's hand came away from her mouth and her arm sank slowly to her side.

They watched Blue's nose go down and her muzzle meet the big mare's nostrils. The pony whickered again almost inaudibly, breathing heavily into the horse's airways. The bay opened her eyes fully for a moment, lifted her head off the straw a little and responded ever so softly before surrendering completely to exhaustion, closing her eyes.

Within seconds, her breathing had become less shallow and more rhythmical.

She was asleep, Blue watching over her.

Pike felt a burden lift off his shoulders.

The big lady would be alright.

Dead or alive.

Chapter 14

"So," Aaron said, ladling thick broth into bowls and passing them out to the three young people sitting next to one another on the long side of the kitchen bench. "I suppose you will be wanting to sleep in the barn tonight then."

Ash, who they'd had to forcibly remove from the stable block and physically push into the house under threats that he was not welcome by the Clydesdale's side any longer if he didn't take a shower *pronto*, nodded emphatically as he reached out for his meal. Properly clean for the first time since Pike had met him and in a fresh set of clothes donated by the collected Hawthorne wardrobes he looked much younger than before and Aaron withheld the food from him for a second, brows furrowed.

"How old *are* you, boy?"

Pike looked sideways at Ash's profile having just wondered the same. He could see a twitch above the other's lip and realised he was considering a lie.

"Truth," Pike hissed.

Ash shut his eyes.

"Seventeen."

When he opened them again Aaron handed him the bowl.

"Bad age for a lad to be sleeping rough."

The surprise on Ash's face was a sight to behold and Aaron chuckled quietly, while measuring out a portion of food for his grandson.

"There's nothing happens in those woods I don't know about. How long have you been on the street?"

"It'll be my second winter."

Aaron sat down.

"You eat now and tomorrow we'll go and get your things."

Ash looked around himself incredulously.

"You lot aren't real, right? You're out of some Dickens novel, ain't ya?"

Wendy who'd been stuffing her face silently during the exchange held up her now empty bowl.

"Wow. *And* he reads. More food? Glorious food?"

Aaron served her a second helping, while Pike swallowed the first spoonful of his dinner.

"Welcome to the family," he stated dryly. "Speaking of which-" His eyes wandered to the girl. "Don't you need to go home some time?"

Wendy's shoulders slumped and she let her spoon sink into her bowl.

"Can't I stay here, too?" she asked the lentils, leeks and bacon.

Pike looked at his grandpa questioningly.

Could she?

Aaron raised his eyebrows and took a deep breath.

"I don't see why not. If your mum says it's alright, then..."

"She's in the Maldives," Wendy informed him hopefully.

"Greaves in that case," Aaron replied.

"In London all week," Pike countered.

"So," Aaron said, frowning deeply, "who's responsible for you in the meantime, young lady?"

Wendy shrugged.

"Dunno. Tink?"

"Well, you had better ring your sister then."

When they got back to the barn, laden with roll mats and sleeping bags to fashion a dormitory out of the tack room, Sarah, who'd been keeping watch during their meal, had little news. Both the big mare and the little roan remained where they had left them, Blue having dozed off on her legs in the meantime.

Pike dumped his baggage, went to crouch down by the

Clydesdale's head and checked her pulse. The beat in the jugular was slow and regular, and so was her breathing. He gently peeled back her lip. The colour of her gums was a little less pale than previously.

Still, he wouldn't allow himself even a glimmer of hope.

Too early.

He watched Blue across from him, drowsing but with one alert eye on the stricken horse. He felt Aaron's big hand on his shoulder and give it a light squeeze. Looking around at his grandfather he saw Ash standing behind the old man, worry making him appear instantly older and meaner again. Pike shrugged at them and got a duet of curt nods back. Aaron squeezed his shoulder again and put his other hand on Ash's arm.

"Don't give up hope, boys. She might well get through this. She is strong. She used to be a police horse before old Bob bought her for his re-enactments. Nerves of steel that one. But," he paused thoughtfully, "he passed a couple of years ago. She must be well into her late teens now. That's old for one of her kind. So don't give up hope but don't kid yourselves that she's definitely going to make it either. I'd sit on the fence on this one."

Pike rose to his feet.

"You know her?"

"Used to shoe her. Don't find many of them around here. Heaven knows how she's ended up in this state. She was well loved at one point."

Ash slipped away from Aaron's touch and knelt down to stroke the sleeping horse's mane.

"She is well loved *now*," he stated softly. "You know her name?"

Aaron nodded.

"Hunter's Moon."

It was well after midnight when Wendy and Ash finally fell asleep.

The girl had curled up on the tattered old tack room sofa and was snoring softly. Pike sat in the dark with his back against the piece of furniture, just by her face. After a few minutes the noise she was making grew louder and he reached over to gently pinch her nose. She shifted and the snores subsided.

Ash lay to her feet on the floor, folded neatly into a sleeping bag. As Pike watched him for a while in the diffused light of the full moon which shone through the Perspex window, he couldn't help but notice that even asleep Ash had a certain tautness about him, a coiled spring poise that suggested he could be up on his feet in a split second. It seemed a painful state of being, a type of sleep without rest that appeared worse yet than Pike's insomnia.

He took his eyes off the stray and looked at the vague shape of the moon through the scratched pane. It had been an eternity since he'd been with so many people for such a prolonged stretch of time. An eternity since he felt whatever he did really *mattered*.

Before Eleanor, there had been months of pure unadulterated solitude, interrupted only by pointless weekly group therapy sessions, not quite so pointless one-to-ones with a counsellor who seemed more depressed than he was, and the occasional brief and uncheerful visit from his parents. Then there had been just him and her, the two of them together paying visits in other people's lives but not *this*. This *thing* that was so familiar yet so alien after such a long absence.

The constant companionship, the living in a mixed herd of humans and animals, all that in the hay day of Hawthorne Barn had been their way of life, all that had got lost but now seemed to be tentatively budding around him again — it suddenly felt almost threatening.

It made him want to get away from it, away from the sleeping bodies, to be in the company of his own thoughts for a while, and he shuffled to his feet.

Ash's eyes briefly flickered open, two silver disks vacantly reflecting the moonlight back at Pike before the part of the other that was keeping watch informed the sleeping entity within that they were still safe and the eyelids closed again.

Pike left the room and crossed the stable block. In the faint glow of the emergency night light he stepped gingerly around the unchanged silhouettes of Blue and Hunter's Moon whose dinner plate sized hooves seemed to be treading water in her dream. A good sign. He briefly knelt by the big mare's side to check her pulse once again and Blue woke from her slumber, watching him intently.

When he left them to open the door the little roan whickered after him and Inigo, roused by the sudden movement in the aisle, stuck his head over the half door to echo her sentiment.

Smiling, Pike headed into the night.

At first he hadn't known where to turn, where to stop and think, but now, feeling the bark of the dead chestnut dig through the layers of his clothing, he knew there had never been another destination. He lay with his arms crossed behind his head on the trunk of the tree, his feet pointing at the paddocks and his head at the cottage, and stared at the sky above him. The round moon was high up and tiny now, barely giving any illumination. If he tilted his head to the right he could vaguely make out the road. In the other direction the twitten lay as a long black tunnel before him.

He turned his face up at the stars again and unharnessed his thoughts.

They immediately wandered back to the feeling that had made him flee out here. The fear of being part of a whole again, part of a tribe of two-legged and four-legged members alike.

He'd written about it for a homework assignment once, just before he'd left primary school. The topic had been life in the middle ages and while others had picked kings and queens and knights and castles to write about, he had chosen the life of a peasant, had described in loving detail how they had lived in the same huts with their animals, how he felt connected to these ancestors by his own family's way of life.

He'd never lived it down.

The flak he'd got from the other boys in his class after the teacher had encouraged him to read it out aloud had been second to none. At some point around then he'd decided to call himself something else, had hoped by reinventing Paytah Hawthorne as Peter Pike he could make a fresh start at the next school.

It hadn't occurred to him that in a town where there were only four secondary schools to choose from, you could change your name all you liked but there was no escaping from who you were. In the end he'd only succeeded in pissing off his father who, born John Pike, as a young doctor had adopted Kimimela's maiden name to be closer to the famous line of medical practitioners he emulated.

Pike changing his name had been like flipping the finger at the man who had donated his sperm to his creation. It had felt good. Now the whole thing just seemed silly.

He sighed deeply at the constellations above him.

He didn't really want to contemplate his parents.

Or names.

Or who he was.

He pleaded with his brain for thoughts of Eleanor but it had other ideas.

It dragged him past the shadow of his father back to the barn, past the pendulum that swung over Hunter's Moon's head to Casta's listlessness the previous day and the question of Inigo's education, into the tack room to the sleeping Ash and Wendy, from Wendy to Straw and over to The Black Horse, from there to the heartless bitch who had driven Hunter's Moon over and finally to old Gladys and right back where he'd started, back to his family.

He replayed the conversation with Gladys in his head.

Tama and the boy with eyes like his own.

Tama, the great-grandmother he knew so little about.

The woman who had named him before she'd died and who he only knew from photographs, looking dark-skinned, tall and square-shouldered with jet-black hair in a tight bun.

A spectre in the family lore, dominating and influential but hardly ever mentioned. Someone he knew his father had loved and adored the way he himself had loved and adored Kimi. An intimidating rebel who had revolutionised after birth childcare and was mentioned in the local history books as the town's principal medic during war time. A fiercely independent human who had worn the Hawthorne mantle of righteousness to defy convention and law in bringing up his grandmother out of wedlock, the child of an unnamed father, at a time in history when such things were simply not heard of. All of that was Tama. Thinking about her like that, he felt a deep connection and wished he'd known her.

But what of the boy?

Who was *he*?

Pike had always suspected that there were things they weren't telling him, things that warranted hushed voices and abruptly ended conversations. It just hadn't bothered him until now. People always had secrets of some description or another. Reasons to whisper. But he had trusted his grandparents and aunt, had always figured they'd tell him what he needed to know in due course.

Now, for the first time in his life, he wasn't so sure anymore.

Another boy with amber eyes.

A myriad of possibilities presented themselves all at once and he felt swamped, breathless under the weight of their magnitude.

A car drove by on the road side, music blaring from within, the beam from its headlights zooming past at the edge of his vision. It jolted him out of his trance and he came up for air, frozen and stiff.

He swung himself upright into a sitting position.

Don't guess, he heard his father's voice inside himself, *investigate.*

He would, he decided, while slamming shut the Pandora's box in his mind.

As soon as the Clydesdale was healed or finished, as soon as he'd found out what was eating Casta, as soon as he'd decided on the next step in Inigo's education and as soon as he had brought Straw home he would go and find out. But for now his little herd had more pressing problems.

He took a deep breath and jumped off the trunk to head back to where he mattered.

When he returned to the barn he found Ash sitting by the wall next to the tack room door, arms folded across his drawn up knees and head resting on top, watching the horse and the pony with one eye and the door with the other. Pike walked over to him and sat down.

"Trouble sleeping?"

"Uh-huh. Where have you been?"

"Outside."

"It's in case she dies, isn't t?"

"Come again?"

"I've been wondering all afternoon why your grandpa made her a bed there, not put her in an actual stable. It's in case she dies, isn't it?"

"Yeah," Pike dragged the word out not really wanting to say the rest but knowing he'd have to give an explanation. "We've had one die in the box before. You can't get them out...without cutting them up."

"Uh-huh. I figured it was something like that."

Ash was obviously trying his best to sound unsentimental but Pike could hear the tremor underneath. He nudged the other.

"Hey, I'm hopeful."

"Uh-huh," Ash responded. "Me too. She had some more water while you were gone."

"What?"

Pike tried to keep the excitement from his voice.

Ash turned to look at him, a big smile lighting up his features.

"Yep. Rolled onto her front, drank half a bucket and flopped right back. I've refilled it already."

"That's brilliant news."

"I know," Ash turned away again and sighed. "I can't stay here, you know," he added quietly. "I'll stick around until she's on her feet again but then I'll have to go. I didn't want to say anything in front of the old man 'cause I didn't wanna piss all over his kindness. But I can't stay. I'll send you some money for her though, as and when I have it. If that's okay."

The anger ball hit Pike so unexpectedly he almost felt winded from the impact.

"No. Not remotely okay. See that there? That's your horse now. She didn't come out of that paddock for *me*, she did it for *you*. And you're not rescuing her from being dumped just to dump her again. And *if* she makes it, she won't need someone who sends money, she'll need someone who loves her. Hands on love. Grooming and feeding and caring. So you will bloody well stay

- 129 -

and look after her. Or you take her with you. I don't care."

"Whoa, chill." Ash put a hand on Pike's back and to Pike's surprise actual calm flowed into his being. It stopped him short.

"I don't know whether you've noticed," Ash carried on wryly, "But she ain't exactly the size you keep on a string and sit in the supermarket doorway with. Where the fuck do you think I could take her?"

"My point exactly. Look, whatever it is you are running from, I really couldn't care less. *She* couldn't care less. She needs you. You're here, you obviously haven't got anywhere better to be, so you effin' well stay here, alright? Or is there an actual reason why you can't? Are the police after you or something?"

Ash retracted his touch, hugged his knees and shook his head. "Mob?"

Ash snorted dismissively.

"I got it. You're being chased by some psycho killer, right? Actually, don't answer that, let me consolidate all my questions into one. If you stayed here, would that pose any danger to yourself, the people and animals around you, the land or property?"

Pike was trying so hard to put an upbeat, teasing spin on the whole thing, that Ash's next response seemed jarringly sincere.

"No," the other answered, seeking eye contact for the first time. "You're all perfectly safe."

"Fine, glad we established that. Then give me one valid reason not to stay. Just one."

Ash let it hang for a long while before he answered.

"I just don't deserve it, okay?" he finally whispered, staring ahead. "Let's leave it at that."

A derisive laugh escaped Pike then.

"Ha! Nobody *deserves* a life shovelling shit and working your arse off for absolutely nowt in return other than a horse farting in your face when you pick out its hooves and occasionally stepping on your foot with its 500 to 800 kilos of live weight but you know what, you don't get a *choice*, mate. Your die has been cast. You'd better accept it. — Seriously, I hate to steal your thunder, man, but you're not the first stray we've had by a long shot. My grandparents and my aunt used to foster. Hardcore cases, too. Kids who'd been through hell and back and some of them had done some not very nice things, you know. Real little shits. But the rule has always been you come here, your slate's wiped clean. You just have to keep it clean. So whatever it is you've done or your family or your mates have done that makes you think you don't deserve a second chance: forget it. It's bull. I've got a foster sister, Charly, lives up in Scotland with my aunt now. Her father is serving a whole life term for armed robbery, rape and murder. All committed in one day. I'll spare you the details. And she was well on the same route, too. Had put a kid in hospital just before she got here. At ten! And I don't mean just a few cracked ribs. We were her last chance saloon. And jeez, did she make it difficult for herself but you know what?"

"What?" Ash was hanging on his every word now and it felt almost uncomfortable.

"Other than Eleanor, she's my best friend. I'd trust her with my life."

There was a long, heavy pause before Ash spoke next.

"This Eleanor? She's a figment of your imagination, right?"

It made Pike laugh out so loud that it woke Blue up. The little pony threw up her head in annoyance, snorting loudly.

"Sorry girl," Pike called across, then got up and turned to stand in front of the other looking down at him. "Nope, she is real alright. And if you stick around long enough you might just get to meet her. Come on." He extended his hand. "Time for bed."

Chapter 15

Ash's sleeping bag was neatly rolled up and back in its case, the roll mat equally tidied and strapped up next to it.

He's scarpered, Pike thought with a sinking feeling, while his eyes adjusted to being awake. But then he heard the other's hoarse laughter from the stable block followed by Wendy's voice giving unmistakable grooming instruction.

"Round and round with the curry comb but always in the direction of the coat with the dandy and the soft brush. Here, no, harder than that, give it some welly. Yeah that's it, now careful with the metal over her ribs, use the plastic one instead, yeah, you got it, keep going."

A surge of energy went through him and he was up on his feet and standing in the doorway before his brain had fully left dream country to catch up with reality, so for the first minute he didn't take the picture in front of him all that seriously.

The Clydesdale was on her feet, her nose buried deep in a bucket of food, which she was polishing off with slobbering delight. The big doors to the barn had been opened wide to let in the glorious autumn sunshine that was gold-dusting the outside world, where Blue, Inigo and Casta were already grazing.

Ash was brushing Hunter's matted coat with single-minded devotion while Wendy was in the process of picking out a hind hoof. Wendy let it down gently, ran a sleeve across her forehead and went to pick it up again. The horse seemed surprisingly steady even on three feet this morning but it was clear that she didn't have the strength or will to keep her leg up for the girl attacking the mud under her soles and Wendy was struggling with the weight she was holding. It was this small detail that convinced Pike he wasn't dreaming and his heart did a little dance of joy in his chest before he flung an exultant greeting at them.

"Morning. Let me get my boots and I'll give you a hand."

Five minutes later, he had taken Wendy's place and, having excavated what appeared to be half a ton of mud, had got down to the actual hoof material. The big mare's feet were in an awful state, overgrown, scraggly, rotten and black with a familiar pungent stench emanating from them.

"Lovely," Pike stated sarcastically. "Nothing like the sweet odour of thrush before breakfast...I need my grandpa's tools. Actually—" He contemplated the huge object in his hands. "I need *him*. I've never trimmed anything like this before. The biggest I've done are Casta's. And they are tiny in comparison. These are massive, aren't they?"

He looked up into Wendy's eyes.

The girl grinned at him, nodding enthusiastically.

Ash, who had stopped grooming and stepped around to look at Pike's handiwork, scrunched up his nose.

"It stinks. That's not normal, right?"

Pike shook his head without looking up and scratched at the decaying keratin.

"No, that's a fungal infection. Comes from not having her feet picked out regularly. She'll be fine after a pedicure and a few days' iodine treatment."

"Did someone call a farrier?"

Aaron had appeared by Ash's side, wearing his blacksmith's apron and was smiling down at his startled grandson.

"Good morning, sleepyhead, we're one step ahead of you. Now if someone would be so kind as to help me fetch my tools and my foot stand, we shall begin."

It took Aaron almost two hours until he'd reached the last foot, with many breaks and occasional help from his grandson whenever the stroke side of his body wouldn't quite obey.

But underneath it all the old man had lost none of his skill.

Pike had always loved watching his grandfather work. There was a rhythm and precision to the blacksmith's trade that strummed a chord deep in his soul every time and seeing Aaron on the tools after so many years made him feel wobbly and small inside in the best possible way. Nostalgia mixed with relief over the great mare's miraculous recovery brought tears to his eyes. He wiped them away with the ball of his hand and suddenly found Ash's arm around his shoulder, squeezing him just that little too roughly for it to be misconstrued as a tender gesture.

"Thank you, man — again," the other mumbled.

Pike slung his arm around Ash's waist and squished him right back. For once, the energy and temperature between them seemed equal and it felt good.

They stood like that until Aaron let the last hoof down. The old man straightened up slowly and painfully, then winked at the two young men. Exhaustion written all over his face and sweat running down his brow, he held a rasp out to his grandson.

"Here, I'm cream crackered. You finish her up. You will need to do her from now on at any rate. My body just isn't up to it any more. Still," he added, mopping his forehead before his face creased in a wide smile, "it's good to know one hasn't completely lost the knack. — I wonder where the womenfolk have got to."

While they had stayed behind, Sarah and Wendy had gone on a reconnaissance mission to find a tack shop that sold rugs big enough for the giantess. The mare, who during the whole fuss around her feet had stood good as gold, munching her way through hay net after hay net, kept stoically eating away while Pike finished up the last hoof then changed the dressings on her legs.

Finally, the girl and the woman returned, carrying two large plastic bags and a rucksack. They set them down by the wall before Sarah went to stand by the horse's head and addressed the mare with a sincerely apologetic undertone, stroking her blaze.

"Now, I'm sorry about the colour scheme, old girl, but your size is not exactly easy to get hold of. Wendy, darling," she looked across to the girl still standing by the shopping. "Take it away."

Wendy unpacked a heavyweight turnout rug in neon pink.

"Oh man." Ash sighed. "I think I preferred the peach."

"I'm glad you said that," Sarah stated dryly. "Wendy, the pyjamas, if you please."

The girl got out a stable rug.

"They call it mauve."

"That's vile," Pike stated the obvious.

Ash made a retching sound but then shrugged.

"Who cares as long as it keeps her warm? How much do I owe you?"

"One-eighty including the wormer," Sarah answered.

"Whoa," Ash responded. "That's a lot of fireworks. Horse's wardrobes don't come cheap, do they? What's in the rucksack?"

"My things," Wendy answered with a shy side glance at Pike. "Tink said I could stay here for the rest of the week, till Rob gets back, if it's okay with you...so I asked Sarah to stop at the house." She turned to face Pike squarely. "Is it?"

Pike frowned.

"Is it what?

"Okay?"

After a moment of sheer confusion it dawned on him what she was asking. He went over to stand in front of her and took her plump, rough little hands into his own then shook them up and down a couple of times.

"Now listen to me good, Wendy Matilda Jones." He had to swallow hard before he could get out the next part. "This is your home. First, last and always. You might need everybody else's permission to be here but you'll never *ever* need mine. You got that?"

The girl snivelled, pressed her lips together hard and nodded.

Pike suppressed the urge to hug her, fearing she'd dissolve if he did.

"So what happens next?" Ash asked into the heavy silence that ensued.

"We dress her up and turn her out," Pike said decisively, half turning towards Hunter. "She can go in a paddock with Blue and we'll take the other two out for a stroll up the path."

He looked back at Wendy.

"What do you say, fancy a ride?"

The girl's eyes, still glistening with unshed tears, turned even rounder than normal.

"On what?"

Pike shot Sarah a glance.

The woman answered with a wink and a faint smile.

"I can't. I'm not good enough," Wendy repeated for the sixth or seventh time since they had got to the middle of the schooling paddock where Pike was holding Casta for her to get on.

He rolled his eyes behind her back.

"You're plenty good enough. And she's not this mythical ride you seem to think she is. Remember what you said? Overgrown pony. You were spot on."

Wendy looked at him over her shoulder.

"I always thought she would be really skittish."

"Well, yeah, she can be." Pike sighed. "Look, just get on her. You'll see what I mean. You'll be fine. In actual fact, in many ways she's a lot like a big version of Straw. Just ride her like you would ride him."

Wendy wriggled her nose.

"Really? Or are you just saying that?"

"No, really. Go on."

"Okay." The girl took a deep breath and put a foot in the stirrup. "Here goes."

She landed gently on the Andalusian's back, leant forward to whisper a greeting in the mare's ear then ran a hand along her crest and picked up the reins. Pike let go.

"Just take her around on—" Pike started but Wendy cut him short, eyes crossed under the peek of her hat.

"A long rein. I *know,* P. I know. Go get your pony."

She pointed her chin at Inigo who was tied up by the fence and rode off, nonchalantly adjusting the mounting stirrup, which she'd made longer to hoist herself up. Pike smiled as he watched her, reins held between her teeth, one leg placed in front of the saddle, both hands fumbling with the strap's buckle yet perfectly centred on the walking horse.

Hawthorne bred, he thought, *every inch.*

He turned to his stallion and a small formation of winged creatures performed a flight exercise around his stomach. He looked at the glorious sky, sucked in a deep breath of autumn air and hummed inside. Today was a good day.

He reached Inigo just as Ash arrived back at the fence, having fetched Pike's riding hat.

"Is that it?" the other asked.

"Yup, that's the one."

Pike took it and turned it in his hands for a few moments.

"I'm confused," Ash said, while letting the stallion lick his hand. "I thought you said he doesn't get ridden yet."

"That's right. He doesn't. Yet. But, you know, my parents — I have some, believe it or not — they work in AIDS research. Terribly important people. The one and only thing they ever took time out enough to teach me? Carry a condom, just in case," he smirked at the other, glossing over the bitterness in his voice then put the hat on and fastened it. "It's sound advice. — Are you coming along?"

Ash shook his head.

"Nah, I'll stay with them." He indicated Hunter and Blue with a jerk of the head. "Might read the paper to them or something. You two have fun."

Pike untied the lead rope that bound Inigo to the fence and the stallion diverted his attention from Ash to him, sniffing the hand on the rope. Pike ruffled his forelock and the horse lightly rubbed his cheek against the young man's shoulder. It was their familiar little ritual but still, today, the feeling was different. Pike hesitated before leading Inigo towards the gate.

"Are you still gonna be here when we come back?" he asked under his breath then sought the other's eyes.

They held fast.

Ash grinned.

"Can't think of anywhere better to be."

Wendy was a perfect riding partner.

As he walked beside his eager stallion up the twitten and out onto the Downs to climb the chalk path that led up to miles and miles of open fields, she followed behind quietly. Occasionally he could hear her murmur words of encouragement to Casta or pat her horse's neck but aside from that there was no chatter, allowing him to concentrate fully on his own four-legged companion. He glanced at his horse sideways, appraising Inigo's powerful chest and the almost square shoulders that were working hard at the ascent. All the walks over the last two summers, up and down the rolling hills, had made him strong. Maturing and filling out had done the rest and if Pike looked properly now, he didn't see a youngster anymore. If he looked even harder he didn't see a carbon copy of Inara any longer either. He saw a stallion with beautifully defined muscles and the character of a gentle leader, with enthusiasm for life and nerves of steel but not with the elegant paces that had made Inara so special. Pike watched the eagerly pricked ears, twitching to this noise and that but ultimately pointing forward and the animal's lively eyes, firmly trained on the horizon. He ran a hand lightly along the horse's neck and smiled.

A battle pony, he thought, *made for adventure, not for the show ring.*

They'd reached the top of the path and started walking along the top where a flat stretch of usually good ground always called for a canter. He breathed to Inigo to stop and turned around to Wendy and Casta, waiting for the much slower pair to catch up. They had fallen behind by quite a distance, the Spanish lady picking each step up the path as if climbing Everest and as soon as they were on the level Wendy asked the mare for a light trot to close the gap.

The girl was beaming when they came to a halt behind Pike and Inigo. The carefree, broad smile lighting up her face effortlessly competed with the brilliance of the sunshine. She patted Casta enthusiastically.

"She is sooooooooooooo comfortable!" she whooped. "You are right, she's just like Straw. She snorted at the same bush he always snorts at and she did a little side hop when a rabbit crossed the path. But if that's all I need to worry about, I'll ride her any day."

"Hm," Pike responded, "You're going to have to get in the queue, I'm afraid. Would you like to take her for a run? Mind you, a run on her is one of the slowest things you'll ever experience at a gallop."

"Are you serious?"

Pike chuckled.

"'Fraid so. You gotta make sure you don't arrive before she does."

"Hell, yeah."

"Okay, she won't go ahead but if you keep her here, I'll walk Inigo to the three-trunk tree and you can meet us there."

"Won't she go doolally if I hold her back?"

Pike shook his head.

"No, she's too well brought up for that. She might feel a bit nervous but she won't do anything. As long as she can see us she'll be fine."

He ordered Inigo, who had started gently tugging at the lead in a bid to stick his nose down into a patch of particularly tasty looking grass, to walk on. A small disappointed grunt escaped the stallion but he followed willingly and they left the mare and the girl behind. The three-trunk tree, an ancient apple tree that presided over the edge of a cluster of wild fruit trees, waited for them a quarter of a mile ahead and once they'd reached it Pike allowed Inigo to graze. He leant heavily across the stallion's back and gave the signal to Wendy to go.

In the distance the girl pushed the mare into canter from the tense stand still they'd been waiting at. Any other horse would have been gone like a bullet from a gun but Casta, true to her natural gaits, approached at rocking horse speed. Half way, he could see Wendy standing up in the stirrups, trying to get the horse to gather momentum but the mare only marginally sped up and they arrived by the tree some considerable time later.

"Flippin' heck! I know what you mean now," Wendy exclaimed when they came to a halt. "How slow??? Yeah, she's lovely." Wendy patted the Andalusian's neck and gave her the full length of the rein so the mare could have a nibble, too. "But she ain't no Strawberry or Blue."

Pike smiled.

"Looks fantastic though."

"Yeah, well." Wendy grinned back at him. "They look good *and* can run. Give me speed over looks any day."

"I worry about you."

"Somebody's gotta," she responded quick as a flash and Pike didn't miss the jaded undertone.

While the horses' noses started grazing closer and closer together, Pike slowly slithered his midriff further up Inigo's barrel, as far as he could reach without climbing onto something, until he was on tiptoes. Once leaning over as far as possible he began pushing his weight down on the horse's back, slightly rocking up and down on the balls of his feet. He'd done this a thousand times in the last year, while grooming or when they were just standing around in the paddock but today was different and he knew the animal knew it, too. There was no visible reaction from the horse, still ripping rhythmically at the grass, but Pike could feel the stallion *wink* inside. He laughed quietly at the thought but there was no other way of describing the feeling he was receiving through his belly. He let his head loll sideways to rest his cheek on the horse's hide, relaxing his muscles for a moment.

Wendy stretched her arms over her head then narrowed her eyes at him as she let them flop back down to rest on her thighs.

"If you are doing what I think you are doing," she said slowly, "shouldn't you at least make some reins out of the lead rope?"

"Probably," Pike replied looking up at her, while spitting a hair from his lip. "I should also be in a school, fully tacked with at least one helper, certainly not standing in the open, under a tree, with you and Casta far too close for safety."

"I'm glad you know what you are doing," the girl replied sarcastically.

"Hm," he responded, "It's just not the Hawthorne way."

"I mean it, P, can the Hawthorne way include some reins, please?" Wendy emphasised the words by gathering her own reins and backing Casta up a few paces. "I'm not big enough to be scraping you off the floor all by my little lonesome."

"Spoil sport."

He grinned at her then did as he was told and fashioned a set of reins out of the lead rope, secured to the sides of Inigo's head collar.

The stallion didn't see the need to interrupt his mid-afternoon snack while Pike crouched around him and soon the young man was back in position, this time holding his brand new reins in his left hand while gently applying pressure to the horse's back again. For a moment he wondered if he could even make Inigo's fifteen hands from a standstill, without running up and vaulting on, before deep inside him he heard his grandmother chuckle mockingly.

'Of course you can.'

A quick release shower of adrenaline pushed the blood through his veins at double speed, making his heart pound in his chest and his lip twitch while giving him all the velocity he needed to get astride the grazing horse. A split second later he landed softly, keeping his body low above the withers.

As soon as his seat made contact he could feel the power.

It was like nothing he had ever experienced.

Something ancient and primeval rose in his soul, pure life force gushing in on him from within and without and saturating his nervous system until he felt like every cell in his body was about to explode. Reduced to a quivering mess, he breathed deeply to control the rush, to form the stream into something smaller, less virile, more *manageable*.

Just then the stallion brought his head up out of the grass, pushing his crest against Pike's lips.

"Whoa," he mumbled into the black and white mane, more to express his awe than to comfort the horse, who didn't seem to need any reassurance. As Pike slowly edged himself into a more upright position the stallion bent his neck around to sniff Pike's legs, first to the left, then to the right, before he looked up at the young man on top of him, let out a long, satisfied snort and finally returned to the business of mowing the Downs.

Pike couldn't help but laugh.

"Wow." Wendy called across in a low voice. "Is that it?"

"Apparently," Pike answered wryly.

"What happens next?"

"Erm…I sit here quietly for a minute or two and then I get the hell off him again? I can't possibly tell you what he *feels* like but let me assure you it has absolutely nothing to do with the picture of the contentedly munching horsey he is painting for you. This is *intense*."

The problem with Pike's plan was that while he'd responded to the girl, he'd looked at her, shifting his weight to do so and Inigo had inadvertently followed the reflex that told him to walk in the direction of that weight.

They were moving.

Pike gathered his wits, picked up his improvised reins and subtly shifted again so they would round Casta and the girl.

"Or not as the case may be." He continued grinning as they passed them by, giddy on the magnitude of the moment. "Do filter in."

They retraced their steps back to the chalk path in complete silence.

Pike sat as still as possible, entirely absorbed in the motion of Inigo's purposeful strides. His eyes remained fixed on the ocean that lined the horizon between the ears of his horse, and his thumbs kept circling the stallion's skin around the withers. All the while his heart fluttered as if wired directly into an electric current.

When they reached the top of the descent he barely managed to breathe his request for a halt yet Inigo obeyed without question.

Pike slipped off his horse hesitantly, a large part of him not wanting to leave the stallion's back ever again. He ran his hand along the animal's spine and over the croup, tears of gratitude gathering in his eyes. Suddenly Inigo's cheek made impact between his shoulder blades and nudged them over the edge as he rubbed against him. Until the tears had turned to laughter. Pike gently shoved the animal's head aside.

"Enough now," he reprimanded lovingly. "There is affection and then there is rude."

He looked over his shoulder at Wendy and Casta who had been following stealthily behind. There was the kind of admiration in the girl's eyes that in the old days he'd thrived on. Now, it just made him feel uncomfortable.

Death, it appeared, had humbled him.

"Wow," the girl finally said. "You did it."

Under the peak of her hat her nose scrunched up concernedly and she indicated the tears still hanging on his cheeks.

"You alright?"

He sniffled noisily, wiped them away with the back of his hand and then beamed at her.

"I'm alive."

"I'm alive. So *alive,*" Pike repeated euphorically for the gazillionth time before he finally realised that the line had gone quiet some time ago.

Eleanor generally didn't talk a lot unless she really had something to say but her present silence was thicker than usual and Pike could almost physically touch the sadness that seemed to be dripping through the airwaves.

"Hey," he added softly, "you still there?"

She didn't answer immediately and while he waited for her to collect her thoughts into one of her characteristically precise responses, he navigated his way across the room from the window where he'd been standing to watch the sunset over the paddocks, back to his bed. He sat down, picked up her pillow and hugged it to his belly.

"Uh-huh," she finally uttered, "I hate this. I'm missing out on so much. When I come back," she added, some feistiness back in her voice, "I'm never leaving your side again."

"I'd like that."

She sighed deeply on the other end before starting to snicker.

"That should be your epitaph, you know."

"What?" he asked mildly confused. "*I'd like that?*"

"No, silly. *I'm alive.*"

Chapter 16

"I don't want to go back tomorrow," Wendy muttered while stabbing her pumpkin haphazardly with a long carving knife. She cut out a second vaguely triangular eye, about half an inch lower than the first one she'd hacked out.

Pike flinched at the clumsy motion but a sharp look from Ash across the kitchen table prevented him from sticking his oar in. He turned back to his own creation, a classic troll face that was coming along nicely, before checking out Ash's masterpiece. Three of the four horsemen of the apocalypse had already been carved into the outer skin of the biggest pumpkin on the table. The fourth was still in progress.

"You're really good at art," Pike stated.

Ash shrugged.

"Where did you learn to do stuff like that?"

"Didn't. Just do," Ash responded curtly, concentrating on Death's scythe.

"What about the fire juggling?"

Ash looked up for a second and smirked.

"Flame throwing for the disenfranchised."

"Pardon?"

"Social inclusion project when I was in year eight," Ash elaborated, returning to his task. "Circus Skills for Inner City Kids. Lasted about, I don't know, two seconds before Health and Safety shut it down or the funding got cut or something but in those two seconds I learned to play with fire properly. Like Dustfinger."

"Inkheart," Pike said. "Brilliant book."

Wendy groaned and crossed her eyes as she impaled the vegetable shell in front of her again.

"Purlease, spare me another book conversation. You two are so boring." She sighed deeply. "I think I preferred it when I knew you separately."

Pike could see Ash smiling down at his art work and felt his own mouth curl up.

Going to get the other's belongings on the evening of the day Hunter's Moon had risen from the mostly dead had revealed another surprise about their similarities. Hidden deep in the woods, Ash's camp had consisted of a small tent disguised amidst a circle of trees with just a few possessions inside, half of which had turned out to be books, soggy and mildew riddled from living outdoors. When Ash had remained reluctant to accept a more permanent invitation to the cottage, Pike had unashamedly used the paper's plight to successfully entice the other with promises of warm, dry shelves.

That day, only a few nights previously, seemed ice ages ago now. The three of them had fallen into a rhythm with each other and the horses so naturally that Pike couldn't bear the idea of either of the other two leaving again. He had returned to his bed in the Watchtower and dreams of Eleanor, once it had become clear the Clydesdale was going to be just fine. But when he lay there at night now, he revelled in the knowledge that Wendy was happily snoring in the yellow room at the foot of the stairs while Ash, still too feral to accept a place in the actual house, was safe and sound in the tack room.

He drilled the last wart into his pumpkin's face, stood up to gather the vegetable guts from the centre of the table and paused for a moment, looking down at the heads of the other two.

My tribe.

His heart swelled double and they both looked up simultaneously, feeling the weight of his stare on them. He caught Wendy's eye and wanted to soothe the lingering despondency there so badly he had to bite his tongue hard not to let anything slip that would give her hope. They had been out on Casta and Inigo a couple more times since their first ride and it had become increasingly harder to keep his mouth shut. But he had managed not to tell her about Eleanor's plan, had bracketed the whole subject of Strawberry from their conversations entirely lest any mention of it jinx the affair.

Superstitious git, he scolded himself, then looked away to the door where an excited Sarah-shaped witch woman was entering, wielding a wicker basket filled to the brim with sweets.

"Oh, how I missed this while I was living in Spain. Such fun," she proclaimed, putting down the basket on the counter and stretching out her arms to show off the full effect of her witch's costume. "How do I look?"

Wendy's nose twitched.

"Not particularly scary."

Sarah's eyes turned to slits as she lowered the fake nose that had been resting on her head over her face and set it in place.

"Is that so, young child?" she cackled, approaching Wendy. "Are you very sure about that now? Not scary, eh? Oh, I'll scare you."

She hunched over the girl and poked her with a long finger. Wendy squealed and the woman straightened up, a satisfied grin spreading across her face.

"And that children," she said in her plummiest accent, "is what a Royal Academy of Dramatic Art education does for you. In actual fact," her normal voice took over, "it's the *only* thing a RADA education does for you because it sure as rain doesn't pay for a pension plan. Right, now, how are these pumpkins coming along? It's getting dark out there. We should have some trick-or-treaters soon."

She turned to the table to appraise the carvings. When her eyes settled on the four horsemen, all theatrics fell from her as she sat down, removed the rubber nose and began looking at Ash's work in detail.

"This is inspired, Ashley. My word, this is amazing," she muttered after a minute or so, running the tip of her finger along the edges of the relief. She smiled. "You made the horses look like ours and the horsemen like...you. Very clever. So you are Death. On my Casta, obviously. The perfect horse for the pale rider. Paytah is Conquest? Very ironic. I like it. I'm amazed he let you get away with that feather crown. Wendy is Hunger and Plague on Blue. Clever. But who is War? Who's that on Hunter's Moon? Also you?"

"My dad," Ash answered flatly.

Pike felt his ears prick up but the subject appeared closed already so he let it go before he even enquired.

Sarah, on the other hand, didn't.

"Is he the reason you left home?" she asked evenly.

"No," Ash stated categorically. It was followed by a short, joyless laugh. "He's the reason I'm not going back."

He looked around the table and shrugged dismissively, nodding at his pumpkin.

"It ain't meant to be clever. It doesn't mean anything. It's just a piece of crappy art work. My dad was in the army, so it works. That's all there is to it."

"You know," Sarah said thoughtfully, "that's a far cry from a crappy piece of art work. You should really consider studying fine art."

"Yeah, 'cause that definitely affords one a pension plan," Ash teased her with a warm smile.

"Touché."

"Hang on a second," Wendy suddenly interjected, crawling halfway across the table to have a closer look, "If it works 'cause he was in the army, how come I'm Hunger *and* Plague?"

Ash grinned at her.

"Well, Hunger 'cause you're always hungry and Plague..."

He let it hang unfinished.

Wendy growled at him.

Ash put two fingers together, touched their tips to his mouth and blew the kiss in her direction.

"You can be my pest any day. Don't you have some devil's horns to put on or something?"

Ghosts and ghouls, witches and wizards, skeletons and zombies, vampires and werewolves came and went. Some just passed through the front garden swiftly, others hung around a while to admire Aaron's decorations in the trees, watch Ash twirl his batons and warm their hands by the fire pit. But by eight o'clock the last visitors had been and gone and it was just them left, still gathered outside and admiring the cold clear night. Pike was sitting on the front steps, watching Wendy and Ash as the other was teaching the girl to walk on her hands.

"Here, have some mulled cider."

Aaron stooped down to Pike and handed him a steaming mug.

"I thought you didn't want me drinking."

Aaron gestured dismissively.

"Fiddlesticks. Just not to excess. It'll warm you up."

Pike took a sip. Apples, cinnamon and cloves huddled his senses. It was good.

Aaron sat down stiffly next to him.

"That's it. I may never get up again."

"Don't say that," Pike said into the distance. "Too much talk of dying from you of late." He turned to look at the profile of the only man in his life who had ever been a father to him. "I can't handle it."

Aaron nodded.

"Noted."

Ash had picked up his batons again, leaving Wendy to do her tumbling on her own and they watched the stray paint his flaming pictures in silence for a while.

"He's good," Aaron stated after a bit. "I've seen a fair few fire jugglers in my life but he is *good*." He took a deep breath. "What do you think he's running from?"

Before Pike could answer, Sarah had come out of the house and seated herself on the top step behind them.

"In my experience," she offered, "people usually run from themselves."

Pike snorted a laugh.

"Wisely spoken, oh wise one." He paused for a moment then shrugged. "It doesn't matter anyway. I trust him. Blue trusts him. Wendy trusts him. He saved Hunter. He's one of us."

The old man next to him sniffled.

"Are you alright?"

"I miss her," Aaron answered.

"Who?"

Aaron's head sunk into his chest and he rubbed the two intertwined horseshoe nails forged into a crude wedding band on his left ring finger with the thumb of the other hand. A sad smile played around the corners of his mouth.

"The woman who just spoke through you." He abruptly put an arm around Pike's shoulder, drew him close and kissed his temple. "I'm proud of you, boy. Ah—" he added, releasing his grandson as suddenly as he'd embraced him and indicating the three foot tall tarantula that was presently rounding the garden gate, "Saved by the bell."

"Ike!" the spider shouted as it toddled towards them, all eight arms flapping. When the creature came to stand in front of Pike the two real limbs among them stretched up in a wordless demand to be picked up. Pike put the mug down, got to his feet and lifted Oscar into a hug. The little boy withdrew and made himself comfortable on the young man's hips.

"Weetie?" he enquired, his little face lighting up expectantly.

"You've got to see Sarah for that," Pike responded.

"Boo?" Oscar carried on with equal enthusiasm.

"Yes," Pike said. "We can go see Blue if your mum and dad say you have time."

Pike looked over the boy's blonde mop at Isabel and Kjell who had just trundled into the garden after their son and were duly admiring Ash's tricks. Isabel looked back at Pike, smiled and started walking towards him.

"I've been waiting for you," she proclaimed loudly half way, as she extracted a fat white envelope from somewhere inside the ridiculously colourful Mexican poncho she was wearing and waved it in the air.

Pike set down Oscar, who promptly proceeded to crawl up the steps and see Sarah about a chocolate bar.

As his girlfriend's mother approached him a familiar, uncomfortable feeling snaked its way into Pike's guts. When he'd first met Eleanor, Isabel and he had played an intense tug-of-war for the girl's freedom to ride and to love. And although to all intents and purposes he had won her over in the end, there still remained some uncleared debris between him and the woman about to hand him the cash to buy Strawberry's safety. He took the envelope from her when she arrived and thanked her courteously.

Gratitude and the ongoing fear of rejection, he noted as he folded the envelope over into a thick wad and stuffed it down his front pocket, made a funny cocktail.

Isabel's eyes sought her youngest offspring, ascertained his whereabouts on Sarah's lap and smiled a greeting at the old woman and Aaron. Then she turned to stand by Pike's side.

"Don't thank me," she stated, watching Ash again. "It's her money. She can do with it as she pleases. He—" She pointed at the man in her life who had started asking Ash some questions in the distance. "Seems to think it's a marvellous idea. If I'd known that in marrying a Swedish dentist, I'd actually be getting a closet horse nut who needs to live out his suppressed wishes to live on a farm and fritter away a lifetime on the back of a pony through his stepdaughter I'd have stayed with the rock stars, but ho-hum."

She nudged Pike amicably in the side with her elbow and indicated Ash, who'd just started showing Kjell a particular baton move, with a jerk of her chin.

"And if I'd known there was going to be a show, I'd have brought my violin. He's quite something. We saw him on the beach a couple of weeks ago. How did you get him here?"

Pike scratched his eyebrow.

"He kinda lives here now."

"Oh. Good stuff. – Do you miss her?"

Pike smiled.

"Like crazy."

"Me too."

They turned to face each other. Isabel's always roaming eyes which never seemed to fix on anything for longer than a second suddenly steadied on him.

"You know," she said slowly, "you could always come and sleep in her bed for the night. Nine weeks is a long time. Would be nice to have at least one of you there for breakfast once or twice."

They didn't hug.

They weren't at that point yet.

Pike didn't know if they ever would be.

But it floored him, nevertheless.

"Careful now, there you go."

Blue gently took a treat from the small hand cupped in Pike's big palm. The little boy on his hip shuddered with delight as the pony's beard hairs tickled his skin, and he quickly hid his face in the crook of Pike's neck, only to look back a second later. He stretched out an arm to touch the mare's ear. Blue blew her nose out and then went back to ripping at her hay net.

"Come on," Pike said, "Lets go find your pappa."

They slipped out of Blue's stable and joined Kjell and Ash over by the box that had become Hunter's permanent bedroom now. The Clydesdale was on the other side of the aisle, opposite Blue, in what had once been the foaling box, the only one big enough to accommodate her. Her large, friendly face was looking out over the half door, while Kjell was stroking her neck with one hand and letting her sniff around the other.

"Beautiful," he stated when Pike and Oscar had joined him. "Makes me want to get another myself."

"Why don't you?" Pike made a sweeping gesture at the eight empty boxes. "It's not like we haven't got the space. And if her introduction to the herd is anything to go by, Inigo and Blue will gladly accept another."

The older man shot him an enquiring look and Pike grinned with pride.

"Yeah, we put them all out together yesterday. I've never seen anything like it. Smooth as anything. No fighting *at all*. As if Hunter had always been part of the gang. Maybe because Blue adopted her first or because she's just so laid back. Doesn't threaten anyone."

"Hm," Kjell said dreamily then shook his head. "No. Not now. Maybe in a few years, when this little man here—" He reached for his son and transferred him from Pike's arms into his own. "Has grown a bit. Ash tells me she was as good as dead three days ago. That's marvellous work, you two." He looked back and forth between the two young men before letting his eyes settle on Pike. "Tidy bandaging on those legs. Compliments to the nurse."

Coming from quiet, thoughtful Kjell who had always had more than a little hand in Eleanor's enterprises of rescuing either Pike, his land or his ponies, the connotation didn't bother Pike in the slightest. Something else did though. The distinct feeling that they had forgotten something hit him with full force. He looked at Ash.

"Damn. We should really have sent Gladys some flowers and a card or something."

Ash grinned.

"Done and dusted, mate. Sarah and I went over there this morning when you and Wendy were out riding. I got her some flowers and some chocolates and brought her the quilt back. Sarah washed it for me. She was very happy to hear Hunter is doing well. I have manners you know. I wasn't raised in a barn."

"I was," Pike quipped.

Just then said barn door opened and Wendy stuck her head around.

"Erm, sorry to interrupt, but I'm supposed to tell you your mother wants to talk to you, P."

Oh joy.

"Why does she insist on ringing the house? Just tell her to ring me on my mobile."

"Actually, she's waiting for you in the sitting room."

Pike felt the blood drain from his face.

"What? She's here?"

Wendy nodded and a wave of nausea washed over him.

"Without my father?"

Another nod from the girl made his stomach bottom out completely.

He was already one step towards the door when Ash touched his arm, concern written all over his face.

"Are you alright, mate? What's happened?"

"Hell's frozen over," Pike replied flatly and left them all behind to find the woman who'd given birth to him.

The way from the stables to the house had never seemed this long.

Thoughts swirled around his head, along with half baked emotions that belied years of pretence towards the man he refused to call Dad yet whose littlest approval, whose tiniest morsel of love shown, could make Pike feel eight foot tall in the blink of an eye.

Alice alone didn't happen. Not here. Not at Hawthorne Cottage.

Something had happened. Some terrible news was awaiting him.

When he reached the twitten he turned right onto the path, towards the high, narrow gate in the flint stone wall opposite, which led to the cottage's back garden. He stepped through it and crossed the lawn hastily in the pitch black. Despite the tragedy that had obviously struck, the party at the front appeared to be carrying on regardless and he could hear Isabel's throaty laughter floating through the night air.

Alice hasn't told Grandpa, yet, he concluded as he opened the back door and let himself into the house, *I'm supposed to be the first to know.*

The kitchen still smelled of mulled cider but it had gone cold and the over-infused scent of spices seemed acrid rather than comforting now. Pike suppressed the reflex to retch while he discarded his boots and hurried through the ominously silent house to the sitting room.

He found his mother standing by the empty fire place, with her back to the door, contemplating the large black and white engraving that hung above the mantelpiece.

Pike had always had a contentious relationship with '*The Widow of an Indian Chief Watching the Arms of Her Deceased Husband*'. There was a romanticised beauty to it that simultaneously enthralled and disgusted him. The blatantly ethnically miscast woman it showed sitting against a tree and staring into the distance with her too milky skin, ill-defined bone structure and round soft shoulders in her late 18th century, studied European pose of melancholic, bare-breasted grief, was an insult to even his barely half an ounce of tribal blood. Yet there was a sense of true wildness to her surroundings, to the storm in the background, that drew him in every time he stared at it for long enough. And for that he loved it.

Right now, with the wiry, evening gown clad figure of Alice standing in front of it, it suddenly took on a whole other meaning, one he didn't really want to face. He gathered his wits and was about to announce his arrival in the room when his mother turned around to greet him.

"There you are," she stated in a clipped tone. "I did tell that girl to hurry. I only have a few minutes. I left John at a charity ball in a hotel some fifteen miles from here. I told him I had a bit of a headache and needed a lie down but he will come and check on me if I don't return within the hour."

She was still talking but the relief flooding Pike's senses rendered him deaf to the next few sentences.

"So, will you come?" was the next thing he heard her say.

They had moved towards each other and Alice was now standing in front of him holding out her arms in a stylized offer of an embrace. They hugged awkwardly, like two wind up toys.

"Come where?" Pike asked as he took a step back.

"Oh for Heaven's sake, Paytah, do listen for once. That is

exactly why I decided to come out here in person rather than call." Alice was seriously annoyed now, her glassy blue eyes shooting icicle arrows at him while she tapped the side of her knee repeatedly with an envelope she was carrying in her right hand. Her nose twitched disgustedly. "You smell of horse. Does nobody in this house ever take a shower?"

"Rarely," he dead-panned, "We try to save on water."

He could tell she was unsure as to whether he was joking or not. It pleased him no end.

"Now, forgive me my momentary lapse of concentration," he continued, mimicking her syntax, "and do repeat yourself in your own good time."

She took a deep breath and sucked in her cheeks before replying.

"As I said, I would like you to grace us with your presence at your father's birthday dinner this year. He's been…how do I put it…a little low. I think he is entering some sort of early midlife crisis. Did you know we were rumoured to be nominees for the Nobel Prize in Medicine this year? We didn't get it, of course, and nobody will know if we were actually on the list for half a century but even being considered in this unofficial manner is a great, great honour. You would think he would have been pleased but not so. He is…questioning certain decisions he's made in his life. And I know he would very much like to see you."

Pike sat down on the arm of a sofa.

"I'm relatively easy to find. I've lived in this house since you weaned me."

The breath she'd taken before her little monologue suddenly came out as a big, honest sigh.

"Why do you always have to be this difficult?" She looked at him with exasperation, handing him the envelope. "Do consider it." Her voice had lost some of its edge. "I know it is weeks yet but such things need early planning so I would appreciate an answer soon. I will make up the guest room for you and maybe you and John could spend some time together the next day. He would like that."

While she was still talking, Pike extracted the formal invitation from its sleeve. His stable-stained fingers immediately left smudges on the embossed eggshell card.

"It says here plus one," he said puzzled.

"Yes. I thought you might like to bring your girlfriend. Are you still with the same girl? That tiny thing? What was her name again?"

"Eleanor," he replied, hanging on to his cool by the skin of his teeth. "Her name is Eleanor."

"Well, bring Eleanor if you like. Tell her it is a formal do. — So, will you come?"

He looked up from the card in his hand.

"She is out of the country till Christmas."

"Pity. *Please* will *you* come?"

Pike could not remember his mother ever having asked him anything with a please attached. Added to her abnormal presence in this house, a place she'd always loathed with a vengeance for reasons that eluded Pike, there was something down to the bone frightening about it. The thoughts of earlier reared their ugly heads again.

"He's not sick, is he?"

"Pardon? Who? John? God, no. Don't be ridiculous. I just know he would love to see his son."

Pike stared at the card a while longer then looked up at her through narrowed eyes. He'd already made up his mind before she'd even asked, round about the moment he'd realised she hadn't come here to tell him John was dead. But he wanted to keep her guessing a little longer, pin her down in her discomfort for just a few more seconds.

"You're impossible," she finally snorted and made to leave. She was almost out of the room when he called after her. "I'll be there."

Chapter 17

When Pike took the first look out of the Watchtower's window on Friday morning, he tried hard to beat down the sinking feeling that immediately took charge of his gut.

Rain was streaking the panes relentlessly, having washed all colour out of the world. The view was a symphony of grey on grey.

Not a day to be facing negotiations with Robert Greaves.

Not a day to ride over to The Black Horse, looking impressive on the back of his stallion, with Ash leading Blue on foot for company, as the two of them had imagined so vividly the night before.

They had gone through various productions in their heads while playing cards and listening to music in the tack room, trying hard to ignore the Wendy-sized hole that had suddenly been cut into their existence by the girl's departure, but this scenario had been his favourite. He'd drawn the line where Ash had wanted to pleat a feather into his hair but truth be told, he could well have done with Inigo's power beneath him, Ash's calm beside him and Blue's wisdom between them when facing Rob. But life was not a movie and though Inigo had come on in leaps and bounds over the last week, taking a young stallion to a whole different yard with a bunch of mares he could potentially incorporate into his herd was asking for a fiasco. Besides, they would have been a pair of hands short to lead Strawberry home.

They'd have to make do with reality.

He shut his eyes and rubbed his forehead with the flat of his palm until his nose got caught by the ball of his hand and squished upwards. He pushed down a little harder, relishing the pain before letting go abruptly.

In an ideal world he would have postponed the meeting with

Greaves but he knew that he'd only get one chance at this and today was the day, whether he felt up to it or not. For a moment he considered asking Sarah to give them a lift although he didn't particularly want her in the mix. Then he remembered that she and Aaron had planned on leaving early in the morning to attend a funeral, not to return until nightfall.

Great. Just Fire and Ash and an envelope full of dough.

Actually, put like that it didn't sound so bad.

He shrugged to himself, got dressed and went to find his designated sidekick.

Ash was already up and grooming Hunter outside her box when Pike entered the barn. A mellow, melancholic vibe hung in the air.

The other had dragged Pike's music player and the little loudspeakers from the tack room out into the aisle and was listening to the last guitar strums of an acoustic song, accompanied by a chorus of happily chewing horses. It was only when the song began anew and Eleanor's voice started filling the air that Pike realised what the piece was. He frowned lightly, not sure how he liked Ash listening to it, evidently on repeat. He hadn't shared it with anyone up to now. His frown dissolved as soon as Ash turned to him, an unsure, almost timid smile on his face.

"Hey. Morning. I didn't know if you wanted them out in this weather, so I gave them all some more hay and filled their water up. Hope that was the right thing to do."

"Perfect," Pike answered.

As he approached further the other returned to brushing the giantess, who had zoned out contentedly under the attention.

"I love this song," Ash carried on talking with his back to Pike. "I've been listening to it over and over all morning. What a voice!

Gets right under your skin. I mean, wow. And the guitar. It's like *it* is singing, too. I mean, I know shit about music but that's serious guitar playing. Who is this? I found it under 'most played' but it just says 'unknown artist'. It's funny 'cause the lyrics could have been written about you. It's like it's you in a song. Weird."

Pike laughed embarrassedly, making Ash turn around again to scrutinise him.

"You laughing at me?"

"No," Pike replied having reached Hunter. He turned away from Ash to run a hand along the Clydesdale's slowly filling out crest. Finally, she'd started putting on enough weight so her neck no longer looked like it was about to snap under the burden of carrying the head. It never ceased to amaze Pike how quickly horses could drop and gain pounds. As he felt the big mare's coat under his fingers, he let Eleanor's voice caress his neck.

"So, go on, who is this?" Ash insisted.

"You ever heard of Jerry McGraw?"

In the periphery of his vision he saw Ash shake his head.

"Nope."

"Supposedly the best guitarist in the world?"

"Like I said, I know shit about music."

"It's his daughter."

"Good for him. And does this daughter have a name?"

Pike faced him again, smiling broadly now.

"Eleanor," he answered, suddenly feeling up to anything Greaves might throw at him today. "Eleanor McGraw."

Maybe it was a good day for business after all.

They passed the architectural disaster zone that was Rob's new house at exactly ten to two, having walked in near silence across the Downs for an hour. The rain had let up shortly after they'd set out, to be replaced by bright sunshine, and by now the two young men were mostly dry again.

Pike had briefly contemplated going on the bike but if Rob agreed to the sale he didn't want to take any chances. He wanted to walk back with Strawberry there and then, without having to worry about how to get the bike home or having to rely on Greaves to provide transport. He checked the wad of money in his pocket for the millionth time since leaving Hawthorne Cottage and nervously touched Blue's head collar, which he'd strapped across his chest.

They would need it. Pike knew already that if the deal went through, they'd be getting the pony and its passport. No more, no less. As his grandma had repeatedly pointed out to him when she'd been alive, people didn't get minted by being generous.

"Fuck me, that's ugly!" Ash exclaimed beside him, his first words since an equally concise outburst when he'd slipped down a bank two miles ago and landed on his butt, leaving white chalk stains caked into the black denim encasing his buttocks.

He'd stopped to admire the grotesqueness of Greaves' domicile.

"That's hideous. No wonder she doesn't wanna live in *that*."

"I think it's the company more than the architecture that bothers her," Pike stated wryly as he grabbed Ash by the sleeve. "Come on, Rob hates people being late. Wendy'll probably be at the yard anyway, so you'll see her in a bit."

"That would be good," Ash said, "No offence, but it just ain't the same without her. She belongs with us."

Pike looked across at Ash's profile as they carried on moving and the other shrugged in response to the question hanging in the air.

"She was the first person who gave me a hug in nearly two years, you know. Like, a *real* hug. No agenda, not a grope from some git wanting...you get the picture."

Despite the gravity of what he was hearing, Pike couldn't help but smile.

"What?" Ash asked after a while.

"You said 'us'."

A car turned from the main road onto the drive and approached from behind. The polished black Range Rover slowed down once it levelled with them and the tinted window on the driver's side went down. A waft of expensive cologne escaped to the outside as Rob's elbow appeared on the door. He steered one handed, crawling along beside them.

"Peter," he stated, briefly sticking his head out of the window and making it sound as if he was genuinely pleased to see Pike. "Right on time. Meet me in the indoor school when you get there."

The elbow retracted, the window went back up and he was off.

"*That* was Wendy's stepfather?" Ash asked, astonished.

"Uh-huh."

"Whoa, I didn't expect him to be this..." Ash's voice trailed off.

"This what?" Pike demanded sharply.

Ash shrugged.

"Good looking. From what she told me about him I imagined this fat necked, red in the face, bald bloke with a belly. You know, the burst veins type. Not Redford's and Pitt's love child, complete with a fucking dimple in his chin and foppish grey hair. Ain't he quite the charmer?"

Pike found himself caught between laughing and snarling.

"Yeah well, never judge a book by its cover."

Ash shot him a sideways glance.

"Is he really that bad?"

They had reached the entrance to The Black Horse and Pike stopped to take in the picture in front of him. The place was heaving with activity. A troop of six riders, about to leave the yard for a hack, were in the process of mounting their horses in an orderly fashion outside the new stable block. In the sand school to the right of the old brick building three young women on jumpers were listening to the instructions of the head groom as she explained the ins and outs of tackling the combination she had put up for them. A small gaggle of teenage girls was leaning against the fence around the school, watching the lesson while on a grass bank on the far side someone was idly hand-grazing what looked like an Irish Sports Horse or some equally athletic, British hybrid type.

'*Indoor school*,' Rob had said.

It was news to Pike that they had one here but in the light of all the rest of the development it didn't exactly surprise him. A bit of bile found its way up his throat at the thought of his grandma and Karen applying for the permission to erect an all weather arena at Hawthorne Barn year in year out, always to be rejected, while it seemed Robert Greaves was allowed to build a whole equestrian village all over the Downs. He scanned the surroundings for a new erection the size of a small aircraft hangar and decided it must be hidden behind the rest of the buildings somewhere.

"Worse," he finally answered Ash's question as he moved towards the riders going out, all of whom were aboard their horses now and coming towards them.

He raised a hand to stop the leader, a young woman atop a liver chestnut mare Pike knew well. A Thoroughbred by the name of Chocolat sans Lait, she was solid proof of the old saying that the blood didn't always come through. Related to a whole portfolio of famous racehorses she'd had only a handful of outings in her day before she had been retired from the track for always reliably finishing last. Though fast when she wanted to be, she had no fighting bone in her body, not the remotest desire to be in front. She was a solid, obedient pleasure ride though and a sweetheart to boot. When his world had still been in one piece, Pike had liked riding her out on the odd occasion, whenever he'd needed a breather, since she was easy to amble along with.

"Hey Coco," he greeted her and let her sniff his hand before he looked up at the mildly irritated face of her rider.

"Can I help you?" the young woman asked.

Pike smiled.

"You certainly can. Could you tell us where we'd find the indoor school, please?"

The woman frowned under her riding hat and her nose wrinkled unattractively.

"You can't go in there at the moment. The boss's daughter is having a private lesson. No spectators allowed."

Stepdaughter, Pike wanted to correct her but stopped himself, wondering why it should matter.

"Rob's expecting us," he answered instead.

The woman's eyebrows shot up and she took an unashamedly curious second look at the two young men.

"It's back to back with the new stable block. If you follow the gravel drive around the side you'll end up in the car park in front of it."

"Thank you," Pike replied courteously, more to Coco who was still nuzzling his palm than to her rider, then stepped away to let them go and follow her directions. He barely noticed the other horses as they passed until the penultimate rider in the line stopped her Haflinger and screeched, oblivious to the older woman on a grey cob behind her rounding on her with a tut after nearly crashing into her.

"Oh my God, Peter! What on earth are you doing here? Are you going to be riding for Rob again? That would so great. Oh please tell me you'll be riding for him. Will you be teaching as well? Please can I be in your group? That would be so awesome." The girl turned her attention to Ash. "He's like only the best rider ever."

"Hi Martine," Pike greeted her, looking up at a girl he remembered as an over-enthusiastic eight-year-old on the lead rein, complete with a Mummy Dippy.

Somewhere along the way she'd grown legs, breasts, a face full of make up and pink streaks in her dark brown hair but her breathless zest for life had clearly not waned in the process. He smiled at her kindly when her eyes moved back from Ash to him.

"I don't think so, Martine. Go." Pike indicated the rest of her company with a jerk of the head. "You're getting left behind."

The girl looked up and, realising how far ahead the rest were, squeezed her pony into a trot. When she'd closed up to the grey cob she turned in the saddle and pointed at her own animal's wide bum.

"Mine!" she shouted. "My parents finally caved in. His name is Nathan. Isn't he gorgeous?"

"Beautiful!" Pike shouted back.

She smiled happily, gave him a last wave and finally turned back into the direction of travel.

"How good are you at this riding lark, exactly?" Ash asked him as they started making their way towards their final destination. "Wendy says you're one of the best, too."

Pike snorted.

"I'm an okay rider. Nobody is ever as good as other people make them out to be. People love a legend and horse people are the worst. They live to mystify. You ask anyone with a horse how they got that horse and they never just bought it, there is always, always, always some big, elaborate story attached."

"Hm," Ash muttered thoughtfully as their feet hit the gravel drive. "So if we're successful today, you're gonna tell people you just bought the pony?"

"Hell no," Pike answered, grinning from ear to ear.

Chapter 18

As soon as Pike laid eyes on the strained horse and rider pair in the manège, he could clearly see what Wendy had been saying about the zero fun factor.

Little Miss Jones and her pearls of wisdom.

He looked around for her, having assumed she'd be here, but other than Tinkerbelle and her gazillion Euro wonder horse, the coach, who Pike guessed must be the famed Frank van den Berg, Greaves, who stood beside van den Berg in the middle of the arena, Ash and himself there was no one else in the building.

The two young men had entered through a door marked 'Spectators', and were now leaning against the partition that sectioned off the raised floor of the viewing platform from the school. Everything still smelled new in here, from the sand to the wooden panels. The lights in the roof hadn't had time to gather dust yet and shone with merciless brightness on the bay Warmblood and the uncharacteristically tense girl riding him. The tall blonde instructor barked something at Tinkerbelle in that unmistakably soft Dutch accent that made everything sound like it started with a 'd' about not letting the horse fall out through the right shoulder and 'getting her seat in there'.

Pike gasped inwardly. To his eyes there was absolutely nothing wrong with Tinkerbelle's seat. There was, however, so much tension in her shoulder and biceps in a desperate attempt to keep her lower arms and wrists supple that it was inadvertently having the opposite effect. Her hands, though soft as anything on the bradoon, seemed practically clamped shut on the curb bit.

'Tension', he heard Karen say in his head, *'Can't be cheated away. If it's there, it's there. Sometimes it might hide in your pinky, but boy can a cramped pinky make a difference.'*

He wondered for a moment if Tinkerbelle was as scared of the double bridle as he had been at the start.

When he'd lost Inara, the mare had been seven and he fourteen, much younger than Tinkerbelle was now, and they had still been learning, seperately, to understand the double bridle. Pike's education had been conducted on old Ty, a kind, rather ancient Hanoverian schoolmaster who they had bought cheap for the very purpose and who forgave many mistakes in trade for his new, stress-free home at Hawthorne Barn. Inara's schooling had been in the hands of Karen who had begun teaching her the signals of the curb from the ground. Pike had never got the chance to ride his mare in it. Later, when Casta had moved in he had at first been loathe to use one on her, opting for the plain snaffle she was ridden out in instead, even when playing at dressage tests in the schooling paddock. As far as he was concerned, the Andalusian didn't need bondage. He could waltz with her in a head collar if he wanted to.

But Sarah had insisted he rode her 'properly' if he was going to school her at all and in Sarah's world that meant curb and bradoon, no discussion. Under the old woman's watchful eye he had lost the last of his fears and made peace with the idea but he still had much respect for the contraption.

"Peter!" Greaves voice dragged him from his thoughts. "Get in here, boy!"

Pike followed the command, walking down the two steps that led from the raised floor to a door in the side panel and into the school. When he met the two men in the middle, van den Berg examined him with undisguised scepticism.

"Are you serious, Robert? You've brought in a horse whisperer?" he enquired, looking at Pike.

Pike frowned, briefly debated the pros and cons of his next action and then stepped up to the man.

"Do I look like a friggin' cowboy to you?"

Rob positioned himself next to them.

"Peter meet Frank, Frank meet Peter," he said evenly. "He is the lad I was telling you about. He has come to talk about a pony today but I thought maybe we could kill two birds with one stone. What do you reckon Peter? Want to have a go?"

Rob had partially turned towards Tinkerbelle and her horse, who were currently practising shoulder-in on the left hand rein. He indicated the pair with a tilt of the head.

"What?" Pike asked taken aback. "On him?"

"Yes."

"Now?"

"Yes. Why not?" Rob looked at him with mocking challenge in his eyes. "Go on. You must want to know what it feels like, riding a horse like that."

"What? One that's overbent, withdrawn and so tightly wound it's painful to watch?"

Pike heard van den Berg take in a sharp breath but could see in the miniature smirk around the left corner of Rob's mouth that he wasn't fooling anyone.

"I'm hardly dressed for it," he added weakly, looking down at his ripped jeans and his chalk, mud and sand caked work boots.

Rob waved the objection off.

"Like that's ever stopped you before. Go on. What size hat are you?"

"Fifty-seven."

"Tinkerbelle, what size hat are you?" Rob bellowed across to the girl who had changed rein by now and was covering the long side of the school at a medium walk.

"Fifty-seven," the girl shouted back without turning her head.

"Turn in at B, halt at X, please," Rob demanded, clearly to the annoyance of van den Berg who was looking none too pleased about the hijacking of his lesson.

Tinkerbelle did as she was bid, halting perfectly just in front of the group of men.

"Hi P, what are you two doing here?" she asked, genuine surprise in her voice.

She glanced across at Ash before letting her eyes return to Pike.

"Get off and give him your hat," Rob said bluntly before Pike could answer her question.

Pike saw her already tight shoulders tense even further but she didn't hesitate in doing what she was told. Once she'd dismounted and silently handed him first her hat and then the reins, she stepped back, folded her arms across her chest and watched him get ready, no emotion showing on her face.

Not that Pike was studying her too closely.

He was presently fully engrossed in the preparations for mounting the biggest horse he'd ever climbed on. Though not as tall as Hunter, Walt the wonder horse stood before him obediently at an impressive, solidly muscled seventeen hands, showing as little emotion and as much tension as his mistress. Pike ran a hand over the soft part of the gelding's nose. Bits of foam that had flown up there from the horse's mouth stuck to his palm. He wiped them off on the seat of his trousers and looked at the animal's almost opaque eye.

'At' is the right word, here, he thought, *there is no 'looking into'.*

The gelding seemed almost entirely oblivious to his surroundings, as if he'd fled so far inside his own soul that he wasn't even registering the new person handling him.

Pike couldn't help but compare the Warmblood's eyes to Inigo's — shiny and alert, always full of mischief and thirst for life, no matter who was standing by his side.

A free spirit, a partner in crime, not a slave or servant.

That was what Pike wanted for his horses, not this.

He shuddered at the thought that Inara might ever have got this jaded.

She'd died but at least she'd died *alive.*

It was a strange moment to finally be making peace with his mare's death fully and truly but he could feel the shift inside him like a seismic event. He laughed inwardly at the absurdity of the circumstances, while he checked the girth on Walt's saddle then took the reins and grabbed the pommel before putting his dirty boot in the stirrup.

Mid-mount he asked himself why then he was about become complicit in this slavery, why then he was getting on this horse and not politely declining. The answer followed rapidly behind, truthful and agonizing, and as far removed from the idea of keeping Greaves happy to smooth the path for the negotiations he'd come for as possible.

The reality was, Rob was right.

Pike *did* want to know what it would feel like riding a horse like this. An animal so valuable it had practically no right to be. There was a burning curiosity to see what made Walt so special, what made him so much superior to Pike's dead overgrown pony with her elegance and panache.

Curiosity beats righteousness, was his last self-deprecating thought before his bottom made contact with the saddle and suddenly the world was all cramped up energy. Within a second of lightly picking up the reins and moving Walt off, Pike had to admit that the myth did not exceed reality.

Where other horses had joints, Walt appeared to have springs.

Even good old Ty, who had taught Pike all the moves of Grand Prix dressage with stoic dedication to the cause and enough remnant buoyancy from his glory days to convince even the more critical eyes around them that Pike had talent, had never come close.

Each step the gelding below him took had such scope and

bounce that for the first minute or so Pike thought he was going to be seasick. But then he found the rhythm in his pelvis that went with this particular horse and the nausea dissolved to turn into pure pleasure. He'd heard people say that trotting on a big horse with this much impulsion made it difficult to keep your bottom in the saddle and suddenly he couldn't wait to find out. Having finished a round at walk with negligible contact on the reins, he picked them up properly and asked the horse to shift up a gear. Walt obeyed, his neck habitually flexing too far down but there was little Pike could do about it immediately while he was busy getting used to the new sensation that was the gelding at trot, while desperately trying to keep the reins supple.

Again, folklore was proving surprisingly close to the truth. Pike could feel his seat being catapulted out of the saddle in a manner he'd not experienced since he'd been a very small boy, when first learning to sit to the trot in a saddle on Blue. The motion though was as different from the pony's as day and night. While trotting on Blue, even when collected, always had elements of riding a bike up a gravel path, this was much like trying to swim atop a wave. Images of the sea crossed Pike's mind before he realised that he was starting to go with Walt much as he would tackle staying afloat in the ocean, letting the motion's build up suck him deeper into the saddle before flinging himself up with the forward momentum of the horse.

Once he'd managed to make his bottom stay glued to the saddle, he could concentrate on his hands, not just staying fluent with the gelding's mouth but actually communicating. He tapped his fingers on the reins, asking the horse to get his head up, out of the automatized hyper-flexion. To his surprise the gelding responded with a short snort, while rising correctly in his frame and at once the dance became easier. More daring now, Pike collected the trot then proceeded down the long side of the school, condensing Walt further towards the passage. But then he decided to push him forward again, rounding the corners of the short side at medium pace before tapping him into an extended trot. He repeated the process a couple of times, Sarah's imaginary voice playing in his ears *'forward and upward, forward and upward'*. Physically Walt was doing everything Pike's body was asking him to do but still the young man could get no real feel for the horse. Aside from the short snort when he'd brought his head up he simply wasn't talking to his rider, was flat out refusing to link. It was much like sitting on a machine that was run by an astute inner metronome. Pike sighed inwardly and asked the horse to slow to a walk. He changed rein by virtue of crossing on the diagonal then took him around to where Ash was standing. Pike asked the gelding to halt and shot his companion a glance.

"Are you alright, mate?" Ash frowned deeply. "What's going on? Don't forget what we are here for, yeah?"

Pike peeled off the head collar he was still wearing across his torso and handed it down to his companion.

"Don't worry. I'm all over it. Tell me, what does he look like to you?"

He didn't have to specify that he meant the horse or what kind of answer he was after and Ash duly scrutinised the gelding's rhythmically chewing face.

"Bland," he finally responded. "Boring. Like he has no personality."

"Hm. Come in here, walk with us."

Pike swivelled the gelding a quarter turn towards the centre of the school, waited for Ash to make his way into the manège and then let the horse walk towards the silent cluster of bodies in the middle, Ash by their side.

As they approached, Rob opened his arms and turned his palms up in a gesture of bewilderment.

"What are you doing, boy? Stop playing around. Go for some moves. The horse is plenty warm. Show what you can do."

Pike stopped by the little group and let his eyes wander over them. He knew what he was about to do was insane. He also knew he was going to do it anyway.

"All in good time," he answered. "He needs waking up first. Tell me, does the racetrack still exist or have you built all over that as well?"

'The racetrack' referred to a corn field adjacent to The Black Horse, which was owned by the eccentric old farmer from whom they all bought their hay and who traditionally let riders use it for fun races in the autumn when the grain had been cut and the straw been baled.

Rob's eyes narrowed.

"As if Mackenzie would ever sell. No, it's still there. You're not serious."

"Deadly," Pike responded with a challenging grin.

"Do you have any idea how much that horse is worth?"

"About five zeros when you bought it," Pike answered dryly. "Currently more like four. It's amazing how much value a bad season can knock off."

Tinkerbelle glared at him but he just winked back at her with a warm smile. Van den Berg had taken a few steps back and was pointedly looking away as if to say 'I'll have no part in this'. The silence grew thicker before Pike finally shrugged.

"Up to you. You clearly think I have something to offer here, otherwise you wouldn't have asked me to get on him. That's what I have to offer. If it's money you are worried about, I'm still insured up to a million on other people's horses. So if I break his neck, you can buy an even better one."

It was meant purely as a snide little tease but he saw a light flicker up in Rob's eyes that made him feel sick to the pit of his stomach. Rob nodded decisively then went to the far side of the arena, where he folded back two sections of the wooden panels to reveal a sliding door to the outside.

He pushed it open and stepped away.

Chapter 19

Pike looked across the soggy field, gauging where the deepest furrows and stoniest stretches were.

Ash was right, my middle name must be Crazy Horse or some shit like that.

As soon as they had passed through to the outside world, Walt had woken up considerably. He was continuously exhaling short, alert breaths while carrying his head high and examining his surroundings with vigour, making the curb chain chime with every move of the head. Pike took the reins in one hand and allowed the gelding as much slack as light contact would allow to let him satisfy his curiosity. He touched the top of the horse's neck with his free palm. Excited energy coursed through the animal's veins in a steady pulsating sensation.

I'm insane.

He selected a stretch.

Totally idiotic.

He wriggled his feet. Having shortened the straps to cross country length he was now acutely aware of the fact that Tinkerbelle's stirrups were a smidgen too small for the width of his boots. Riding in the arena on his toes rather than the ball of the foot when all he'd had to do was sit pretty was one thing, standing to the gallop on this powerhouse of a horse was going to be an entirely different ball game.

He divided the reins between both hands again and shortened them up.

I'm gonna die.

He sat deep and gave the aids.

If he had expected Walt to go silly in the face of freedom he was to be sorely disappointed. Well brought up to a fault, the Warmblood set off across the field at a measured, slightly unbalanced working canter. Here and there flint stones flitted away under his heavy hooves and Pike could feel the gelding struggle with the uneven ground, could sense how unsure he'd suddenly become on his feet in these conditions. But there was also another sensation.

Self carriage having become difficult under the circumstances, the horse was suddenly seeking his rider's hand, was outright asking for Pike's guidance. For the first time since getting on Walt, Pike got a taste of the gelding's personality and he realised that underneath the dancing, withdrawn wunderkind was a soul as sensitive and timid as it was desperate to please. He gave the horse a reassuring pat then rose onto his toes to make himself light on the animal's back. His knees automatically sought the knee rolls that weren't there and he nearly unbalanced himself, inwardly cursing the fact he was doing this in a dressage saddle. The gelding promptly slipped a little beneath him. Pike steadied himself with the balls of his hands against the withers, found his position and urged the horse on.

Something finally loosened in the animal and within seconds Pike could feel the horse throw caution and education to the wind as they gathered speed at a breath-taking pace. It was nothing like flying along on a thoroughbred bullet or sailing on a swift little hunting pony but majestic and eye-watering in an entirely different way. He was racing an ocean liner.

Halfway across the field, when his toes where starting to get numb from the strain of balancing in the stirrups, Pike realised that the sound ringing in his ears was his own laughter. A little further on his toes really began caving in and with much regret he took the gelding back into a canter, settled himself in the saddle again and gradually brought the horse down until they'd reached walking pace.

He patted Walt with joy and leant forward to whisper to him.

"We must do this again sometime. In the right tack. Thank you, boy."

Walt answered him with the longest, most voluminous snort Pike had ever heard a horse breathe out. They turned back towards the back of the buildings, where Pike could see the tiny figures of Rob, Tinkerbelle, van den Berg and Ash standing in the distance. He took his aching feet out of the stirrups, crossed the straps over in front of the saddle and rode the gelding back at a leisurely, long rein walk.

There was a swing in the animal's hips now to complement the natural spring in his step that hadn't been there before. Clearly chuffed as pie with himself, he snorted loudly every few paces until he had his rider chuckle, lean forward and pat him again.

"Aren't you proud of yourself?"

Pike laughed mockingly as he sat back. Suddenly, Elvis began singing in his head.

The invitation couldn't have been clearer if it had been written on card and he gratefully accepted, picking up the reins in time to change tempo with the imaginary tune.

They trotted toward a large patch by the edge of the field, where the temporary storing of straw bales had flattened the ground and coated it in a soft layer of straw.

Once they reached it they danced in earnest.

Pike had no idea what they looked like to their observers, what number value a panel of judges would have granted them and he couldn't have cared less.

All he knew, when they had gone past passage and piaffe and finished on a canter pirouette, was that he'd never felt so drunk on dressage in his life. Walt truly was phenomenal and, Pike understood that clearly now, *loved* his job.

Especially to an Elvis soundtrack.

As they made their way back to the small cluster of people still gaping by the edge of the field, Pike had to fight the urge to just pass them by and carry on riding, to simply take this horse home with him.

When he reached the others, the difference in the expressions on Rob's and van den Berg's faces was laughable. While Rob was beaming like the cat that had got the cream, van den Berg's features were brewing something akin to a thunderstorm.

"Wonderful! That's what I was talking about, boy!" Rob exclaimed enthusiastically.

"Irresponsible," van den Berg growled. "You cannot expect a horse like this to perform on ground like this without asking for injuries."

Pike shrugged at the Dutchman, "Fiddlesticks. Dressage came from military training. Do you reckon just before Waterloo, Napoleon and Wellington had the battleground flattened and backfilled with sand? Just 'cause he's worth a bit of money doesn't mean you have to treat him like a Fabergé egg. He's still a horse and he needs some fun. And we had fun, didn't we boy?" he added to the gelding, patting him one last time before swinging himself out of the saddle. "But I do agree that we need to keep him moving, so he doesn't get cold," Pike carried on, while sorting out the stirrups then unbuckling the girth straps and sliding the saddle off Walt's sweaty back. He shoved it at van den Berg, who happened to be closest to him, with a disarming grin. "Here, hold this, I might break it. Tink, come around this side."

He ducked under Walt's neck to call Tinkerbelle over who was standing with Ash on the far side. Before she had managed to get to him, Rob stepped up to his right.

"So, do you want to take the ride?" Greaves asked bluntly.

There was no mistaking what he meant.

Tinkerbelle had just arrived by Pike's left and was looking at Rob aghast.

"What?" she barely managed to utter under her breath.

"Chill," Pike told her then turned to Greaves.

"No. I don't. You have a rider. She's right here." He jerked his head at Tink. "And she's your much better bet because she *wants* to do it. I don't. I have no interest in doing this for real anymore, *whatsoever*. Least of all for you. And Tink is better than I would have been at sixteen by a wide margin. But—" He handed the reins he'd been holding to the girl so he could stand back and form a semicircle with her and Greaves left and right of himself. Then he angled his body so he could look into her eyes while carrying on talking to the man. "She is also *only* sixteen and you would all do well to remember that occasionally. To quote Karen — you know, that woman you pissed all over — riders are like horses. They need to mature. And when they are still young they need to have the breathing space to feel insecure and stupid sometimes and they need to be allowed to make mistakes."

An unsure smile played around Tinkerbelle's mouth while her brown eyes, so much like her sister's in that moment, started brimming with tears. She let go of Walt's reins and threw her arms around Pike's neck, sniffling quietly.

"I'm sorry, P," she breathed almost inaudibly.

"We're cool," he whispered back and squeezed her brief and hard. Then he twirled her around to stand between Rob and himself before stepping out of the embrace. "Now get on your pony, lady! He's gonna get a cold if we carry on yacking."

He positioned himself to offer her a leg up. She looked at him wide eyed.

"Bareback?"

"Yeah, bareback."

"Outside?"

"Yeah, outside."

"I can't."

He straightened up and frowned at her.

"Of course you can. You're Tinkerbelle Jones. I know. Wendy told me he tanked off with you on a hack and it knocked your confidence. But it can happen on any horse. You know that. You've come off a billion times before. Only difference with him is, if you fall off you need to put in another roll midair. So don't give me 'I can't'. Get over it, get on with it, have some fun with him."

He cupped his hand again and this time she placed her shin in it obediently. He threw her up onto the horse and, when he saw the still worried look on her face as her bottom made contact with the gelding's hide, placed a hand on her thigh.

"I'll stay by your side. Now lightly pick up just the curb rein, leave the other on the neck, relax your shoulders and let's move."

They walked towards the indoor arena, Pike flanking the horse with his long lost friend aboard to their left, Ash guarding their right. The two men trailed behind them at a distance.

Halfway, Pike looked up and saw that the girl's shoulders still hadn't softened. He smiled to himself as he hollered up to her.

"Now give us a propeller forward."

He could see her face break into a grin as she let go of the reins and began rotating her arms.

"Backwards," he demanded and her arms changed direction.

"One forwards, one backwards," he continued after half a minute and was pleased to hear Tink erupt in a giggle fit.

She'd always been dismally inept at this and nothing had changed. She stopped flapping her arms about and picked up the reins as they passed back into the indoor arena. Once inside, Pike told Tinkerbelle to halt for a moment.

He looked up at her.

"That's what you need, Tink, what he needs. He's a fantastic performer but he needs variety and just silly fun sometimes. Even

Olympic gold medal horses get hacked out, you know. And whenever people buy them and put them in gilded cages, that's always the beginning of the end. And you, too. You need to stop being so tense and serious. You already *are* a person in your own right," he echoed her sentiment from the night on the beach. "Now, carry on warming him down. I'm gonna get those two idiots to stay out of here for a bit, so you can spend some time with him *alone*. Oh—" he added with a broad grin while he stroked the horse's neck and patted the girl's thigh one last time, "and did you know he *loves* Elvis? Off you go."

With that he turned and walked back to Ash who was standing in the entrance. Together they folded the wooden panels back into place and pulled the sliding door shut, just in time to close it in front of Greaves' and van den Berg's noses.

"Sorry, gentlemen, but give them some privacy for a bit, eh?" Pike grinned.

The coach shook his head in total disbelief and turned to Rob.

"We'll have a talk about this later," he stated abruptly.

Then he hurried off around the building, presumably to find a tack room for the saddle he was still carrying. Rob stared after him for a few seconds before turning his attention to Pike.

"You sure know how to make friends, Peter."

"One of my many talents," Pike agreed dryly. "Now, let's talk about Strawberry."

"Yes," Rob began, sucking a breath in through his teeth, "I can't really sell him to you, I'm afraid."

The planets suddenly seemed to ground to a halt.

"Pardon?" Pike asked sharply.

"Fact is," Rob said, "the pony was already as good as sold when you rang me. They picked him up yesterday. Good buyers, too. I could hardly pull out just because—"

The universe imploded around about then.

If Rob ever did get to finish the sentence Pike was never to know.

The next thing he remembered was Ash's hot breath in his ear and his friend holding him in a vice from behind. Pike strained against it but Ash was stronger and better positioned. Pressed up against the other's relentless calm, Pike felt his own rage more acutely than ever before.

"Don't." Ash's voice bored itself into his ear drum. "Let it go. Breathe. It's not worth it. You don't want to end up like me. Calm. Easy. Relax."

As Ash kept murmuring soothing nothings Pike slowly felt it taking effect. His vision cleared and he saw Rob still standing in front of him, clearly taken by surprise by what was happening but entirely unharmed. It looked like Ash had been so fast in his intervention that Pike had never even managed to land one punch.

Ash loosened his grip and, when he was sure Pike wasn't going to try and lash out again, released him completely. He stepped around to Pike's side and tugged at his sleeve.

"Let's go," he said. "We're done here."

Pike followed him numbly.

Chapter 20

He'd failed them all.

Strawberry.

Eleanor.

Wendy.

Blue.

He was vaguely aware of the tears running down his face in a steady stream but didn't care enough to wipe at them. Borne from anger, frustration and loss, he saw no need to feel embarrassed for them in front of Ash.

They were three quarters of the way home already, neither of them having said a word since leaving The Black Horse. Dusk was settling in fast now, smudging the line between sky and ocean on the horizon and Pike was glad to see the three-trunk-tree looming in their path, just a short distance ahead.

He shot Ash a side glance. The other had sucked in his cheeks and was chewing on them rhythmically, a symphony of frowns playing on his forehead, amplified by the strange light. Pike lifted his sleeve to mop up his tears after all. Ash briefly looked over at him.

"He played you," Ash said hollowly as if his mind was really on something else, immediately turning his head in marching direction again.

"No shit."

"He dangled the pony in front of your nose, so you'd come and ride that horse. But why?"

"He wanted me to take the ride," Pike answered then realised that it wouldn't mean anything to Ash and added, "Be the horse's dedicated competition rider."

"Hm." Ash made a long pause before carrying on. "Why not let you buy the pony to sweeten the deal though?"

Again, his voice seemed to come from far away, like the interest was genuinely there but entirely feigned for the moment.

Pike answered anyway.

"I guess he didn't want me badly enough to let me have the carrot." He shrugged. "Second-guessing Robert Greaves is a futile past time, trust me. He ticks on money, status and sex. You never know what other players he has on his board. Maybe it wasn't about me at all, maybe it was about getting a reaction out of van den Berg. Or to have a dig at Tink, rouse her competitiveness, make her perform better. Maybe neither. Maybe he would have sold Straw to me but genuinely couldn't get out of the deal because he was laying the woman. Or because the family are stockholders in his company. The Black Horse is just a hobby for him after all. Real business always comes first. The guy honestly has no soul. He— "

Pike stopped himself mid-rant although it would have felt good to let rip now. But Ash clearly wasn't listening, still lost in thought and by the look on his face not the pleasurable kind either.

Pike changed tack.

"What did you mean when you said I don't want to end up like you?"

A faint, ironic smile interrupted the grinding of Ash's teeth and the creasing and uncreasing of his forehead. He kept walking though, staring ahead.

"You heard that, huh?" His face went back to performing its contortions. "Ah, fuck it. I'm gonna have to tell you at some point. Might as well do it now. Might help ya keep that temper of yours in check, 'cause, mate, do you need anger therapy or what? I'd like a word with your therapist some time. You're nowhere near ready to be released into the wild. Anyway. Right. You know when people go all 'yeah, man, when I land a punch the other guy doesn't get up again'?"

"Uh-huh."

"For me that's true."

Pike took a second to process the sentence.

"What? You punched someone and they didn't get up again?"

"Uh-huh. Ever. — He's dead."

Ash had said it in the same withdrawn manner in which he'd conducted the rest of the conversation and as they kept moving without missing a beat there was a moment when Pike questioned that he'd heard correctly. Although deep inside of himself he had no doubt at all.

"*You* killed someone?"

"Yes."

"Huh. — Did you mean to do it or was it an accident?"

Ash's pace quickened as he answered.

"No, I didn't fucking mean to do it. Although the guy was a bully." He paused. "Not that it's an excuse. He was taking advantage of this kid at school. Not very bright but sweet. Wouldn't harm a fly. I caught him touching her up, dragged her away from him. He came after me. Like I'd taken a toy from a pit bull. He swung the first punch. I swung one back. Only I kinda forgot I wasn't in the ring and that concrete is hard. But that's why I got off. Self defence. Open and shut. But, no, I didn't mean to kill him. I just threw a punch back. One punch, man, and he didn't get up."

"Fuck."

Ash stopped abruptly and turned to face Pike.

"So? Deal breaker?"

It seemed such an absurd question that in the first instant Pike didn't think it was meant seriously. The intensity in Ash's eyes told him otherwise.

"Don't be daft," he answered. "We all have our albatross to bear. Don't fancy yours much but it doesn't change a thing."

"You're not like other people are you?"

"Don't know. To the best of my knowledge I've never been other people."

Ash scrutinised him long and hard through eyes like slits.

"You sure?"

"Doesn't change a thing."

"Good," the other stated. "'Cause we got bigger problems."

Pike was confused.

"Have we?"

"Yeah, we do," Ash said, walking on. "Let's just hope she's run back to yours. Keep on moving."

"Who?"

"Wendy, you numpty. Why do you think she wasn't there? Ten to one she's scarpered."

"What are you talking about?"

"Oh, man, would like me to send you a text or something? If they sold the pony, she's taken off, mate, one hundred percent."

Wendy wasn't at the cottage when they got back. Anxiously they put the horses away for the night and then waited around in the kitchen for news. It was funny how even without a shred of evidence Ash's assumption had almost immediately become their accepted reality but in his heart of hearts Pike had known the other was right as soon as Ash had voiced it. He'd felt around the ether for her but it was as if she'd cut off all connection. He'd tried calling her in the real world but her phone was switched off and there was nobody picking up at The Black Horse now. Any attempts to reach Tinkerbelle remained equally in vain and Pike didn't dare dial Rob's number. It was 10pm when the Cottage phone rang and made them all jump. Rob asking evenly if they'd seen Wendy at all today, confirmed their fears.

The girl had gone.

Chapter 21

"Hey, you, open your eyes."

Eleanor's voice softly wormed itself into his subconscious and Pike snuggled deeper into the pillow, clinging to the illusion of her cool hand stroking the side of his face, tracing scars.

He didn't want to wake up.

He'd slept badly, lying awake well into dawn, tossing and turning until sheer exhaustion had claimed him for a couple of hours of fitful dreams.

After the brief and awkward phone conversation with Rob, Ash and he had set off into the woods. When that hadn't conjured up the girl, they'd gone into town to prowl the seafront and search doorways and playgrounds for her. Ash knew every nook and cranny, every crack in the pavement a person could fall through but they had had no luck. They'd given up in the end, too tired to put one foot in front of the other anymore, and had gone home.

At some point during all of this, sitting at the foot of a slide in one of the parks, Pike had called Eleanor. He could tell she was gutted by the turn of events but she'd soothed him nevertheless, telling him to keep his head up and his heels down. It had made him laugh. She was good at that, making him laugh in the midst of despair. She was also good at cooling his fire with her soft touches and he happily let himself be engulfed by the memory of them for the moment, in favour of getting up and facing another day's worry.

Eleanor's hand ran through his hair, exposing his neck. She kissed the skin right above the jugular vein then let her fingers trail along his arm. They reached the top of his hand and she laced them through his, shuffling up against his back.

"Come on, open your stupid yellow eyes and turn around."

It was the 'stupid yellow' that did it.

It was then that he allowed his nose to find her scent underneath a cloud of stale tobacco, dry ice and beer hanging on her clothes. Gig smell. *Real* gig smell.

He opened his eyes and turned to look at her.

"You're here. You're actually here."

Olive green irises danced with joy around sleep-deprived, inflated pupils, while her nose twitched amusedly. During her absence she'd cut her hair even shorter, getting rid of all artificial colour in it to sport her natural honey brown in a pixie style. He reached for it, running his thumb along her temple.

"Of course, I'm here, you stupid boy," she said, snuggling her cheek into his palm. "You end a phone call with 'I need you back' and I come back. – You like it?"

He didn't answer but slipped his hand around to the nape of her neck and pulled her into a kiss. He hadn't meant for it to become everlasting but, as always, once their lips touched, existence itself became fluid around the edges and for the next few minutes there was nothing but sheer lust, desire and hunger for more.

He'd always been careful not to overstep the boundaries he'd set for them despite her pushing them constantly but after so many weeks apart he found it difficult to refrain from just gobbling her up whole. Her delicate small limbs writhing all around him in equally hungry responses didn't make restraint any easier and for once it was her who pulled the plug.

When she retracted, she was sitting on top of him, straddling him firmly between her black denim clad thighs. Her naked torso was breathing heavily under his touch as his hands rested on her waist, his thumbs circling the soft skin left and right of her belly button. From this angle, in the shadowy twilight and only half decent with the remnants of the previous night's make up still lining her eyes in kohl, she looked every inch the rock star's daughter that she actually was.

A far cry from the shy little sprite who stole my land, my pony and my heart.

Her eyes narrowed and her lips curled into a bemused smile. "What was that look for?"

"Just thinking how shy you used to be."

"Uh-uh," she smiled. "Never shy. Just small and quiet. Big difference." She stretched her arms to the ceiling, arching her back to push out her tiny breasts to the best of their perfection. "Look at me now though. Five foot. Who would have thought. Almost ready to be backed, don't you reckon?"

She leant forward with a quietly dirty laugh and kissed him softly before he could say anything.

"Come on, come downstairs, meet my dad."

She got off him, collected her skimpy vest top off the floor and put it back on before stopping for a minute to admire the new additions on his wall. "Decent poem. Hell of a drawing. Nice pleats. You must seriously like him to let him get away with that."

She looked over her shoulder at him and grinned then turned back to the collage. She let her eyes rest on the pinned up photograph of John and the young woman on horseback for a moment. Pike could see a shiver wander down her back.

"Who's the pretty lady with your father?" she asked, then went across the room to pick up his trousers from the back of the chair and threw them at him. Watching her stand there, framed by the dull light of morning coming through the window, Pike suddenly realised that one side of her jeans was covered in grey hairs.

"Not sure. — You went to see Blue first, didn't you?"

She looked down at herself, frowned and brushed at the dusting of pony coat.

"Of course." She grimaced. "You did better than Mum though. She doesn't even know I'm back in the country yet."

"So you've met Ash?"

"Yup. Hunter's Moon, too. She is huuuuuge. — He's a good guy, I think," she answered the unasked question. "Bit freaked out by me appearing in the stable all of a sudden. And worried. Really, really worried."

It was like having a bucket of ice water emptied over his head.

He knew this sensation well from the various deaths in his life: the waking up to everything being alright for a few minutes before reality slapped you around the face and made you want to sleep a thousand years.

Eleanor had turned around to rummage in his wardrobe and a minute later a clean t-shirt followed in the flight path of the trousers. She sat down at the end of the bed and watched him get dressed.

"Don't freak. It hasn't been mentioned in the media yet. That's a good sign, I think. We were keeping an eye on the news all the way here. When we weren't singing 'I drove all night'. We actually do sound really good together, Dad's right." She took a heavy breath. "Don't worry, we'll find her."

The penny dropped while he pulled the t-shirt over his head.

"Did you just say, 'meet my dad'?

"Yup."

Pike's mouth went dry.

He had never met Jerry McGraw.

The man was a legend. A legend whose entire recording history had been in Pike's possession long before he'd met the man's daughter. A far, far away legend who lived in Australia and who he was supposed to meet at the end of the present tour, in a few weeks, in a controlled environment, somewhere in a faceless hotel room in London.

Not here, not now, not under these circumstances.

"He's here?" he asked dumbly.

"Yes," Eleanor said, getting to her feet and taking his hand. "But only for another ten minutes or so. They pretty much need to turn around and head straight back to the port if they want to stand a hope in hell of making the gig tonight."

"You came by ferry?"

She dragged him out of the room and onto the windy staircase leading down from of the Watchtower. She had to let go of his hand to navigate the narrow path between the stacks of books that lined the steps and she bounded ahead. He watched the muscles move between her shoulder blades as she bounced and talked at the same time. She was still small, still so much more like a creature from a fairytale than an ordinary human, but she'd grown alright.

"Yup. Didn't really have a choice. There weren't any more flights last night and Dad gets it. He knew I couldn't just hang around doing nothing till the morning. I know I keep moaning about him but he's a good guy, really. He grabbed a driver and a car and we headed for the ferry. But, like I said, they've got to turn back pronto, otherwise there'll be a few thousand very angry people in Brussels tonight."

She held the heavy door to the first floor landing open and smiled up at him, while rocking excitedly on the balls of her feet.

"And for the record, I've been this size for a while. You just couldn't see it. Absence clearly makes the eyes grow wider."

He stopped in front of her and leant down until his forehead touched hers, stilling her.

"Stop fishing around in my brain."

"Can't help it." She grinned. "It's just too interesting in there."

Out of the corner of his eyes he could see goose bumps form along her naked arms.

"You're cold," he stated, rubbing his hands over her shoulders.

"Wrong." She detached her forehead from his and slithered

around for her mouth to find his ear. "I'm hot," she breathed, barely suppressing a mocking chuckle, "So very, very hot."

He quickly straightened up and ran a hand through his hair. "You've got to stop doing that."

She laughed at him then, a proper taking the mick laugh, while crossing her arms in front of her chest, leaning back and putting a foot out. The cool chick's pout.

"Really? Why?"

Great. Carry on exactly where we left off, why don't we? Five minutes and we're straight back in the thick of it. Hallelujah.

"Because we're still not ready," he responded heavily, looking away. "You running off for a few weeks doesn't change anything."

He heard her take in a sharp breath and found her eyes again. They were shooting daggers at him in no uncertain terms.

They'd had this argument so many times in the last two years, Pike could recite the script. Next she'd ask him, 'When? When we're a hundred and eight? What are we waiting for?', then he'd counter that all things had a natural rhythm and that everything always went wrong if you tried to mess with that rhythm. She'd call 'horseshit' and so on and so forth.

He sighed heavily.

"Horse—" she started, obviously skipping a part of the routine, but he got in there before she could finish the word.

"Okay," he interrupted then added very softly, "*I'm* not ready, alright? I told you a long time ago that you need to be a bit more patient with me and that still stands."

Her face lit up.

"You concede that I *am* then?"

She searched his eyes and he knew he didn't really need to answer the question as her stance changed and she threw her arms up in the air.

"Progress! Huzzah! That's all I was after. — Come on." She grabbed his hand again. "We don't have time for this. We have people to send off, a girl to rescue, a pony to find and personally I could really do with my jumper. I'm flipping freezing."

Jerry McGraw was standing at the bottom of the stairs, already bidding Aaron and Sarah goodbye when Pike and Eleanor descended towards the ground floor.

The man looked up to smile at them broadly.

"Hey, there you are. I wasn't sure if you were going to make it down in time." He winked at his daughter then held out his hand to Pike who'd just made the last step. "I'm Jerry."

Pike took the hand and shook it.

"It's a pleasure to meet you, Sir."

Close up, Jerry was even smaller than the pictures that Pike had seen in the past had suggested and he took a step back, so the man didn't have to strain his neck as he looked up into his eyes. Jerry McGraw's long trademark mane of greying ash blonde curls began shaking in an uncontrolled bout of raspy laughter as he released Pike's hand and looked over at his daughter.

"Did he just call me Sir?"

Pike felt Eleanor step up to his side. She slipped her hand into his and gave it a small squeeze.

"Don't be mean to him, Dad," she said evenly.

The laughter subsided and Jerry's eyes narrowed, taking the two of them in soberly. He looked back and forth between them.

"Oh shit. You two are fucked."

He cleared his throat then snatched Eleanor from Pike's side to give her a brief hug.

"Right, I'm off." He let her go. "Thanks again for the tea," he said to Aaron and Sarah before smiling at Pike with genuine pity. "Beware of the Payne women, young grasshopper. Once you give them your heart you'll never get it back." He laughed again as he turned to leave. "Good luck finding your friend. Keep me posted. See you in London, baby. I already know that you ain't coming back out to join me."

Jerry winked again and a second later he was out of the door.

Chapter 22

Ash had brushed Hunter to within an inch of her life.

The big mare was tied up in the aisle, gleaming from the tip of her nose to the bottom of her tail but he still kept running the soft brush over her manically. Pike could see in the horse's half turned ears and her twitching tail that she had long ceased to enjoy the grooming session and was now just patiently waiting for it to be over. If it had been Blue, Ash would have had a hefty nip in the butt by now.

The little roan, Casta and Inigo were all still in their stables and didn't appear as if they had been tended to, although Blue looked distinctly more contented than she had in recent weeks. Inigo, on the other hand, kicked the door as soon as Pike had entered the barn and Casta whickered at him impatiently. They would have to wait a while longer for breakfast and freedom.

Pike walked up to Ash from behind and put a hand on the other's shoulder.

"Stop."

Ash kept brushing.

"Seriously. She isn't enjoying it anymore. Time to stop."

Ash's action slowed and finally halted. His forehead sank against the mare's ribcage and a violent shiver went through him.

"The stupid girl. She's gonna get herself killed. Stupid idiot."

He snuffled helplessly.

"She's not going to get herself killed," Pike said with conviction. "Don't be a drama queen. She's tough as old boots, our Wendy. She'll turn up and she'll be just fine, you hear me?"

Ash shook his head, still facing the horse.

"You don't know the half of it, mate. You know how I met her?"

Pike nodded behind him.

"Yeah, on the beach."

"No." Ash turned around, ridding himself of Pike's touch in the process. "I never said that. No, I woke up in the tent one morning and there she was. She'd just crawled in, in the night, and decided to sleep in my tent. With me in it. I could have been anyone. A pedo. Some arsehole who gets off on little kids. Or just some random arsehole. Whatever. I mean, what kid *does* that? She might be tough but she ain't that clever. I gave her such a bollocking. Told her to go home and stay home. Not that she listened. Started turning up at the beach after that. Fucking pain in the fucking neck."

He'd thrown the brush back into the grooming box on the floor with the last sentence and was now looking at Pike again, pure desperation oozing from him.

Pike did the only thing he could think of. He pulled the other into a hug.

There was a moment of resistance but ultimately Ash relented and clung to him like a limpet for a few seconds.

"She'll be okay," Pike whispered and let go, smiling at Ash reassuringly.

"You're wrong, you see. She *didn't* crawl into anyone's tent. She didn't find a pedo, she found you. She is *that* clever."

"Bull," Ash answered back.

"Maybe. But that's exactly what we are going to believe until we're proven otherwise. Come on, help me get these horses fed and turned out. And let's think about where to look next."

Ash looked around as if waking from a trance.

"Where's the pixie gone?" he asked with a frown.

"Sprite, actually. She'll return. She's gone to tell her mother that she's back in the country. Come on, we need to keep the world moving."

When Sarah came to help them fifteen minutes later, she told them that Wendy's disappearance had just been on the local news.

It seemed surreal.

The police turned up an hour later.

Sarah had gone back to the house, leaving Pike and Ash to muck out the stables, when four coppers in uniforms came marching across the paddocks. Ash spotted them first, while wheeling a barrow out of the door. He stopped and called to Pike to come out.

Together they set off towards the officers, three men, two of which seemed to be setting out already to scour the grounds, and one woman. Pike and Ash stopped in front of the woman and her partner.

"Good morning," she said briskly, "I'm Sergeant Sally Ward, this is Constable Jack Phillips. We're looking into the missing persons case of Wendy Jones. Which one of you is Peter Hawthorne?"

"Paytah," Pike corrected her, "If it's official, it's Paytah. P — A — Y — T — A — H."

She frowned inquisitively and he sighed.

"It means fire in Siouan."

She turned to Ash who was doing a double take at Pike. "And you are?"

"Ashley Parker. Ash."

"You live here, too?"

"Yes," Pike answered for him. He could sense an edge to Ash that had never been there before. It wasn't the wisest thing to give off right now. For a brief moment he wondered just how many police interviews the other had been subjected to between the 'open' and the 'shut' of his case.

"We understand Wendy stayed here for most of last week?"

They both nodded numbly.

"In the house, yes," Pike clarified.

"We've already been in the house," she informed them. "Right now I'm interested in the stables. Do you mind?"

She indicated the barn with a tilt of the head.

Pike stepped aside, turning towards the building.

"Go ahead."

Within the movement he caught sight of one of the other officers who was poking around the muck heap with a long stick. All blood drained from his body. He could feel it pooling down in his feet.

"Ash?" he whimpered.

"Uh-huh," the other replied equally wobbly, his eyes having followed Pike's.

"I feel sick."

Sally Ward was almost subtle in her refusal to let them out of her sight, while having the stables turned upside down by her two unnamed minions who seemed barely older than Pike and Ash. After they'd checked out all the boxes, she sent them back outside then leisurely ushered the two young men into the tack room. All the while she was gently probing them, interlacing relevant questions with more general chit chat.

While she let Jack Phillips do most of the active snooping once they had entered Ash's domain, she asked the two young men to park themselves on the sofa and began interviewing them more openly.

"So, you say you last saw Wendy Thursday afternoon, just before she was taken home by Ms Osbourne and that neither of you has seen her since?"

"That's right," Pike answered, looking up into her face. She was quite a soft looking woman underneath the uniformed exterior and quite young. In her late twenties or early thirties, Pike guessed. They locked eyes for a moment and in the same instant

Pike understood that she wasn't just some bot. She was good at what she did and she knew it.

"Hm." She picked up the book Ash was currently reading from the old mounting block that served as Ash's nightstand and twirled it in her hand. "Gaiman. Bit dark, isn't it? I'm more of a Pratchett person myself."

She was trying to put them at ease and to his annoyance, Pike realised it was working.

For him.

Ash was another matter.

Pike could feel the other next to him getting wound tighter and tighter with every second that passed and with every object Jack Phillips began scrutinising in the background. His right leg had started shaking restlessly and without looking, Pike's hand found Ash's thigh. He gave it a squeeze.

Chill.

The motion stopped.

Sally Ward's eyes narrowed slightly as they caught the gesture. Her focus shifted to Ash.

"So, how would you describe your relationship with Wendy?"

"She's a friend," Ash answered hoarsely.

"Bit young, isn't she? What do you do together?"

Pike was up on his feet in an instant, slipping in between Ash and the Sergeant, blocking her view.

"Look, lady, you're barking up the wrong tree here. And you are wasting time. Ours and yours. We should all be out there looking for her. So stop harassing us and go do your flipping job."

Sally Ward hadn't moved an inch. Jack Philips on the other hand had swiftly crossed the room in two paces to stand by her side. She held a hand up, signalling for him to back off before she smiled up at Pike, almost sweetly.

"I'll ignore that. Sit down."

Pike could feel Ash getting ready to pounce behind him.

"No, he won't," a cool, slightly rough girl's voice interjected from the doorway. "You, on the other hand, will leave my guys alone now and, to say it with him, go do your flipping job. *Somewhere else*."

No one had heard Eleanor come in and both Sally Ward and Jack Philips turned around on their heels. Pike couldn't see the police woman's face but the shift in her neck as she cocked her head slightly told him that she was somewhere between put out and amused by the interruption, clearly mistaking it for the misguided gumption of a little girl. At first glance, Eleanor still passed for a lot younger than her actual age. Pike could hear that he was right once the Sergeant opened her mouth.

"And who might you be?"

Eleanor leant back against the door frame.

"Eleanor McGraw. And I'd like you to leave now, please."

Pike could smell instant rage dripping off Jack Philips like sweat off a race horse. The man clearly didn't take kindly to youths who did not come with blind respect for authority figures.

Sally Ward appeared to have a similar problem.

"Excuse me?" she said sharply.

Eleanor smiled.

"You have no right to be here unless you have a warrant or my permission," she said matter-of-factly. "As far as I know you have neither."

"*Your* permission? *Excuse me?* Who do you think you are?"

"Eleanor McGraw. Didn't I say that already? Sorry, it's been a long night. And, yes, *my* permission. I own this land and unless you *do* have a warrant you can show me, I'd like you to leave now. But—" She grinned with true delight all of a sudden. "As I was coming to tell you, you might need my guys to help your guys to get out."

All Hawthorne horses played nose ball from foal.

It was a fundamental part of their early learning regime, according to Pike's grandma the bread and butter of educating any trick pony. But, like any other discipline, some liked it more than others. No pony passing through the Barn had ever adored it as much as the famous Blueberry Mouse though, with Inigo following a devoted third, just behind Blue's late mother Bracken from whom the little roan had inherited the love of the game. Once a human picked up a ball they would stand attentively, waiting for the two-legged animal to start the match.

So it was no wonder that the very object they had picked up to defend themselves with was the thing keeping the two young policemen trapped against the big elder tree in the little herd's paddock. While the bodies of Hunter and Casta, taking their midday naps under the sparse autumn canopy, blocked at least two escape routes to the rear, the little roan and the stallion had planted themselves firmly in front of the men to the left and right, eyes fixed on the ball. Oblivious to the horses' expectations, the two officers kept passing the ball between them to use it as a shield and were threatening to lob it at the animals whenever one tiptoed closer. Both Blue and Inigo, on the other hand, were delighted with the sophistication with which these two humans appeared to be starting the game.

It was a funny sight but it didn't last. Shortly after stepping out of the barn Pike saw that Inigo was beginning to get impatient with the feinting of throws. A few seconds later, the stallion's front feet began rising off the ground, not high and not close, but to the already frightened men it must have seemed threatening enough.

Pike took pity.

"Just throw the ball as far as you can!" he shouted across, then added to be on the safe side, "Not *at* them though!"

He could see the taller of the two men, who was currently in possession of the ball, hesitate before hurling it away with all his might. Both Inigo and Blue were gone in a cloud of dust, the little old pony shooting ahead, not having lost any time with silly antics. Casta briefly looked up from her slumber before letting her head sink again into sleep stance.

Eleanor's elbow poked Pike in the side.

"Hah! Mine's still better than yours. That's what he gets for prancing."

"Why didn't *you* just tell them what to do?"

Eleanor shrugged.

"Wanted to show you. Thought it was too funny to miss. Good thing, too."

She turned to Ward and Phillips who were standing on her far side, watching their men scramble over the fence with ill suppressed smiles on their faces. She caught the Sergeant's eye. They stared at each other for a moment and something passed between them, something distinctly *female* that Pike couldn't quite fathom but that seemed weirdly amicable. Whatever it was, to all intents and purposes it appeared to end in Eleanor winning out. Without further ado, Sally Ward gathered her troops and left the premises.

Chapter 23

"You're taking *him*?"

Eleanor looked up sleepily from slumping sideways across Blue's freshly groomed body as Pike brought Inigo into the stable block. She'd gone ahead to spend time with her pony while Pike had stayed outside, helping Ash adjust the seat and handlebars of Eleanor's mountain bike.

The surprise in her voice made Pike turn to the stallion and contemplate his choice. The animal looked back at him expectantly, making Pike chuckle. He ruffled the horse's forelock. It hadn't even occurred to him to take Casta. If it hadn't been for Eleanor's raised eyebrows right now, he wouldn't have given it a second thought. This was a search and rescue mission, an adventure, and this was his adventure horse. Inigo blew out his nose softly and Pike tugged on the lead rope.

"Absolutely. Come on, boy, they're ready and we haven't even started. Do you want a saddle?" he asked Eleanor while he tied Inigo up and started unbuckling the stallion's rug straps.

"Heavens no," her voice came from behind. "It's cold. I want seat heating. Also, we need to get going if we want to make it to the quarry and back before dark. Ash is going to slow us down and the police cost us a lot of time."

Pike looked out through the open barn door into the misty, dark noon where Ash was circling the yard on the bike that even with all the adjustments was still comically too small for him but would have to do. She was right. He began hurrying up without more chat.

Twenty minutes later they rode out of the main entrance, filtering into heavy weekend traffic and heading towards the woods. As soon as car after car started passing them, some more slowly than others, some with more of a berth than others, Pike knew he had definitely taken the right horse for the job. Green though he was where understanding the aids was concerned, Inigo's unflappability on the road was far superior to Casta's nervousness around anything with an engine. Nevertheless, Pike couldn't wait to get away from the vehicles.

He breathed more freely once they'd slipped away into the woods. They joined the main track, a gentle incline wide enough to ride two abreast, and he shouted for Ash to cycle ahead to the fork in the path then signalled for Eleanor and Blue to join him. They trotted up silently. He glanced down across at her, taking in her profile under the riding hat, the look of concentration on her face, her eyes firmly trained ahead. He'd missed her so much his heart was still aching from the bliss of having her back. Her mouth formed a smile under his scrutiny.

"Stop staring at me. Look ahead. You know what my riding instructor always says? Look where you're going."

She tipped her head sharply and he turned his attention back onto the path, just in time to duck and avoid an overhanging branch sweeping him off his horse. Inigo mistook the sudden lightness on his back as a signal to go and broke into a canter. At first Pike wanted to rein him back in. They hadn't gone faster than a trot yet and this really wasn't the day to further Inigo's education but as he felt the power and the beauty of the stride beneath him, accompanied by a cry of joy from Eleanor who appeared to think they were intentionally going for it, he couldn't resist. He threw caution to the wind, let the aids follow the motion and urged the stallion on. Inigo's response to the trust instilled in him was immediate and complete. Pike would never have thought it possible to be sucked into a connection so deep and limitless, so absolute. As the trees whizzed past them the lines between him and the stallion dissolved entirely.

He had to gather all his wits to force himself out of the mix of their soul soup again, to collect his own being into a separate entity and bring the horse back down to a trot and then a walk. He patted the stallion, laughing and crying at the same time, knowing full well the gesture wasn't remotely needed for Inigo to *know*. A couple of minutes later Eleanor and Blue cantered leisurely up to their side.

"Oh, man, I missed this sooooooo much! What a thrill!" she exclaimed happily, just before their eyes fell on Ash. He was standing by the fork in the path, leaning heavily on the handlebars of the bike, facing them. They both let their gazes sink like naughty children and looked at their hands as he glowered at them angrily.

"Having fun, are we?" he snarled.

They stared guiltily at their horses' withers.

After choosing the left path to check out the old fort first, they rode on in solemn silence. As long as the path sloped up gently Ash cycled ahead but once they left the woods and got back onto open ground the hill became steeper and he started lagging behind. The mist of earlier in the day had become denser with the advancing afternoon and fog had gathered across the hills, not so thick it impaired their vision of the immediate surroundings but opaque enough to obscure the next hilltop along, home to the fort, a small mound of medieval earthworks. Despite its comparatively unspectacular nature it was a favoured summer picnic spot, with a neat circle of trees at the top providing both a tethering opportunity for horses and shelter and shade for humans.

A perfect hideout, Pike thought, his heart speeding up in hopeful anticipation.

It had been Eleanor's idea to check out the various destinations of their favourite rides for the missing girl, arguing that if she were a twelve-year-old on the run, she'd head for somewhere she knew, not some shop doorway in the centre of town. Pike hoped and prayed to all that was or wasn't there that she was right.

Images of broken, dead Wendys kept intermingling in his brain with fantasies of happy reunions and for once in his life he wished he had a less vivid imagination.

She's going to be just fine. Just keep the world moving, he reminded himself.

They came to a halt, letting their horses graze while waiting for Ash to catch up.

"That's where we're going," Pike said to him as soon as he stopped beside them, pointing across into the fog. He indicated the steeply declining path in front of them that would get them down the hillside and to the next slope up.

"You go ahead. Down, then up, and when you get to the top there is a little track to your left that leads to the fort. Wait for us there — if we don't overtake you first."

Without so much as catching his breath, Ash nodded grimly then freewheeled down into the mist. Seconds later he'd disappeared out of sight.

Pike was about to ask Inigo to get his head up out of the grass, when the stallion abruptly stood to attention of his own accord. The animal's focus shifted instantly. Whereas before Pike's purpose had been Inigo's purpose, suddenly the horse clearly had his own agenda. Pike could feel a nicker so low it wasn't audible shiver through the body beneath him.

"Eleanor," he said loudly, "There are other horses ahead. Keep her together. I don't know what he's going to be like."

A quick look across told him she'd shortened her reins already.

"Forget about him, he'll be cool," she answered urgently as she rode past him, starting the descent. "But if there are other riders ahead, it's an accident waiting to happen. Ash is hurtling towards them at a thousand miles an hour. Let's go."

It wasn't a gradient that could be negotiated at anything but a walk. Especially with an ancient pony, sure-footed though Blue was, and a young stallion still learning to balance a rider, perfectly centred though his rider was, and by the time they got to the bottom, Eleanor's prophecy had long come true.

They heard the voices before they could see the scene and both hurried their horses on when they realised one was Tinkerbelle's, swearing at panic pitch.

"You idiot! You could have killed us. Dumb luck you didn't. What do you think you're doing? Who the heck goes –"

She stopped mid-sentence when Pike and Eleanor rode into view then did a double take at Ash who was sitting by the chalk bank, looking at a gash in his right calf through a tear in his trousers. He had evidently swerved to avoid Tinkerbelle and Martine, coming off the bike in the process. Tinkerbelle was unharmed, still sitting on Coco, but her riding companion had had less luck. Martine wasn't mounted on her Haflinger anymore. She had her bottom firmly parked on the path a little way off, holding her pony's reins from her perch by its front hooves and was laughing good-naturedly.

"Oh, it's you!" Tinkerbelle exclaimed and swung herself out of the saddle to walk over to Ash, dragging Coco behind her. Beneath him Pike could sense Inigo sniff the air, appraising the new mare's scent. He put a flat palm on the horse's shoulder blade.

Not now, boy. Bigger fish to fry.

He emphasized the thought with a light half halt to bring the horse's attention back around. Inigo gave off a small, disappointed grunt as he gave in to Pike's command and stood obediently.

Tinkerbelle in the meantime had reached Ash, dragging Coco behind her, and was berating him from a closer vantage point now.

"It's your fault! All of this! If she hadn't met you she'd never have thought of running away. But you just had to come along and make it all look such fun, didn't you? If she dies, I'll kill you."

Ash got up to stand in front her and everything went quiet. Nevertheless, his voice was such a deep growl that when he spoke, Pike nearly missed it.

"Don't worry. If she dies, I'll help ya."

"Right," Pike shouted brightly. "Enough of the blame game. Martine, are you hurt?"

The girl in question had stopped laughing and risen to her feet.

"No," she answered equally upbeat, dusting herself off. "Learned to fall from the best of them."

"Great. Hold Coco for a minute then, so Tink can come and grab Inigo off me while I take a look at Ash's leg."

"I'm fine, it's just a scratch," Ash said. He had already picked up the bike, examining it for damage.

"Brilliant news," Pike answered back sarcastically. "I'll take a look at it anyway. Now, come on people, just get on with it, please, we're losing time and daylight."

Once they all complied, Pike had them sorted in record time.

Ash's wound was indeed not very deep and the blood was congealing already. Nevertheless, if they continued the journey it would start bleeding again and it needed wrapping. Eleanor, perpetually cold and layered up in a gazillion vests, t-shirts, jumpers and jackets, donated a t-shirt to the cause and Pike tied it around the leg best as he could. When he was finished, he went to take Inigo back from Tinkerbelle.

Without Pike's influence the stallion became more interested in Coco again and Tink had moved him away a little, using Eleanor and Blue as a shield. When he got to them Eleanor was in the process of redressing herself garment by garment, fishing them off Blue's neck in front of her, which she had utilised as a clothes horse. To Pike's surprise the two girls were talking in low, friendly voices.

From the moment they had first met, there had been no love lost between these two, Tinkerbelle having thrown down the gauntlet the minute Eleanor had moved to their snoozy little town. They were in the same year at school and on day one Tink had treated Eleanor in a pretty nasty manner, surprised to find that the 'midget' could hold her own in a word fight. Pike had never been able to figure out quite what the bone of contention had been — other than Tinkerbelle being a bit of a cow. Listening in on the conversation now, though, one wouldn't have known. They were talking about where Eleanor had been for the last few weeks and although there was an undisguised tone of envy in Tink's questions about the tour it all seemed quite civil.

"It's alright for some, isn't it? While the rest of us get to do our work placements in supermarkets, you get to go off around Europe with a rock band," Tink finished the conversation with a dejected air, handing Pike the reins of his horse.

Suddenly he felt guilty. He knew he hadn't exactly helped the atmosphere between these two up to now. His refusal to let go of his silly grudge against Tink and his tendency to always stoke the fire of jealousy when Eleanor felt twinges about his past with Tinkerbelle as a riding partner was shaming him now.

He'd liked the grudge and, even worse, he'd liked the jealousy.

You're a git, Paytah Hawthorne.

He cleared his throat.

"Right, do you two reckon you could bury the hatchet for the time being, at least as long as we're all still looking for Wendy?"

Both girls frowned at him in disbelief, then exchanged a look between them and burst into laughter.

"You really need to get with the program, P." Tink snorted as she as she passed him and touched his arm lightly then hollered over to Eleanor, "You tell him. You're the girlfriend."

Pike slung Inigo's reins back over the horse's neck and jumped on him. Once seated he leant over to Eleanor and Blue.

"Tell me what?"

"We've been cool for ages. We did a science project together before the summer and it was good. We had a good time. She's alright. Wouldn't exactly exchange make up tips but we're okay."

Pike was stunned.

"Why didn't you tell me?"

"You weren't ready," she grinned sweetly.

Girls!

Before Pike could say anything else on the matter, Ash interrupted their little tête-à-tête by cycling to Pike's other side and braking noisily.

"Hate to interrupt but are we going or what?"

Pike turned, nodded sharply at Ash then looked over his head at Martine and Tink, as they mounted their rides.

"I take it you've checked out the fort already?"

"Yes," they replied as their seats made contact with their saddles.

"So? Quarry next? Ride together?" he asked into the round.

"Lead on," four voices replied.

Pike would never speak to anyone about what happened at the quarry.

That night, rubbing Eleanor's legs, sore from the long ride, with aluminium diacetate he came close to telling her but couldn't find the words.

How did you describe something that was not even the nucleus of a feeling, not even the shadow of the ghost of an idea yet so strong it made you nauseous enough to nearly fall off the edge of the world?

He chewed it over as he watched Eleanor gently drift off to sleep beneath his kneading hands.

The five of them had made it to the old sandstone quarry in good time, approaching it from the road at the bottom and finding quickly that it was another dead end. The giant excavation in the side of the hill which humans had left behind decades ago lay as deserted as ever. A few empty beer cans and remnants of washed out bonfires told tales of summer parties that nobody had bothered to clear up after but there was no sign of current life. They had ridden away silently, taking a short cut, which meant climbing up a narrow, windy bridle path. It ended near the top of the artificial hole in the ground, close enough to the sheer drop into oblivion for Eleanor to shudder and tell them all to come away quickly.

They had already started the journey home, ready to escort Tinkerbelle and Martine to The Black Horse before making their own way, when Pike had suddenly felt a pull. Something was tugging at his soul, whispering at the edges of his consciousness to *come back and look.* Without a second thought he'd told Eleanor to take the lead and turned Inigo back towards the quarry. The others had all looked at him inquisitively as he passed them by going in the opposite direction but he'd just mumbled to them to carry on, that he'd catch up in a sec, was just quickly checking something out. Looking back, he had no idea what words he'd actually used. They had happened purely on the outside, as if his vocal chords were detached from his true being.

He wondered what would have happened if it hadn't been for Inigo's grounding presence. He might just have walked into the abyss. But with his horse looking after him, their journey had stopped at the edge, where the stallion had stood fast and used his own pull to glue his rider firmly to his hide. While Pike had stared down into the foggy grey below, looking for something he couldn't name, something he somehow knew wasn't there *anymore*, he had thought he could almost hear a voice but then again, *not*. In the end, Inigo had woken him from the trance with an impatient stomp on the ground. In the real world, the other horses were getting away without them and he wanted to go.

Pike had turned him around abruptly and fled the spot as fast as the stallion's hooves would carry them.

Chapter 24

They were woken by a soft knock on the Watchtower's door the next morning. Eleanor was snuggled up tightly against him, smelling enticingly of girl flavour and he had to force himself to take his hand off the soft skin around her belly button to slide up the bed and prop his torso up into a presentable position. With a disapproving grunt, his sprite wriggled further beneath the duvet until her head had disappeared entirely.

"Come in," he said loudly and Isabel stuck her head around the door.

"Good morning," Eleanor's mum replied, startling the burrowing animal by his side. Eleanor gave off another guttural sound in her hidey hole and then slithered out to sit up next to him.

"Hi Mum." She blinked sleepily. "What are you doing here? Oh man, I ache. Remind me not to go on another three hour ride after not being on a pony for weeks."

"Well, if the mountain will not come to the prophet, the prophet will go to the mountain." Isabel smiled. "And the prophet has brought cake for breakfast. Apricot. New recipe. Very breakfasty."

It made Pike feel all warm inside towards the woman who'd walked over to them and had sat herself down on the edge of the bed, but also acutely aware of their situation again. One thing he had learned about Eleanor's mother in the time he had known her was that Isabel turned into a domestic goddess of all things ovenborn only when she was worried or trying to distract herself. So the next sentence she spoke hit him like a sucker punch.

"There's been a development," she said soberly. "Nothing bad. But it's not good news either. They've picked Wendy out on CCTV footage from Thursday night. At Kings Cross. It's on the news."

"In London?" Pike asked somewhat idiotically.

"Yes."

"Crap," Eleanor swore under her breath. "That's like the last station you want to be roaming around as a twelve-year-old, at night, on your own. Why couldn't she have gone to Victoria?"

Pike knew exactly what she meant.

Of all the main London stations, Kings Cross was the sleaziest and most dangerous to hang around, complete with street hookers of all five genders and kerb crawlers adhering to little or no age of consent.

When he and Eleanor had gone up on the train to see Karen in Scotland in the summer they had caught the Stirling service from there and some greasy guy had promptly tried to pick up Eleanor, despite the fact she'd been walking by Pike's side. And that had been in the middle of a bright, sunny day in July.

Eleanor and he both sat up a bit straighter.

"Karen!" they shouted out at the same time.

Their moment of exultant joy, having realised where Wendy must have been headed when she'd been caught on camera, didn't last long. It was Sunday morning and if the girl had left home on Thursday night, not Friday morning as everyone had assumed until now, she should have turned up at Pike's aunt's place long since and they knew she hadn't.

The remote farm where Karen lived was located between Callander and Loch Lubnaig about twenty miles outside Stirling. A bus ran between Stirling and Callander but after that it was a case of hitch hike or hike in the freezing temperatures. Scotland in late autumn was a cold and wet affair. That was, if she had ever made it that far in the first place.

When Eleanor and Pike joined the others in the sitting room

they found them glued to the continuous news loop running on the little TV in the corner. It was obvious that all present, except little Oscar who was happily stuffing cake into his face, were equally concerned with the new timeline.

The short reel of grainy footage the broadcasters were sharing with the public showed Wendy at the turnstiles coming out of the part of the station where the service from the South would have spat her out. There was no mention of her having crossed to the other side where the trains to Scotland ran from or indeed if she had purchased a ticket or boarded another train. The whole coverage was notably compact and unsentimental. There was no press appeal from Jenny or Rob, no speech by a senior police officer, no sense of urgency in any way. Just a quick, half a minute slot before the news started rolling from the top, reporting the same wars, disasters and pile ups, sporting events and media embarrassments they'd just covered all over again.

Pike looked at the round of anxious faces.

Ash, who they had forced to camp inside the house the previous night, was sitting on a sofa in an upright foetal position with his knees drawn up to his chin and eyes so red from crying they probably glowed in the dark. Nameless, the tom who had become a more regular feature now they were heading into winter, was curled by his side.

Aaron and Sarah occupied another settee, sitting close together and holding hands. Aaron looked ashen, his thumb rhythmically, absentmindedly stroking the side of Sarah's hand. When she caught Pike's eye, he had to suppress a gasp of horror. Her ageless beauty seemed to have evaporated overnight, worry having eaten all of what she often called her fairy glitter. In her place sat an old woman with all her seven decades of life etched deeply into her face.

The only people in the room sustaining something akin to an

aura of normality seemed to be Oscar and Isabel, who had left Pike's room before Eleanor and him to let them get dressed, and was now kneeling by the coffee table with her son hovering next to her near the cake. Looking at her solid shape in the middle of the room Pike truly appreciated Eleanor's mother for the first time for the rock that she was outside of her own chaos. She turned when she felt his eyes on her back and smiled wanly at him and at her daughter standing by his elbow.

"Not much, is it?" She voiced loudly what everyone in the room was thinking and suddenly the stale air was whirled around in the fan of opinions.

Rob was trying to keep it out of the news to save face.

The police were purposefully withholding information.

The police didn't have a clue.

The press were deliberately holding out for a body before making a meat feast out of the story.

The police weren't taking it seriously yet.

The press just wasn't interested in a measly missing pre-teen on a weekend when three young adults had been stabbed in one town and eight killed in a horrific minibus crash.

And on it went.

Their helplessness drove their vocal chords.

The only one not saying much was Ash as he stared blankly into the room. Pike felt Eleanor detach herself from his side and watched her walk over to the other side of the room, ruffling her little brother's hair on the way and snatching a piece of cake from the coffee table. She sat down gingerly next to Ash on the side not flanked by Nameless and nudged his upper arm with her shoulder. Ash shot her a quick glance, tears gathering in his eyes again and then buried his head in his crossed arms. Eleanor put an arm around him and held him lightly while nibbling on her breakfast in the other hand. She looked back at Pike.

I got this.

Pike cleared his throat, bringing the conversation between the three elders to a momentary standstill.

"I'll go make some more tea."

In the kitchen, waiting for the water to boil, he stared at the worktop trying with all his might to elicit a moment with the universe, a glimpse into the fabric of life that would help them find Wendy.

But it didn't work that way and he knew it.

Frustrated he gave up and began rinsing the dirty mugs in the sink instead, scrubbing the tea stains out of the china with single-minded devotion while his blood raced around his veins in fear.

Three days, he thought, *she's dead. Definitely dead. Or hiding,* the voice of hope insisted, *But where? How long can she survive out there without help?*

Suddenly everything inside him went dead quiet.

He put the last mug down on the draining board, found a tea towel to dry his hands and took his phone out of his back pocket. He scrolled down to C and hit Charly's number. His foster sister's phone rang for a long time. He looked at the kitchen clock. It was half past ten in the morning. In all likelihood she was out riding or mucking out, earning her keep as Karen's second in command with honest graft.

Or she is busy looking after a little girl she's always had a soft spot for.

The more he thought about it, the more he was convinced that Charly was not out and about at all but sitting in her bedroom up at Karen's new yard, staring at his name on her phone's display and decidedly not picking up.

He cut the connection and typed.

Pick up the fucking phone.

He hit send, awaited delivery confirmation, counted to ten and rang again.

Charly picked up on the first ring.

"I hate you."

"I love you, too. Seen the news at all?"

"Yup."

"There are trains to Stirling from Kings Cross."

"Indeed."

"Char?"

"That's my name."

"Charly?"

"I hate repeating myself."

"Charlene! I'm crapping myself here. Sarah looks like she's about four-hundred years old. And Ash, I won't even go there. He's falling apart, one eyeball at a time. I know you haven't met him yet but we like him, we're keeping him. And he *adores* Wendy. Even Tink's losing the plot. We were out together yesterday looking for her and you know what? Transpires Tink really does actually care for her sister."

"Good for her. Glad to hear you've made up."

"And Aaron…" he carried on undeterred by her sarcasm but then let it hang deliberately.

"What about Aaron?"

The gruff voice of his 6ft3 giant foster sister, who could pick up a hay bale in each hand as if they were empty cardboard boxes, suddenly sounded like that of a dormouse. She knew that without Aaron Pike and the Hawthorne women, she would have ended up in prison or worse, and though to the outside observer her relationship with her foster father would forever appear contentious with a continuous soundtrack of bickering, taunting and arguing, she was as fiercely protective of the old man as a dragon of its eggs.

Pike decided to sink in the knife.

"He looks like he's about to have another stroke."

"Shit! No! Look, she's here, okay? She's fine."

The sense of relief was like nothing Pike had ever experienced. Like every drop of blood in his system was clapping with joy. Once the initial rush was over he could feel a tear run down his cheek. Or maybe it was condensation. The kettle had been boiling for some time now, steaming up the kitchen. He went to pick it up and poured the water into the teapot, then sat down at the table, head in hand.

"Oh for heaven's sake, Char!" he hissed into the receiver, suddenly concerned the others might hear. "You stupid idiot. You're gonna get yourself into so much trouble. Is she actually there with you? Stick her on."

"No. I'm not that stupid. She's up with the Shetlands. I get her food and stuff and check on her twice a day."

Despite everything it made Pike smile. He could picture it easily. In the farthest corner of the estate was a field full of small fur balls — some Shetland ponies, some sheep — with access to an old barn and largely left to their own devices. Eleanor and he had ridden to it a few times in the summer holidays. The little barn had seemed cosy enough and Pike could see Wendy huddling in there, warm and safe among the animals, a sheep as a pillow and a couple of ponies for blankets.

"How on earth has Karen not noticed?"

"Hah! K's got pregnancy brain. I could probably hide a herd of zebras up there and she wouldn't cotton on."

"She's got what?!"

"Oh. Ooops."

Chapter 25

There was more than one moment in the twenty-four hours that followed Charly's confession when Pike thought being the president of the World Health Organisation negotiating a common approach to a deadly epidemic would probably be the easier task.

For some reason it had fallen to him to persuade Wendy to come home and to make up a story that would keep Charly out of trouble. Once the missing girl had miraculously been found on Karen's doorstep he also got the short straw that was ringing The Black Horse with the offer Wendy had put on the table.

Her demand was simple. She'd come back and promise not to run away again only if she was allowed to move into Hawthorne Cottage, period. Fired by the euphoria of hearing her voice Pike had promised her the moon and stars.

Once he'd hung up though, ringing Rob and Jenny was the most uncomfortable phone call he'd ever had to make. To their credit they took the news with appropriate gratefulness, and the challenge Wendy had laid down with much dislike but ultimately some grace. Pike would never forget Jenny's last words in that conversation, which lasted almost two hours and included much tit-for-tat before ultimately always coming back to the issue at hand.

"You know," she'd sighed flatly after the marathon of accusations and counter-accusations had finally come to an end. "I always knew she'd go back to you lot eventually. She should have just asked. She's a strange child."

For the briefest of moments something in her tone had made Pike remember the savvy, spade-a-spade, unpretentious best friend Karen had once had. That slightly chubby young woman featuring in his childhood called Jennifer Jones — before permadiet, breast implants, fake nails and the dedicated quest for a man with money. He'd quite liked her.

Still it had taken him by surprise that she and Rob had given in so willingly in the end while the resistance that still needed to be broken even now, an hour or so before everyone would turn up at the cottage for the final drawing up of a treaty, had come from Aaron, of all people.

As welcoming as he had been of Ash, as reluctant was he to agree to Wendy moving in. He was old, he claimed, not fit to foster a young girl any longer. Pike hoped that once Karen, Charly and Wendy actually arrived, his grandpa would change his mind.

Karen had called from not far away a little while ago. It had been Pike's signal to inform everyone else, including Rosemary Wrage, the local social worker who had been assigned Wendy's case.

At least this part of the aftermath of the girl's reappearance had been handled by Karen. She had made all the necessary official calls to the police and social services. The agencies had been only too happy to let her provide safe transport for the girl back down South and for the families to sort out a deal between them. One headache off the list, one missing person's, one *potential dead girl's* case closed.

Pike shuddered violently as he thought about all that could have been, and counted their lucky stars. He scrubbed the body brush with which he had been grooming Casta against the curry comb and turned to Eleanor who was leisurely separating Blue's tail hair by hair with her fingers.

Outside, the next biblical flood had been staging a rehearsal all morning with cold, dense rain playing the lead. When they had turned the horses out first thing all three mares had remained by the gate, looking back longingly at the stable block. Only Inigo in his youthful exuberance had embraced the waterworld outside but after a couple of hours Pike had accepted the majority vote and brought them all back in for extensive pampering sessions. Ash had finished with Hunter a while ago and had left, mumbling something about needing to take a bath, so they were alone in the aisle.

Looking at his girlfriend now, lost in her task, his bad conscience suddenly started nagging at him rather loudly.

"Hey you."

She looked up dreamily.

"Yeah?"

He laid the grooming kit on the floor and went over to her.

"Come here for a sec."

He pulled her away from the pony, laid his hands on her waist and hoisted her up to sit on his hips.

"Hi."

"Hi," she smiled back.

"I'm sorry," he said.

She frowned.

"What for?"

"Scaring you *that* much."

He didn't need to explain to her that he'd just rewound time around twenty-six months. She knew he was referring to a night when he'd left her worrying, left her thinking he had gone to kill himself.

"Apology accepted," she pulled a face to cover up a silly grin. "Just don't do it again."

"Never," he answered gravely.

She kissed him then, all sweet and innocent, before slinging her arms around his neck and finding his ear.

"I love you, Paytah Hawthorne."

The tension in the kitchen was palpable, all eyes on Aaron who had not as yet given his consent.

Unlike everyone else who was squashed around the kitchen table, the old man was standing with his back to the Aga and looking at the crowd, an inscrutable expression on his face. Sarah, Ash, Karen, Charly, Wendy, Jenny, Tink, Eleanor, Rob, Rosemary Wrage, who had turned out to be a fairly young, colourfully dressed woman with purple dreadlocks, killer boots and a number of tattoos crawling up her arms, and Pike himself were all waiting with bated breath.

Sarah was staring at the old man with raised eyebrows.

Ash was quietly examining his hands. He'd been odd all morning and even odder once the Scottish contingent had arrived. He refused to speak to Wendy or show any emotion, in total contrast to his initial reaction when Pike had told him the girl had been found safe and sound.

Karen was radiant and seemed somewhat bemused by the whole situation. Sitting at a table with her ex best friend and her ex fiancé who had done the dirty on her to decide the fate of a girl they all loved clearly hadn't been on her to do list for this month but she seemed to be enjoying it in a warped, laid back, Karen sort of way.

Charly, beautifully large scale person that she was, had recovered from the feeble stomach punch Pike had delivered upon her getting out of the car more than enough to devour most of the contents of the biscuit tin on the table by herself.

The only one helping Charly with the consumption of the snacks supplied was the object of discussion herself. Wedged between Charly and Jenny, who barely looked at her daughter, Wendy nervously kept stuffing her mouth, looking around as if she was trying to determine who in the room was going to deliver the inevitable telling off. The most she'd got so far had been from her mother, hissing at her to 'stop snacking'.

By and large, Jenny already looked like she had somewhere better to be. After a last ditch attempt at talking the girl into coming home with her after all, an exercise, Pike had thought, purely designed to save face in front of Rosemary Wrage, Jenny now clearly just wanted to go and get on with her life.

Tink appeared to be just sad.

Eleanor seemed like Eleanor. Watching from the background, having faded almost into the wallpaper, she didn't miss a beat, not a twitchy eyebrow or a fluffed line. One day, Pike thought, he'd have to ask her how she did that vanishing thing. It looked useful. It could come in handy next time Rob scowled at him as he was now.

Greaves seemed the least keen on the solution presented and it tickled Pike.

Stallions! It suddenly occurred to him. *We're just stallions and I'm stealing one of his mares.*

The thought made him laugh out so loudly, it broke the tension in the room as all eyes shifted away from Aaron to look at him instead.

Pike got up and walked over to stand next to his grandfather, facing the room. He cupped the back of Aaron's hand that was resting on the work top next to the Aga in his palm then pressed down on the old man's wedding band.

"You," he addressed Aaron under his breath without actually turning to look at him, "promised me less talk of dying. So if you're not dying, there is no reason not to foster Wendy." He retracted his hand and stood taller. "Come on, release these people."

Aaron finally nodded.

"She can stay."

Chapter 26

When Pike walked back home the next morning, it was one of those rare moments when life was nearly perfect.

He had left Eleanor to breakfast at her house, from where she was going to have to go back to school, now her work placement had ended early. He felt a small twinge of guilt for he knew she was going to find it difficult to keep her eyes open today.

They had talked and snuggled until way after the witching hour, finally getting the chance to catch up. She'd wanted to hear about rescuing Hunter all over again and he'd happily recounted the story, basking in the glory of a horse saved. After she'd already long drifted off in his arms he'd still lain awake, thinking of his other charges. He'd wondered once again what the matter was with Casta lately, before lingering over finally trying to diagnose the strange sense of disorientation he had picked up from Strawberry during their walk in the storm. The thought of the little gelding, lost out in the world without his protection, had made him feel angry and frustrated, so he'd stopped himself there and had opted for sleep instead.

As he'd reached over to switch off the bedside lamp, something inside him had clicked so loudly it was deafening to his inner ear. The fundamental knot that he had been picking at for months, only to succeed in drawing it tighter in the process, had suddenly come apart of its own accord. Astonished by the simplicity of it, he'd wrapped Eleanor against him and mumbled happily into her ear.

"A vet. That's what I am going to be. I am going to be a vet."

Then he'd quietly laughed himself to sleep.

Now, walking back home, his new found purpose carried on humming inside him with such certainty it surprised him.

He was just about to ascend the front steps to the Cottage when Wendy came out of the door, dressed in her school uniform and still chewing on a piece of toast. She beamed at him as she skipped down.

"See you after school," she said, then added hopefully, "Pick me up on the bike?"

Pike raised his eyebrows.

"You'd need a lid first. Ash spoken to you yet?"

A shadow passed over her face as she shook her head. He kissed his fingertip and put it to her nose.

"He will. Give him time. You scared the living daylights out of him. Now scram. If you fall behind in school, they'll take you away from us again."

She was off in a flash and he grinned to himself as he proceeded to head into the house and towards the kitchen.

He'd expected to find more than one person in there but when he entered there was only Karen. She was sitting at the short end of the table, drinking tea and reading a book. She looked up when she heard him, shut the paperback in front of her and contemplated him with sparkling eyes.

"Ah, favourite nephew of mine, come in, sit with me." She patted the seat on the bench next to her. "I've got something to tell you."

Pike slipped up the long bench to settle by her elbow.

"I..." she started with a big breath.

"...am pregnant," Pike finished for her.

She looked at him, stunned, then pulled a face.

"Charly! Blabbermouth! I wanted to tell you myself. I'm going to throttle her."

"I wouldn't bother." Pike winked at his aunt who was barely three inches taller than his girlfriend. "I don't think you could reach. Besides, I think I would have noticed anyway. You're not exactly showing but you kinda glow, your hair's all shiny. And you seem, I don't know, sort of detached but happy. Plus you don't move the same way."

"Really?"

"Straight up. Bit weird to watch, actually. Bit like the difference between—" He stopped himself there to hit his forehead against the table top. "God, I'm such an idiot. She's in foal!"

"What? You lost me."

"A bit like the difference between a dressage schoolmistress and an overweight pony I was going to say. Casta. She's in foal. I swear. So much for barren."

"Well," Karen said, raising her mug, "Maybe she just needed the right stallion. Congratulations to the both of us."

Pike smiled.

"So, how far along are you?"

"Fourteen weeks." She beamed. "Early days, so don't mention anything to Dad just yet, yeah? They want to do some tests because I'm getting on a bit. I'll tell him when I've had the all clear."

"Agreed," he said just as it hit him. "You are never coming back, are you?"

There was a long pause before she slowly shook her head.

"Not if I can help it. All of this—" She made a sweeping gesture. "It's all yours. I'm happy where I am."

Pike swallowed. Part of him had suspected as much but another part felt sad for her. David Allaway, the man who had given her a new life in Scotland, was a nice guy. Small, stocky and dark haired like her, he was softly spoken and most of all an empathic rider and a kind human. But something, Pike had always thought, was missing between those two. His aunt could have done — nearly had done — much worse, but she could also have done so much better. He could feel her watch him and smirk before she put her mug down with a deliberate clang.

"Look, P, here's the deal, that thing you and Eleanor have, that thing Mum and Dad had and John and—" She stopped there, took a breath. "It's just not meant for me. Or at least I haven't found it. And by now I don't want to find it anymore either because a) all it seems to bring is heartache and b) what I *have* found is real happiness. When I wake up, even in the pissing rain, and trust me, there is a lot of pissing rain where we are, you've only seen it in the summer, and I go to the bedroom window and I look out into that beautiful, wild landscape stretching out as far as the eyes can see, knowing nobody will ever bloody well build all over it and I get called back to bed by the man who gave me *that*, I am happy."

He registered the finality in her speech but really he'd only been half listening for most of it, having got stuck somewhere at the start. A thought had occurred, one that came with goose bumps on his arms and a shiver down his spine. He looked her square in the face and he knew his eyes were burning as he spoke.

"John with whom?"

"Pardon?"

"You heard me."

His aunt just kept staring at him, like Mowgli mesmerized by Kaa.

"Let me help you," Pike heard himself hiss. "There is a photograph. Old. Of John. On a horse. Taken here. In front of the barn. And there is a young woman sitting behind him on the horse. Pretty, tall, long legs, dark skin, hair cut in a bob. In other words, not Alice. And he looks *happy*. Ring a bell? I can go and get it, if you like. It's in my room."

"Not necessary. I know the picture," Karen answered quietly.

"Who is she?"

His aunt looked away.

"You need to ask John."

"I will, given half a chance. But since you are here, you will do. She is his 'and', right? Not my mother. Not Alice. She's more like a 'with'. John with Alice. Alice with John. Not to the exclusion of all others, to the exclusion of *her*. What's her name? And who's the other boy?"

Karen faced him again. There was a pained expression on her face but her voice was steely when she spoke next, her instructor's tone, reserved for particularly stubborn children and ponies.

"I don't know what other boy you are talking about, but honestly, you'd have to ask your father. Subject closed. – Now, will you ride Inigo for me before I go? I want to see how you two are doing."

The ground in the schooling paddock was soggy and deep from the torrential downpour the previous day, so Pike and Inigo had to keep it frustratingly simple. When they had fled the quarry, the stallion had followed the canter aids immediately and Pike was itching to see if Inigo still remembered. Some horses learned on the first go, others needed time and repetition but Inara's son seemed to be of the former variety, doubling the responsibility on Pike's shoulders. A horse that was quick to learn was also quick to learn wrong.

Either way, today there was no going faster than a dainty trot for danger of slipping, so he concentrated on showing Karen how nicely the stallion was learning to stretch already, how beautifully he stepped under and how obediently he would stand and rein back.

Karen was impressed. Pike could see it in the deadpan face she was deliberately trying to maintain when he slipped off his horse's back and they walked towards her. Once they came to a halt in front of her they both looked at her expectantly and she laughed, her eyes darting back and forth between horse and nephew. A slow grin melted her features.

"Good work, you two. I knew it was the right choice to leave him with you. What are you planning on doing with him?"

The question threw Pike a bit. He hadn't really thought about a career for Inigo. He'd had enough on his plate contemplating one for himself. Shrugging, he turned to the stallion and scratched the animal's cheek. Inigo leant in gratefully.

"Nothing. He hasn't got Inara's paces and I don't think he'd enjoy the show ring at any rate. He's not a dancer, he's an adventurer and a player. He likes playing nose ball and he likes it when there is, I don't know, purpose in the ride, I guess. It's hard to explain. He's old fashioned. He would have made a good battle pony or a stock horse or a doctor's fine steed in the days before cars. You know, racing to save a patient's life. That would have been his bag."

He turned back to look at Karen who was smiling in amusement and frowned.

"What?"

"Oh, just wondering which one of you you're talking about," she probed gently.

But for now, it was his secret to keep.

Chapter 27

Over the coming week Ash thawed a little towards Wendy but mostly he remained awkward and distant. It was painful to watch and after a few days Pike decided he'd had enough of the atmosphere between them.

He went to accost Ash in the stable block after breakfast.

One aspect of shunning the girl was that Ash had stopped coming to the house in the mornings, waiting for Wendy to leave before he'd go in and grab a cup of tea and a bite to eat. On the morning in question Pike pre-empted him, preparing a sandwich and a flask and taking it over to the barn.

Ash was already up and fussing over Hunter who was looking glorious. The scabs were coming off the legs now with the new pink skin underneath looking healthy and good. She'd need continuous extra care of her legs as was normal with feathered horses but they had beaten the infection for now. The rest of the big horse looked amazing, too. She'd carried on filling out and by now her neck looked entirely normal and her ribs had stopped showing. If Pike ran a hand over them he had to apply at least a modicum of pressure to feel them. Her top line was still triangular and her rump the epitome of a bony arse but she was getting there and with exercise the muscles would build up eventually. She was old but she wasn't past it and the sooner she started a bit of light work, the better.

He handed Ash the food and the thermos. The other accepted the offerings gratefully and sat down on the upturned crate that he stood on to get better access to Hunter's back while grooming. Pike appraised the Clydesdale's shape further then made his decision.

"Right. When you are done eating, it's time you got on your horse."

"Pardon?" Ash asked around a bite.

Pike suppressed a grin.

"See the sticky out spine? All the food in the world is not going to fill that out. That's muscle wastage. She needs exercise as much as she needs fodder."

Ash looked up at him as if he had lost the plot.

"You do remember I can't ride, right?"

"Nobody can when they first get on a horse. And this lady here—" Pike stepped up to Hunter's head, slipped a hand under her throat, put his flat palm on the cheek on the other side and turned her to look at Ash. "Seems like the perfect beginner's horse to me. Provided you are not scared of heights. But just to be on the safe side, I'll test her out first. Bear with me."

With that he left an astonished Ash behind, and went to find some bits and bobs for kitting Hunter out.

The best he had been able to cobble up to make sitting on the big mare possible was an absolutely ancient, thick saddle blanket of the variety Kimi had used in the 1970s when still working in Wild West shows, plus Casta's sheep skin numnah, both of which he secured to Hunter's back with a roller. They didn't have a proper bridle or a bit that would fit the big mare but Pike trusted her temperament enough to go with the head collar variety of steering.

While the other three equines watched with interest from the adjacent field, they led her out into the schooling paddock and Pike got Ash to give him a leg up while Hunter stood docilely.

The concoction of various padding materials beneath his bottom did make the horse sufficiently bearable to sit on without giving Pike the feeling he was breaking her spine but he still tried to make himself as light as possible. From above she still seemed quite fragile. The impression changed instantly when he picked up the lead rope reins. A shift went through the big lady, a sense of purpose and pride as she picked up her head and looked around herself, alert. Her ears started playing and suddenly Pike could really sense the police horse underneath: she would have been a formidable partner in patrolling the beach or in crowd control but she was also a survivor of one of the hardest jobs in the horse world. The moment of grandeur didn't last and as he gently asked her to move off she did so at a lumbering pace. He took her once around the paddock on each rein, asked her to halt, rein back and turn on the forehand and she obliged. Her reactions were slow but true and he was more than satisfied that Ash would be safe as houses on her. He turned her back towards the centre of the school where the other was waiting, halted and slid off her back. He took his hat off and pushed it down onto Ash's head.

"Here, try not to need it," he said, fastening the chin clasp for Ash as if he was a little kid. "It's a long way down and I need to buy a new one if it gets knocked."

"I'll give it my best shot," Ash replied hoarsely, looking at his mare with new respect and patting her shoulder nervously.

"Right. You ready?" Pike asked.

"No," Ash said while bending his left knee nevertheless, so Pike could give him a leg up.

"Up you get then."

Pike slung the other onto the big mare's back and Ash landed with all the poise and grace Pike had expected of him.

"I can feel her bones," he said uncertainly after a second, stroking the mares neck, "I'm not hurting her, am I?"

"No. That's why I put the blanket and stuff on."

As if to reassure her rider, the Clydesdale blew out of her nose happily.

"But if after today you want to learn to ride her properly," Pike carried on, while reaching up to arrange Ash's hands correctly around the reins, "we'll need to find her a saddle. Get the weight off her spine completely. If she ever develops a decent topline again, you can try her bareback but at her size, you'll probably always want proper tack. Are you ready to walk yet?"

"Let's go for it."

Pike didn't need to tell the other much in terms of how to sit. Clearly Ash was someone who learned by eye and he'd watched a lot of riding recently. He sat well with great balance from the off, which was important considering the state of Hunter. Pike took one look at the expression of total concentration on the other's face then let them get on with it undisturbed, silently walking by the great mare's head and letting Ash find his own rhythm. After ten minutes he called it a day and smiled when he saw disappointment rather than relief wash over Ash's face.

There we go. Tick. Another one in the bag.

Suppressing a grin he took a step back to examine Hunter's head.

"Yeah," he mused, "We'll need to measure her up for a bit as well. We'll do it when the dentist comes. I'll ring him later. Get him to come and do her teeth. That'll help her with putting on weight and all. Should probably have done that earlier in the game but with everything else going on it slipped my mind."

"Dentist?" Ash enquired from above.

"Uh-huh. A horse's digestive system starts in the mouth. Well, anyone's does, really, but the thing with horses is, their teeth keep growing throughout their lives and they become scraggly and get sharp edges because they don't remotely eat what they would have eaten in the wild to keep 'em smooth. And when the teeth don't meet properly anymore, chewing doesn't break up the food the way it should any longer and then half of the calorific value can't be absorbed by the gut and goes straight out the other end.

So you get the horse dentist to file their teeth. We get ours done once a year. It's good practice. It's not cheap but not doing it is false economy, especially with older horses like her. You'll just end up shoving in more food and that costs, too, while they still don't get all the nutrients."

"How much?"

Pike waved it off. With the weather and Wendy going missing and the townsfolk getting used to the resident firefly and no tourists outside the holiday season, Ash hadn't had a chance to make much by way of coin in recent days.

"Don't worry about it. We'll pick up the tab between us all." He grinned. "Wendy'll need something to ride, so you'll probably need to share Hunter with her at any rate. She won't be able to carry on riding Casta as of a certain point and in one respect Rob was right. She *was* way too big to be riding Strawberry, which makes her too big for Blue. And even if she wasn't I don't think Eleanor would share. She's pretty possessive of her pony."

He'd thought making Ash and Wendy share a horse was a pretty good ploy to get the two of them to sort themselves out, so he wasn't remotely prepared for what happened next. Ash hugged Hunter from above, then slipped down off the mare's back, undid the hat, took it off and stared at the lining for a minute before shoving it at Pike.

"She can have her," he mumbled, looking at his feet.

"Pardon?"

Ash cleared his throat and looked up.

"She can have her," he repeated. "I'm leaving. I'm already packed."

"What?! Is it because of the crap Tink slung at you? Don't listen to her. We both know Wendy had already tried to run when she met you. It's not your fault. It's their fault for being idiots."

Ash put a hand on Pike's shoulder and once again Pike could

feel true calm flow from the other but also, he thought, a strange kind of fear.

"Chill. It's nothing to do with that. I...when she was gone and we didn't know if we'd ever see her again, I realised something. I have a mum and she's my mum. And I have a dad and he's an idiot but he's my dad. And I have two brothers. One older, one younger. The older one's in the army and I don't even know if he's still in one piece. The point is, they haven't heard from me in almost two years. They probably think I'm dead. It's time I went back."

They sat silently on the empty platform with the sharp wind sweeping around them, each bent forward with elbows resting on spread knees and staring down. There were only minutes left until the train would roll in and take Ash and his belongings away to London.

"Are you nervous?" Pike asked around the lump in his throat.

"Very."

"You know you can always come back, right?"

In the corner of his eye, he saw Ash nod.

"Yeah I know."

"What is he like?"

"Who?"

"Your dad. You said once he was the reason you weren't going home. Are you going to be alright?"

Ash straightened up and laughed.

"Don't worry, mate. He's a kitten, really. In a hard as nuts, ex-army, runs a martial arts gym kinda way. Chances are he's gonna cry rivers when he sees me. It's my mum who's gonna slap me, make no mistake. Nah, he's a good man. Just an idiot."

Pike looked at him sideways enquiringly.

In the far distance the train appeared on the tracks and an

announcement on the tannoy told them that their time was running out.

Ash shouldered his rucksack.

"He bragged about it," he said as if it was an explanation.

Pike got up, too.

"Come again?"

"After I killed Mark. That was his name. Mark Lawson. Anyway, few months later I came home and Dad was there, drinking with one of his old army mates, bragging about his new life on civvy street. How well he was doing and stuff. It's a big thing with those guys, the release. Anyway, I heard him brag about me. About *it*. About how I was going to be *the* future UCMMA featherweight champion for sure and how if I land a punch the other one doesn't get up again. I mean, you know, I was fifteen. I'd just *killed* someone. I was having nightmares every night. I was pissing the bed like a little kid. Didn't know what to do with it. And people didn't want to hear about it either. They'd just, I don't know, either be afraid of me or do the justification for me, tell me to forget about it, move on. That it was okay. Like something like that is *ever* okay. But for Dad? It wasn't just okay, it was something to be proud of. How fucked up is that? So I packed my bags and I fucked off."

The train arrived next to them and slowly opened its doors.

They hugged.

Time was up.

Chapter 28

One of the things in life that could surprise Pike over and over again was the resilience of young girls and little ponies. Out of all the inhabitants of Hawthorne Cottage, Wendy appeared to be the one who took Ash's departure with the most ease.

He'd feared her return from school on the day he had taken Ash to the station and, after nervously checking with Eleanor what to expect, had braced himself for a meltdown requiring hugs, chocolate cake and binge watching terrible American tween movies all night. But Wendy had taken the news with a nod and a 'so that's why he's been so weird all week' before seamlessly changing out of her uniform and into her jodhpurs to catch the last hour of daylight for a ride on Casta. While she still talked incessantly about Strawberry and lit a candle for the pony in her room each night, she hardly ever mentioned Ash.

The entity truly competing with Pike in missing Ash over the coming weeks was Hunter. Though they all took turns in taking care of her, the great mare pined notably, at least until the day Sarah strolled in with the saddle fitter.

She had found tack at a second hand sale that would fit the big mare with a bit of tweaking and had decided that riding Hunter might just be the thing for the both of them. When the vet had come to officially scan Casta in foal and had given her the all clear to be kept in light work for a few months yet, he had also taken a look at the Clydesdale, only to concur with Pike's assessment. Dr Halland, a burly Cornish man with an always slightly flushed but smiling face and hands like shovels that despite their size could give an injection to any horse without it so much as twitching an ear, had prescribed gentle hacks, no longer than half an hour and at a steady walking pace.

So most days, if he wasn't at college knuckling down for his exams with new found enthusiasm, Pike would get Inigo, Blue and Casta ready in the time it took Sarah to groom Hunter and they would go out as soon as Wendy and Eleanor got in from school.

Hunter was thriving on being brought back into work by Sarah and despite her age the mare turned out to be so light in the mouth that Sarah couldn't have wished for a horse kinder on her wrists or her nerves. Inigo, too, loved these rides with his whole herd out together and so did Pike, though he felt the hole in *his* herd deeply every day.

He hadn't heard from Ash since saying goodbye but in his heart of hearts he was certain the other had made it to his destination and was doing alright back with his family. Still, he missed him like mad. In a way it was worse than what he'd felt when Eleanor had been away because he'd known she'd return to him. It had been a sweet kind of longing, a romantic pain certain of relief. With Ash he had no idea if he'd ever see him again and it just hurt, raw and true.

Where Strawberry was concerned, on the other hand, he soon realised that they still stood a chance. All they needed to do, he reckoned, was to find the little gelding and make his new owners an offer they could not refuse. Much as Pike despised the reality of it, horses were commodities that could be bought and sold and there were few things in consumer world that couldn't be obtained by raising the price tag.

"Good plan," Eleanor agreed when he ran it by the rest of the cottage population one foul late November afternoon, sitting around the table in the kitchen. "But where are we going to get enough money for this 'offer they cannot refuse'? I came home half way through the tour, remember? So the record company is only going to pay me half as well. That wouldn't be nearly enough."

"No," Pike agreed. "But it would be a start. I haven't worked the details out yet."

"Clearly," Sarah interjected.

She glared at him angrily with a surreptitious side glance in the direction of Wendy who'd been hanging on Pike's lips, hope written all over her face.

Aaron shut the National Geographic he'd been leafing through while his grandson had been talking and cleared his throat. All eyes wandered to the old man's chair. He slowly pushed the magazine away and folded his arms on the table before wriggling his eyebrows mischievously.

"We let Rob pay for him," he suggested with a small, satisfied smile.

"Pardon?" four voices replied incredulously.

Aaron shrugged and looked straight at Wendy, "The keep they have to pay for you is set by *their* earnings, *their* life style. I could probably feed us all until next Easter on what you bring in a month now. Not that that is what it's for, mind. It's for you and I was going to put what you don't need now for clothing, food, phones, school things, pocket money and such aside for later. Kimi and I did the same for Charly, not that hers was as much because the authorities paid for her. Still, it set the girl up for college in the end. But from where I'm sitting it looks like this here, right now, is more important than a future that may or may not happen. So, what I am saying is, if you are prepared to live our kind of life, look after what you have, buy your clothes second hand, have your hair cut by Sarah, not have the newest phone, computer or whatnot, then I'm happy to ask the bank for a temporary loan and pay it back through your maintenance."

There was complete silence for a moment while Wendy stared at Aaron, her eyes brimming with tears.

"And Straw would be mine? For good?" she asked.

"Yes," Aaron smiled.

She got up and dashed around to him, so quickly her red hair seemed like a streak of flames crossing the kitchen. The next thing Pike saw was that she'd somehow managed to get the old man to move his chair so she could clamber onto his lap and that she was hugging him tightly.

"Thank you. Thank you. Thank you," she mumbled against his shoulder. "You're the best. And I promise, I won't ask for anything. Ever. I'll do exactly what you said."

Aaron's right hand came up slowly to stroke her hair.

"I know you will. Now—" He grabbed her gently by the shoulders and pushed her back a little. "It's up to you and them," he tipped his head to indicate Pike and Eleanor, "to find the pony. Scram. Go do your thing. Leave us in peace."

They located Strawberry in no time.

A quick search later they were staring at a picture of Odelia, Lilly and Straw on Pike's computer. Taken at some low level country show somewhere near Ipswich, the little gelding stood good as gold in the autumn breeze, his neck arched prettily in a perfect pose for the camera. His rider and her mother, however, were looking out of the picture stony-faced. Underwhelmed would have been the understatement of the century.

"Oh dear."

Pike pointed at the purple rosette flapping in the wind on Strawberry's bridle.

Eleanor, who was standing by his right, leant forward to take a closer look then turned her face to him.

"What does it mean?"

He stole a kiss before he answered, high on the rapid success of their search and loving the fact she'd been with him so long, riding all this time yet still caring so little about the show circuit she had no idea what the colours signified.

"Yuk, get a room," Wendy chirped from his left.

"We're in my room."

"Well, then stick to the task at hand. I don't want to see that."

"Yes, mam." Pike focused his attention back on the girl he could still taste on his lips. "It means they didn't place. Purple is like sixth and below. Participation ribbon."

"Hm," Eleanor answered, frowning at the computer while her eyes skim read some of the text underneath the picture. "Didn't you tell me he was a dressage pony?"

"You know he is."

"Well, maybe they didn't want to enter him in a jumping competition then."

She was jabbing a finger at a sentence on the screen. Pike went pale. Straw had never been the best of jumpers but if he was right and the pony's eyesight was starting to fade, pushing him over jump courses could be lethal for all parties involved.

"Oh no, those friggin idiots," he muttered but Wendy stopped him with a raised hand.

"Whatever," she said soberly. "Doesn't matter. Let's not go in all guns blazing. They are strange people, so let's go carefully. Let's just ask them how he is doing generally first." She pulled the keyboard over to her side. "I'll send them a message to ask how they are getting on. They know me. They know I used to ride him. So it won't be weird. Let's go in easy. See where they are at."

Both Pike and Eleanor looked in astonishment at the girl's profile as she typed. Her sudden level-headedness had surprised them so much they nearly didn't notice how very slowly she chose the keys for forming the words, typing hesitantly with two fingers. When she'd finished, the two simple sentences in the message body were riddled with spelling mistakes. Pike corrected them, hit 'send' and then grabbed a miscellaneous paperback from a pile on his desk that Ash had left with him. He shoved it at Wendy, blurb side up.

"Read the back to me."

The girl blushed scarlet.

"I'm not very good at reading."

"Yeah," Pike said gravely. "I figured. Do you get extra help at school?"

She shook her head, avoiding his eyes.

"So how have you got away with it so far? Why haven't you said anything?"

"I wing it," she said quietly. "They already think I'm a klutz, didn't want them to think I was stupid as well."

"*Not* telling is stupid. About as stupid as running away is. Right, if you want us to help you with this," Pike motioned at the screen, "you promise you will let me sit you down for reading lessons every night. I'm not having it. It's like the most important skill ever. If—"

"And Wendy?" Eleanor said softly, having elbowed him in the ribs not so softly to shut him up. "You're neither a klutz nor stupid, okay?"

Wendy didn't get the time to respond because just then a message pinged up on the screen. It seemed the weather in East Anglia was just as dull as it was in the South and Strawberry's new humans were busy wiling away the dreary day online.

In contrast to Wendy, Odelia Smith on the other end was clearly a ten-finger typist. In the time they'd had their little exchange she had written a five hundred word essay on the unworthiness of Strawberry Mouse. Pike's eyes flew over the lines until they arrived at the last bit of information and suddenly he could feel the biggest smile since losing Ash pull at all the muscles in his face at once. He snatched his keyboard back, typed, hit send, leant back on his chair, folded his hands behind his neck and waited.

Seconds later an answer arrived.

Agreed. Saturday 2pm suits us. Will send exact postcode once money has arrived. Electronic transfer acceptable. Pleasure doing business with you. OS

Wendy frowned at the screen.

"What does it say?"

"You read it yourself."

She scowled at him but relented. It took her a long time and Pike could feel impatience eating away at him but he wouldn't budge. This was important. Eleanor, who had spotted the conclusion to Odelia Smith's tirade at the same time as him and knew what the deal was, was bursting in her skin with joy already, trying hard not to let on. He could sense her curling her toes in her socks in anticipation of Wendy joining the party. Wendy finally crinkled up her nose unsurely.

"Okay. I've read it. But what does it mean?"

"It means—" Pike answered while slinging an arm around her waist and pulling her closer. "We've just bought a pony."

Chapter 29

It was a big showing Saturday for the South and all The Black Horse transporters were unavailable, so they ended up with Mackenzie's old livestock trailer along with the farmer's mud-encrusted Subaru for towing.

Pike's mouth went dry when he saw the contraption. Inara had drowned in a trailer like that, though one made for horses not cattle, and he still couldn't bring himself to trust another tow bar. But beggars couldn't be choosers and Sarah was nervous enough about driving a towing vehicle without any stories of tragedies past, so he buttoned up and thanked Mackenzie kindly.

"No worries." The farmer laughed over the noise of the tractor that he'd left running in the yard. "I've called on you often enough in haying season." He slapped Pike's arm with a grin that turned his face into a moon crater landscape. "And looking at what the agricultural college is sending me *this* year, you can expect my call again in August. So I hope you're not planning on going on holiday. They just don't breed 'em like you anymore."

He looked across to Sarah in the driver's seat of the Subaru, familiarising herself with the dashboard, and turned to Aaron who was standing next to his grandson.

"Are you sure the woman can drive it?"

"The woman can drive it."

"Good luck."

Mackenzie raised a hand, went back to his tractor and climbed aboard. They let him drive away before going to join the others in the car. Pike slipped into the back seat next to Eleanor and looked over at Wendy on the far side, impatiently staring out of the window. He sighed as he buckled himself in and let his hand seek Eleanor's.

It was going to be a long, tense ride.

The yard where the Smiths kept Strawberry was a friendly, small, well-kept affair with a thirty-something owner by the name of Victoria Buttons, who lived in a caravan on site and who greeted them kindly enough, although with a more than questioning side glance at the trailer. She seemed a little more reassured once Eleanor and Wendy had scrambled out of the car.

"Long drive?" she asked noncommittally as she shook all their hands in turn. "I'm afraid the Smiths aren't here today. They've given me his passport and signed a receipt for you, so as far as I'm concerned you can just load and go..."

Her voice trailed off unsurely while she took another look at their vehicle.

Pike grinned widely when she turned to him, about to take his hand as last in line. "Don't worry. Straw has been transported in that thing before. He actually used to quite like it because he gets to travel loose, which he prefers. He likes it better when Blue is with him but he's going to have to wait for her till we get home."

He could feel her relax through the connection of their palms.

"Oh, so you know the pony?"

Pike realised in a flash that she'd taken them for meat traders.

"Yes. Look, you really don't need to worry about him. He should never have been sold to the Smiths in the first place. He belongs with us. As a pony, not as sausages, if that's what you were thinking. It's a complicated story but I promise you once he's back home he is never leaving us again."

The woman laughed a little embarrassedly then led the way to the stables, a traditional u-shape of twenty wood-built loose boxes cradling a concrete slab yard. Most of them were empty, their inhabitants grazing in the surrounding paddocks or out on rides, but even in this quiet state it was obvious that this was a good place. The individually styled name plaques on the doors ranged from funny to a-bit-up-themselves, the head collars on their hooks from bling to could-really-do-with-a-new-one but all in all the air felt like that of a happy yard. As they walked towards the last box on the left arm of the U, the heads of three horses popped over various stable doors, all whickering softly at Victoria as she passed. If she hadn't already shown concern for Strawberry's future this would have been all Pike would have needed to know about the woman. It made the darkness that fell on her features just before they got to the box they were heading for, over which no pony head had appeared, so much worse. She'd suddenly turned around to face them and spread out her arms out to stop them all in their tracks. She searched their collective eyes apologetically and finally settled on Pike's.

"Wait a second. I just want you to know that I have already told the Smiths that I will not let them keep another horse here. I'm hoping they'll get bored of the whole idea now." She stepped aside and pointed at Strawberry's box. "He's in there. It might be best if only one of you goes in. Be careful. Watch the teeth. I don't know what he was like when you had him and I don't know what the Smiths did to him but he took a chunk out of the girl's arm last week. He's been tricky to handle ever since. None of my girls wants to muck him out or feed him now. I do it myself but, truth be told, it's scary business. He'll go for you if you get too close. It might be best if some of you come to the caravan so I can give you your paperwork and only one or two people try to load him."

A quick, silent exchange of glances later they did as she suggested and spilt up. Victoria Buttons, Sarah and Aaron walked away. Pike took Wendy's hand and Eleanor hung behind respectfully while the two of them made the last few metres towards the stable door. The words he'd just heard were echoing around in his brain, trapping him somewhere between disbelief, jaded anger and caution. Although more easily spooked by natural predisposition and a more accomplished ride than Blue, who would always take her cue from her rider's ability, her little red roan partner had always been a gentle soul. Biting had never featured as part of the Strawberry Mouse experience. In his mind's eye he saw Lilly's crop coming down on the pony's hide again, with no rhyme or reason, and shuddered.

The picture that presented itself when they reached the half doors let tears well up inside him but he swallowed them down. The gelding stood pressed against the back wall, in the darkest corner of the box, his head held low, his muzzle resting against the side panel. He'd been dozing but when he heard Pike and Wendy lean on the door his ears immediately went back. Worse, as soon as Wendy softly called his name, he pinned them against his poll properly and turned his head in their direction with all teeth on show, snapping at the air.

"Whoa." Wendy took a step back and looked at Pike dumbstruck. "What was that?"

"They've broken him," he said flatly.

It had escaped his mouth before he could censor the words and the girl's face promptly fell. He grabbed her by the shoulders.

"But nothing we can't fix."

Hopefully, he added in his mind.

Wendy looked slowly back and forth between the stable door and him.

"So what do I do?" she asked.

There was no fear in her voice, he noted, just a straightforward request for advice and much as he wanted to tell her 'nothing, you let me handle this' he knew she needed this. He gave her his best smile.

"We do it like they do it in the movies," he answered. "We pack you in padding."

An idea hit him as he spoke. He beckoned Eleanor and she walked over to take a peek across the door.

"Oh. That really doesn't look friendly."

"Is that the jumper you were wearing when you groomed Blue this morning?"

"Uh-huh."

"Excellent. I love girls that don't wash. Hand it over."

Eleanor did as she was told, muttering something under her breath about why it was always her who had to strip off. Despite the other eight or so layers she was wearing underneath today, she started shivering immediately and Pike shrugged off his jacket and hung it over her shoulders.

"Right, Wendy, hold out your arm."

He wound the jumper around the girl's offered limb, taking great care to get the part that would smell most of Blue onto the outside of the wrap.

"Perfect. Now when you go in, I'll hold the door, so you can dash out if you need to. Provided he doesn't go ballistic and turn his butt on you as soon as you enter, try and approach him so he can find Blue's scent on the jumper. That should help. She was his first herd after mummy mare, she's home. Go confidently, don't freak. If you start sweating fear, it'll overpower everything. By all means, talk to him but leave your ego at the door." He could see in her expression that she didn't know what that meant, so he changed the wording. "It means, don't expect him to recognise your voice. I'm sure somewhere in there is the Strawberry who loves you but he's so far gone where his trust in humans is concerned at the moment, right now we all sound the same to him. Talking monkeys. And it's not a good sound. Got it?"

"Yes."

"Ready?"

She nodded and he opened the door for her.

She entered and Straw pulled his face back even further than before, the white showing in his eyes now, his teeth clacking inches from the girl's face as she approached. Wendy stood her ground. She advanced further and for a moment the pony's hind started edging around towards her body.

"Don't you dare! Pack it in!" she commanded firmly, her automatic response to any horse playing up. It was brave and Pike felt proud of her. She was acting exactly as he would have done and though it didn't miraculously transform the gelding back to his normal self Pike could see a jolt go through the pony's body, making him unpin his ears a little and stand up taller. Wendy raised the wrapped arm towards his nostrils and slowly began approaching, soothing tones emanating from her now.

"There you go, there's a goooood boy. Have a little sniff."

She left the arm hovering in the air, an inch from the gelding's nose. It took quite a while until anything else happened but the girl had patience. Finally the pony's muzzle edged a little closer. His nostrils twitched as he inhaled in hectic short breaths and suddenly his lip curled up.

"Smells good, doesn't it?" Wendy murmured.

Straw took another step towards her, his ears playing a fraction friendlier now. A small grunt escaped the pony's throat as he sniffed more intently now, up and down the jumper, too immersed in the sensation to keep up the threatening stance. For a second he seemed almost like the old Strawberry but when Wendy brought her other hand up to try and stroke him, he stopped examining the jumper and his ears went back again. She let the hand sink down. The pony's face relaxed a little once more but he wasn't nuzzling the jumper any longer. Wendy didn't take her eyes off him nor did she shift her arm but a tiny shrug in her shoulders told Pike that she didn't know what to do now.

Stalemate.

Next to Pike Eleanor suddenly started humming. Pike was about to put a finger to his lips when he realised it wasn't simply an absent-minded action. It was a deliberate effort. She hadn't just chosen any melody but a particular one. It was the tune that had accompanied Blue's and Straw's most successful routine, the one Tinkerbelle and he had awed the show circuit with for nigh on two years when they'd been little, the one Eleanor knew from the videos.

He watched as Straw's head went up and his ears found the notes in the air, pointing firmly forward to where they were coming from. The tautness on the gelding's face softened and suddenly he nickered. His eyes cleared and he took a look at the girl standing in front of him, his lips finding her face again but without bared teeth this time. He gently nibbled at her hair above the ear then let his muzzle wander down her now relaxed arms, inhaling Blue's scent again in little snuffles before proceeding to find Wendy's trouser pocket, nudging it lightly.

"P?" she called, laughter in her voice.

"Coming! You're a genius," he added in a whisper to the girl by his side. "Keep humming."

He dug around his pocket for a treat, grabbed the pony's head collar from the hook by the door and went in. There was a sudden sharp movement from Straw when he entered but Pike was certain the pony could hear them for who they were now.

"Hey, boy," Pike reassured him, slipping the treat into the hand Wendy was holding out behind her back.

Never one easily fooled, the pony's eyes stayed on the prize until it appeared on the girl's outstretched palm in front of him. He took it and crunched happily, instantly looking at Pike for more. Pike laughed with relief.

"And he's back in the room. Here—" He held the head collar out to Wendy. "Put it on and let's get him the hell out of here!"

Chapter 30

Compared to the task of introducing Strawberry to the current Hawthorne herd, negotiating Wendy's return to the fold had been a walk in the park.

Pike spent sleepless nights over the next week, thinking up strategies then finding catches in any plan he could come up with, while Strawberry remained in isolation. Although his human impulse had been to put the frightened little pony in with Blue immediately, the equine reality had hit him when they'd got back home.

As soon as Inigo had seen the new male of the species unload, he had started prancing around the perimeter of the paddock in an entirely unwelcoming fashion. None of the mares had been allowed anywhere near the fence line. Not even Blue, despite her alpha mare status and her obvious desire to get to her old friend, stood a chance against Inigo's guard. The two Mice had neighed to each other loudly as soon as they had seen each other and Blue would spend her days now wistfully looking at Strawberry from afar. Half a paddock away was as close as the stallion would allow her to get.

Inigo's behaviour under his rider had changed, too. The ever shortening days meant no more hacks out after school, so during the week Pike's work with the stallion was confined to the schooling area on those mornings that he didn't have to attend to his own education. The sessions had turned into a permanent discussion between him and his horse about what was more important, learning or keeping an eye on the mares. In the end Pike always won out but Inigo continued to test his patience with his inability to concentrate.

Even small jobs like which horse to turn out first or bring back in last became a case of careful negotiation if Pike wanted to avoid

Inigo kicking the stable door in, running the fence down or churning up the field.

For the first time since having him around Pike really appreciated the headache that was having a stallion run freely with a herd. Although he still despised the idea, he was starting to understand those who kept an ungelded boy separate from the rest of a yard by double fencing and generous exclusion zones.

"Why don't you just put Straw and Blue together on their own for a while first?" Wendy asked while she was grooming Strawberry one afternoon, "It worked with Hunter."

As if I hadn't already thought of that.

Pike and Eleanor were seated on a straw bale outside the tack room door, cleaning and waxing a seemingly endless supply of leather items. He reattached a cheek piece to Inigo's bridle, inhaling deeply. Everything smelled of damp horse, leather soap and beeswax.

Winter smell. Winter rhythm.

It was dark outside already, all horses were in and Inigo's head was hanging out of his box, watching the red roan who had been tied up at the other end of the aisle. The mares were nowhere to be seen. Having come in from a fairly miserable day of intermittent sleety drizzle and gusts that blew up their rugs, they had been instantly more interested in hay and warm bedding. A little earlier Blue had briefly stuck her nose out to wicker at Straw but it had earned her a threatening face from Inigo accompanied by a hoof tattoo on the door and she had retreated obediently.

Pike looked up, back and forth between Inigo's watchful stare and Strawberry's meek stance under Wendy's deft curry combing.

Other than being a bit lonely, for the most part the pony they'd brought back seemed intact in his soul again, having clearly put the Smith ordeal behind him as a nightmare he'd woken up from. Pike counted their blessings that they had found and got him back before any lasting damage had been done. But it didn't change the conundrum everyone seemed to be expecting *him* to solve. There had been no constructive input from either Aaron or Sarah, aside from things he already knew. Karen, for her part had simply laughed down the phone at him, told him to sink or swim and rung off with an amused 'Welcome to proper stallion ownership, P. Good luck and let me know if you find a solution'.

"Hunter is a mare," he answered Wendy's question with a big sigh. "She was one more for the harem, so it was okay for Blue to bring her in. Strawberry is a boy. If I put him and Blue together, chances are we'd have to split the herd up for good because to Inigo's pea brain it would look as if Straw had stolen one of his ladies. So if we split off the Mice and then tried to introduce both back in, Inigo would probably kill Straw. Look at him, look at the way he's staring, he's itching for the fight."

Eleanor stopped waxing the saddle on her knees and looked ahead dreamily.

"You know, I used to think Straw was a girl. Back when we first met and Strawberry Mouse was just a name to me." She glanced at Pike, gathering her thoughts back into the present. "You're kidding, right? You don't actually mean kill? As in *kill*? I thought you told me that a stallion will sometimes allow a spare male at the fringe of the herd."

Pike sucked his upper lip in through the chip in his tooth and chewed on it for a bit before he shook his head earnestly.

"No, I'm not. It happens. And yes, they do but only after some serious fighting." While he spoke he watched Wendy as she stopped brushing and turned to lean with her back against Strawberry's side, bracing herself for a lecture. "The second stallion is sort of trapped between a rock and a hard place from the off. He can't be as strong as the boss, obviously, but if he shows himself as too weak, he is deemed not worthy as a back up and run off just the same. The problem Straw would have in a fight is how weak he is. Aside from Inigo just being bigger, stronger and younger I'm certain now that there is something wrong with Straw's right eye. If you watch him you'll notice he keeps turning his head to look at stuff with his left. I've already called the vets to take a look at him but Halland is on leave at the moment and I want him to check Straw out himself. The others are all fine for routine stuff but for this I want Halland himself. I like him. He's got good hands. So we wait till he's back. Point is, if Inigo charges Straw on his blind side Straw may well get flattened." He laid the bridle he'd finished putting back together on the floor and dropped his head between his knees to address the flagstone beneath him. "I don't know. I really don't know what to do."

He let himself hang in space for a second, feeling Eleanor's hand on his back, rubbing it gently.

"It's alright. You'll think of something."

He raised his head, exhausted and clueless, and looked slowly to and fro between Eleanor and Wendy.

It had been a long autumn.

"No I won't. I've been racking my brain for days. I don't know what to do. You all seem to think I'm this big sage for anything horse related. I'm not, people. I'm eighteen, not eighty. I wasn't born with this magic knowledge or anything. Most of what I know comes from watching others and from books and films on animal behaviour because it *interests* me. The last person I knew who could handle this died when I was eight. And you know what? We didn't exactly discuss herd dynamics beforehand. She was busy trying to finish reading *Harry Potter* to me before our time ran out. But you all seem to think I can just run this show like that." He clicked his fingers in the air. "I can't. I don't know what to do. I haven't got the faintest." He drew in a long, helpless breath then breathed out sharply. "Maybe we should just split them up for good. The Mice in one paddock, the other three in another. Job done. When the foal comes things will change again anyway. But I don't want to do that. I want them *together*."

"Maybe you should give them a task *together* then. Worked for us," Tinkerbelle's voice joined the conversation loudly from the entrance. "Didn't it?" she added more unsurely.

They had been so absorbed in their little round they hadn't noticed her arrive. She stood inside the doorway, just far enough in to escape the drizzling rain, folded back the hood of her fashionably tailored oilskin parka and waited. Wendy's face lit up.

"Hey Tink. What are you doing here?" she welcomed her sister kindly.

Tinkerbelle took a step into the barn and sought Pike's eyes.

Permission. I can't believe she's actually seeking permission to come in. It's her bloody home, too. How much of an arse have you been, Paytah Hawthorne?

He beckoned her over and watched her raise her hand in greeting at Eleanor before walking towards Wendy and Straw.

"I wanted to check on Straw. You seem to forget that he was my pony first. I wanted to make sure he's okay."

"He is *now*," Pike said and Tinkerbelle flinched almost imperceptibly.

She stopped midway and looked at him unsurely. He held up his palms.

"Not that I'm making you responsible for their actions anymore."

She relaxed, smiled the smallest of smiles and carried on walking.

"Just so you know," she said more to her sister than anyone else, having reached the gelding's nose and letting him sniff her hands. "Mum didn't know either. Rob deliberately waited until she was in the Maldives to shift him. They've had the most massive rows over it. I think coming home from holidays to find you were missing was one of the worst experiences of her life. Other than having us in the first place."

Strawberry inclined his head to offer her an ear for scratching and Tinkerbelle obliged.

"Is that why you're here? To make me feel guilty?" Wendy asked dejectedly.

She'd started curry combing again, biting her bottom lip ferociously.

"No. Just thought you should know. I also came," Tinkerbelle continued, looking over across the pony's back at Pike now, "because I wanted to say thanks. Walt and I came second at the weekend. You were right. He needed some fun and he *does* love Elvis. How do you come up with this stuff, P? You know *that's* why everyone is so in awe of you, don't you?"

"Hm," Pike replied. "They shouldn't be. You should look to your sister for that. The fun part at least. She put that thought in my head. Who knows if I'd seen it without her saying so beforehand. You should listen to her more."

He could see a shift in Wendy's shoulders as he said it that made him grin.

"I'd love to but it's a bit difficult now that she isn't there anymore," Tink retorted acidly, flicking a strand of damp hair from her face, just before her voice became smaller. "Which is why I thought maybe..."

She didn't finish the sentence.

Wendy stopped brushing.

"Maybe what?"

"Maybe we could all go out riding together at the weekend? Meet half way? Or if they're busy —" She tipped her head to indicate Pike and Eleanor. "Maybe just you and me? Or just hang out?"

For a moment edged into eternity the Jones sisters looked at each other over Strawberry's withers. Sometime amidst it, Pike could feel Eleanor tugging gently at the back of his shirt. He dragged his eyes away from the two girls in the aisle to find her smiling at him with damp eyes.

"Come on," she whispered through a sniffle, "Let's take some of this stuff back into the tack room."

Chapter 31

A task together.

The words had etched themselves into Pike's brain immediately. He'd been too scared to use his grandma's trick of introducing a new herd member, unsure of how exactly it worked. That was the information he'd tried to get out of his aunt on the phone but she had just repeated what he already knew.

On the surface the method was simple. Freeschool the new horse together with the rest of the herd, making them run until it looked like the recent addition had been there all along. Put out as a group. Watch. Hope for the best.

It had always been an impressive, exciting sight, whenever Kimi had stood in the centre of the school, flicking her whip and directing a whole herd to run this way and that until the animals' individual shapes blurred into one body.

A task together.

Pike had never thought about it in those terms but now it dawned on him that it wasn't some kind of supernatural power his grandma had possessed which made her approach work but exactly that, the fact that she had been giving the animals a common goal.

Still, he wasn't quite sure enough of himself to do it alone.

So he gathered his tribe.

On a Sunday morning, as friendly a day as November would allow, he stood with his stallion by his side in the centre of the schooling paddock and watched each of them lead in a horse or pony, past Aaron who held the gate for them.

Sarah and Casta came first, followed by Tink leading Hunter and then Eleanor with Blue. He let them all line up parallel to Inigo, as if preparing a company of riders for mounting. He could feel the stallion on the other end of the rope get restless long before Wendy brought Strawberry out of the stable.

As soon as they entered the arena, Inigo's tension became tangible. He started pawing the ground and giving off little grunts while Pike breathed deeply and deliberately, more to exhale his own nerves than to communicate calm and peace to his horse. But as two were one it worked both ways.

And we are one, he thought lovingly.

He loosened his grip on the rope and touched the bay patch on Inigo's side.

Be kind.

He could be a friend.

Images of Ash flashed through his mind and he allowed a wave of sadness to wash over him before he concentrated on Inigo again. A sudden surge passed between the animal and him. For the first time since Strawberry's arrival they were truly communicating again. Pike could feel the animal's upset and insecurity, the two hearts beating in the stallion's chest. His programming to protect and defend his herd versus his naturally friendly, curious and quite laid back character.

"What do I do now?" Wendy called across.

She had stopped Straw just inside the school and Aaron had shut the gate behind them. Much to Wendy's dismay the old man had made her wear a hat and body protector for the exercise and looking at her padding now, Pike truly realised the danger he was putting her in but also the trust he had in her.

Little Flame, we should call you. Because you are that other me I wanted around so badly. Just a bit younger and female. Goes with the hair, too.

On that note, he told her to bring the little gelding over.

They let them meet nose to nose.

They sniffed and with a screech Inigo kicked a front leg out. Straw didn't retort, just as Pike had feared. The pony simply stood there, making himself small in his frame. Inigo reared a couple of feet off the ground then came down heavily, inches away from the gelding. Straw's ears pinned back and he bared his teeth. Pike could see a light flicker up in Inigo's eye as he pulled a similar face. As the stallion put on his best dragon act and started sweeping the space around Straw with air bites, Straw responded in an equal fashion.

They had chosen their fight style. Low and with teeth, not high and with hooves.

Pike was relieved. It was going to be as fair as Straw's limitations would allow.

"Right, everybody other than Wendy release your horses and get out of here," Pike called aloud then focused on Wendy. "You are doing great, keep the lead loose so they can carry on snaking at each other but don't let Straw's teeth make contact. When the others are out, take his head collar off and get out of here, too."

He tugged sharply on the lead as Inigo's teeth were getting too close to their target. Out of the corner of his eye he saw Sarah, Tink and Eleanor leave the arena.

Casta and Hunter stood where they had been left. Only Blue took a couple of steps around the other mares to watch what was going on, head and tail held high in the air, alert and ready to get involved. Inigo clocked her, too, and his air biting immediately became more intense.

Pike nodded to Wendy and she set Straw free.

"Go," Pike commanded.

She left hurriedly.

As soon as Straw was unhaltered, the pony retreated a step from Inigo but didn't run. Suddenly Blue neighed loudly and both males answered her. When they looked at each other again, the expressions in their faces had changed.

The fight was on.

With his heart beating in his throat and a last thought willing him to be kind Pike released Inigo then walked backwards out of the fight zone.

It was swift and brutal to watch.

Strawberry had a lot more gumption left in him than Pike had given him credit for. As the air filled with grunts and attack squeals the little gelding went straight for the side of Inigo's neck and bit down hard. Once stuck there he didn't let go again, no matter how much Inigo shook and moved, trying his hardest to get him off. It was a clever move, preventing the stallion from changing the fight style to attacking from above, where he'd have the advantage of height.

Once Inigo realised that Straw was there to stay he gave up trying to break free and bit down himself on the gelding's crest. They stayed like that for minutes, moving around in circles, interlocked and neither letting go. On the sidelines, Casta and Hunter had moved closer to one another, the big mare sliding her body protectively between the pregnant horse and the fighting males. Blue, on the other hand, had jogged closer to the adversaries, alarm written all over her body, making her seem instantly younger and fitter than her twenty-seven years.

Eventually Straw's grip slipped and Inigo had the upper hand. Without further ado he wrestled the pony to the ground, letting go of the crest once Straw was down to hold him there with his forehead against the gelding's barrel. Straw's head flicked up trying to get his teeth at Inigo and his legs kicked wildly but nothing reached anywhere close. Pike could see that the pony was getting more uncoordinated with his good eye to the ground but also that he would fight until the bitter end.

Suddenly Inigo stepped back, releasing Straw momentarily, only to rear up above him before he could get up. Pike heard Wendy scream by the fence at the same time as Blue giving off a

loud, panicked whinny. Then his own voice penetrated the mix.
"No!"

Inigo didn't listen to any of them but to his relief Pike saw the stallion's hooves come down on the ground, just below Straw's belly line. The intention had not been to kill but to demonstrate he could. He gave Straw time to scramble to his feet and the feisty little roan kicked up both legs at him before he scarpered. Inigo turned to round up his ladies but soon found that his challenger hadn't really gone away. With no room for Straw to run off over the hills he had tried to hide in the farthest corner of the arena but he was clearly still there. Pike took the break in the fighting to go and grab a whip, so when Inigo and with him the rest of his herd charged at the little gelding he stood prepared. Before they could get at Straw, he cracked it loudly, forcing them to run past the gelding and suddenly the animals found themselves trapped in an eternal chase off without a target. Pike let them circle the arena once and when they passed Straw again, made the gelding join the group at the back. After that it became a game, letting them run, urging them on whenever they flagged then letting off for a little while until Inigo started hassling Straw again which would inevitably lead to Pike putting on the pressure once more. While he was standing in the centre, commanding them in this direction and that, Pike suddenly felt like a conductor, sure of his notes and sure of his musicians. An hour went by and the breaks in the symphony became longer and more peaceful. When not running, Straw was allowed to hang at the fringe of the group now until Inigo would suddenly half-heartedly attack again. Presently they were having a rest in the bottom half of the school, the mares huddled together in a cluster and the two boys a little off on either side.

Pike looked at the mares and began to worry. Though healed and fitter than Pike could have hoped for after the short time she'd been with them, Hunter was starting to show signs of serious exhaustion, Blue similarly so and pregnant Casta also had only marginally more energy left. All five animals in the arena were glistening and steaming with sweat by now and it was cold. They couldn't carry on for much longer.

Just then Inigo's head rose again, preparing for another charge at Straw but Pike could see that the stallion, too, was concerned with the wellbeing of his herd now. The horse looked back and forth between his ladies and his human and when Pike whistled to him he came over without hesitation.

One eye still on Straw he let Pike rub his forehead, pat and scratch him until he relented, forgetting about the gelding and delightedly scrubbing his cheek against the young man's shoulder.

Pike laughed and gently pushed Inigo's head away.

"Too hard boy. But I appreciate the sentiment. Now — " He let the stallion's head collar slip from his shoulder and slipped it on the horse. "Do you reckon we can finish this nicely? Come on, walk on."

As he spoke the command he tugged on the lead and started moving towards the other animals. Half way he clicked his tongue to ask Inigo for a trot and together they jogged in a circle around Strawberry and the mares. Pike changed direction and they rounded the whole herd once more before he called over to the fence where tea and biscuits had started happening in the meantime.

"Right, everybody back in here, please. Grab your horses, we need to walk them dry. Otherwise by tomorrow our problem will be solved permanently by five cases of equine pneumonia. – Grandpa, could you fetch us some cooling rugs, please?"

He met Aaron's eyes and felt showered in love and pride.

The old man winked at him.

"Certainly can. Haven't seen a show like that in a few years."

They walked the horses around for a long time then exchanged the fleece rugs for turnout ones and set them loose in the paddock.

They stood at the fence to watch with bated breath, Pike holding Eleanor's ice-cold hand tightly in his own, Wendy standing in front of Tink who had slung her arms around her little sister's waist and was resting her chin on the smaller Jones' head, and Aaron by Sarah's side, an arm around her shoulder, rubbing her gently to keep her warm.

Nothing happened in the field and after a couple of minutes Pike squeezed the side of Eleanor's hand lightly a couple of times.

"Come on. Let's go inside. You're freezing."

"You don't want to wait a bit longer?" she asked, astonished.

He took one long look at the herd, the way they were grazing, where their bodies were in relation to one another and shook his head decisively.

"No. There'll be scraps for a few weeks to come but no carnage. Inigo's not going to try and chase him off now, just keep him in his place. Time to sink or swim. In my case, swim in a bath. I stink with adrenaline. Come." He grinned down at her. "If you're lucky you get to wash my hair for me."

Without further ado, she dragged him away.

Chapter 32

His prediction had proved accurate and by the end of the following week Pike had as peaceful a herd as could be expected. Occasionally Strawberry was even allowed near Blue for a quick nuzzle now, without Inigo immediately asserting his authority.

Teaching the stallion, too, had become a pure pleasure again. Pike was starting to ride him under saddle now, doing as much flatwork as the ground conditions would allow and he was doing beautifully. Quick on the uptake as Inigo was, Pike had to stop himself occasionally not to ask too much too soon but if in doubt he would consult Wendy.

As another eye on the ground that he could trust, who understood what he wanted from his horse and who wasn't afraid to set him straight, she was everything Pike could have wished for. He deliberately waited with Inigo's schooling sessions until after she came home each day, squeezing the last half hour of twilight from the day to work with his horse under her guidance.

As a literacy student she was much less of a success but he hoped that with growing confidence, her reading and writing would eventually start to take shape. At the very least she was sticking to her promise and was letting Pike sit her down after dinner each evening to practise.

Things should have been good.

But whichever way he turned, Pike still felt the lack of Ash.

More so in moments like this one, having just come back from a Saturday ride with Eleanor and standing in the tack room to put saddles away. Although it had been completely reverted to its original function, it still felt of Ash's presence in here, still faintly smelled of wood smoke, kerosene and camping.

Pike inhaled deeply, chasing the sensation, then looked down at Eleanor and reached out to take Blue's bridle from her. She held on to it and searched his face with worried eyes.

She had softened her approach since she'd come back from tour, had stopped pestering him about sleeping with her, even when they were huddled together at night and he was at his weakest.

She'd finally agreed to let him carry on dictating the pace.

It bothered him.

He didn't want to be treated like a wounded animal.

"Ah, but you are," she said with a light in her eyes, finally releasing the bridle.

"Are what?" he asked, turning away to hang it up.

"Whatever it was you were thinking. I didn't quite catch the actual words. But I've got an image of a seriously pathetic puppy holding up its paw."

He faced her again, not quite sure what to say.

"See," she continued, "You, *you*, would have been indignant at that. You're eyes should be going all firecrackery and stuff. But you're not. He's taken your anger."

"Who?"

"Are you kidding me?"

Pike cupped her cheek in his hand and bend down.

"Is that such a bad thing?" he whispered.

"No. Maybe not. But I don't like that he's made you sad instead."

"Hm."

He didn't want to talk about it, didn't want to admit how deeply it cut that he still hadn't heard a word from Ash.

So he kissed her, trying to distract them both and when she slung her arms around his neck he thought for a moment how much more he wanted her now than when she had been pushy. He lost himself in her mouth, in the sensation of her body against his and let himself just want her for once.

She detached.

"Ah," she mumbled against his lips, panting but somehow still rational. "But you're still not ready, I see that now." She pulled back a bit more and added with more volume, "Parker's."

"What?" Pike straightened up.

"Parker's Academy of Combat Sports."

"Come again?"

"Parker's Academy of Combat Sports," she repeated with emphasis. "SE18. Woolwich. I say when we go to your parents' stupid do next weekend we take the train up early and do a little detour."

Very slowly it dawned on Pike what she was talking about. She would never cease to astonish him. He ran a hand through his hair.

"How? How...How do you know where he is?"

"Interweb."

"What? You've heard from him?"

"No. I just did a bit of research."

"Right. But how did you even know his dad runs a martial arts club? I haven't told you. I know I haven't told you."

She frowned, looking at him as if he was a bit slow.

"*He* told me. — We all spent a week together before he legged it, remember? And unlike some people I ask questions and stuff."

She turned towards the door to go back into the stable block where the horses were waiting for their dinner.

"Did he tell you the whole story?" He nervously addressed her back.

"What?" she asked over her shoulder. "That he killed some poor kid? Yes, he did."

"And?"

She looked ahead and carried on moving, shouting the rest of it into the air above her.

"And nothing. If you ask the oracle, it checks out exactly as he tells it. End of. I'm not interested in the past, I'm interested in the present. And in the present I want to go and see if we can get your friend back. If Inigo had actually killed Straw we still would have kept him, right? Same difference. We didn't fail Blue and we are bloody well not going to fail you."

His girl had spoken.

Chapter 33

In between his sporadic visits to the capital, Pike would always conveniently forget how much he despised the city and how thankful he should really have been to John and Alice for abandoning him on his grandparents' doorstep as a baby.

The place was distinctly too loud, too hectic and too dirty for his liking. Though there was next to nothing by way of litter and the beach at home usually looked infinitely worse on a Saturday morning, there was a London-specific kind of grime. It surreptitiously clogged up your pores and coated your hands in a fine film of black grease within seconds of arrival, which made him feel claustrophobic in his skin.

There was also a remarkable lack of horses.

Or cats or dogs for that matter.

He snorted at the thought as they headed out of his parents' apartment building where they had already narrowly avoided a citizen's arrest by the porter for being an unsightly blemish in this tower of glass, marble and all things sterile. They had walked here from the station to drop off their bags, a ten minute stroll across the Thames during which he hadn't seen a single animal aside from other furless monkeys, not even one of the famous London pigeons.

How could people live like this?

Eleanor was bouncing along next to him across the lobby, undisturbed by their clinical surroundings and still amused from her short exchange with his mother who had foolishly tried to suggest sleeping arrangements in different rooms. Pike was relatively sure that by now Alice was regretting having asked 'the tiny thing' to come along.

The tiny thing grabbed his hand and pulled him impatiently out of the glass doors.

"Well, that was fun," she said once they were outside.

They looked up and down the street.

It was doused in cold, silvery December sunshine, the tall buildings throwing stark mid-morning shadows. There were few people about. This was a road where people had living quarters but didn't actually live. They were either busy being important elsewhere or spending the weekend in their country residence or their second, third or fourth global homes.

The two Doctors Hawthorne fell firmly into the former category, dividing their time evenly between travelling and the lab of the honourable educational establishment that employed them, a stone's throw away, just across the river. The apartment, bought for proximity and convenience, was a space for sleeping in only, where John and Alice were thoroughly out of place. If Pike's mother hadn't originated from debutante orbit, the sole offspring of a family that swam in wealth, a flat here would have been unaffordable on the comparatively paltry salaries their research posts brought in. It was one of the few redeeming features of his mother, one of the handful of truths about her that Pike respected deeply. She hadn't married for money or status and most definitely not to have children. She had married for love. Whether for love of the man or for love of the job Pike was never quite sure but as a symbiotic whole her devotion to John and their shared work was beyond question.

Eleanor nudged him.

"Hey, are you growing roots?"

He contemplated the piece of pavement between his feet.

"I don't think that's possible."

"Come on." She tugged impatiently at the arm of his leather jacket. "Let's go."

Woolwich was a world away. One that felt instantly more

comfortable with its standard British medley of architecture through the ages, from tall and modern to ancient and quaint and with people busily to-ing and fro-ing on their Saturday errands. There was actual life here, pigeons and even the occasional dog, but they soon left the hustle and bustle behind in their quest to locate Parker's Academy of Combat Sports.

They found the club in an industrial estate right by the Thames, wedged in between nondescript warehouses and factory outlets. It wasn't anything like Pike had imagined. No dingy, dark room full of shady characters standing around a ringside while two guys were beating each other to a pulp but a large, bright space with four separate training areas, only one of which was a classic boxing ring. The others were made of simple mats on the floor, all populated with pairs of training partners. Above was a mezzanine balcony where people were busy cycling nowhere, pumping iron or thrashing punchbags.

Pike and Eleanor stood in the entrance for a few minutes, being thoroughly ignored until a Chinese whisper of nods in the upper echelons ended at a boy of about sixteen. He stopped kicking the crap out of a punchbag and leant over the railings to stare down at them. Even from afar he looked ridiculously similar to Ash, only shorter, squatter and weirdly ripped for his age above his black boxer shorts, and Pike's heart did a little jolt.

They'd definitely found the right place.

He waved and the boy made his way down the steel staircase towards them. They met him at the bottom.

"Hi," he said, giving Pike the once over while jittering on his feet. "If you want to enrol you're going to have to wait for my dad. He's gonna be in around one." His eyes drifted over to Eleanor. "No offence, you look fit enough, but you're too young. We don't take anyone under fourteen."

"Actually, I'm sixteen. Not that it matters 'cause I have

absolutely no interest in beating up inanimate objects. Or animate ones. That's not why we're here. We're looking for Ashley."

The boy froze, his face darkening instantly.

"What d'ya want from my brother? Look, he's only just come back to us. We don't want any trouble. Let bygones be bygones, eh?"

It took them a moment to work it out.

Pike shook his head.

"You misunderstand. We're friends of Ash's. Genuine. He might have mentioned us. I'm Pike and this is Eleanor. Pleased to meet you."

He stuck out a hand and the boy touched it with his glove, clearly drawn in by the anachronism of the gesture.

"Aiden Parker. Sorry but he hasn't mentioned you. To be honest he hasn't said a lot since he's come back. I mean, he never talked much anyway but now it's difficult to get more than two words out of him a day. All he does is sit in his room and draw and make little horses out of clay. Horses! I mean, seriously? Mum says to give him time but I don't know…"

He shrugged, looking up over his shoulder at his punchbag calling to him from above then turned back to Pike. A flash of realisation suddenly illuminated his features.

"That's why I thought I knew you! I thought you were, like, from another club and I'd seen you fight or something. But that's not it. You're one of the people he draws! I thought you were made up."

Pike grinned, happiness spreading through him like wild fire. He'd been missed.

Ash's brother turned to Eleanor and examined her more closely then frowned.

"But you are definitely not the girl he keeps drawing."

"No." Eleanor smiled wryly. "We left *her* at home."

The three-bedroom brickbuilt mock Victorian terraced house Aiden led them to was situated in an estate not far from the club. As soon as mini-Ash had put on some regular clothes, a funny transformation had taken place. Once his unnatural physique was covered up, he seemed like a pretty normal, if verbally overactive, sixteen-year-old, intrigued by the visitors and curious about everything they could tell him to do with his brother. Even Pike with his limited understanding of fellow human beings realised quickly that Aiden was torn between some kind of hero worship and not being particularly happy about said hero's return in the flesh. It seemed the brother he'd created in his head during Ash's absence had been acutely better than the real thing. Although, to his credit, underneath Aiden seemed to have a pretty good grasp of who Ashley Parker really was. When Pike told him a little about Hunter and how they'd saved her, Aiden laughed at first at the idea that his brother should have a horse but then quickly conceded that it kind of fitted. Ash, he told them, had always been the one out of the three brothers pestering their parents for a pet and once when they'd been little and he'd accidentally run over a baby rat with his bicycle he'd cried about it for days.

"About a stinking rat!" Aiden exclaimed just as he was putting his keys in the front door.

The house greeted them with the odours of a fry up just eaten, summer meadow scented washing powder and permanent damp. It also came with the noise of a couple arguing good naturedly somewhere in a room to the right of the hallway.

"He needs a job, is what he needs," a hoarse male voice stated.

"He's trying, Scott. You know how difficult it is around here. And people still remember who he is. They haven't forgotten."

The female sounded slightly exasperated, like she wanted to move on from the conversation already.

"He could always work for me. Or he could sign up."

"Don't even go there." The woman's voice took on a vehement edge. "For God's sake let him find his feet first. I've not got him back just to lose him to the army now. Two years I've spent wondering if he was dead or alive. I'm not doing that again. One son we agreed. No more. The other two do something else."

"We've done alright out of the forces. Adam's doing alright."

"Yes, of course he is. Because he's like you. Ashley is —" The woman appeared in the hallway, dressed in a pink terry cotton bathrobe over white flannel pyjamas and carrying some dirty dishes. "Different. Oh, hello."

She looked inquisitively at her youngest son, Pike and Eleanor who were standing under the light of a dim energy saver bulb.

She was reassuringly ordinary looking, skinny with shoulder-length dyed black hair that showed chunks of grey-blonde at the roots, a narrow oval face that lacked chin definition and mercury eyes exactly like Ash's and Aiden's. There was something youthful underneath her heavily lined forehead, saying that she'd aged before her time but wasn't quite prepared to give up and grow old just yet.

Pike instantly liked her.

"Hi Mum. These guys are here for Ash. Friends of his."

The man appeared behind her in the door frame, fully dressed in blue jeans and a white shirt. He was the complete opposite of his wife, all angles and beef, much better preserved and tougher looking but also infinitely more jaded behind his baby blue eyes.

"Friends?" he enquired gruffly, considering Pike and Eleanor. "I don't remember either of you."

"Not *old* friends, Dad," Aiden added urgently. "*New* ones."

"Oh," both Parkers said in the same breath.

"Well, friends are good," Ash's mum decided and carried on taking the plates to the kitchen at the end of the hall. "Feel free to go up. Second door on the right."

Pike's blood pumped faster around his body with each step up the avocado green carpeted stairs. By the time he knocked on the door his heart was hammering in his chest and he could feel his top lip beginning to vibrate nervously.

What was he going to say?

"Come in."

As soon as he heard the other's muffled voice, he felt calmer again but he didn't push down the handle until Eleanor poked him gently in the side and jutted her chin in the direction of the room.

"Go," she whispered, "I'll wait here." She took a step back and leant against the banister. "Go!"

He went in.

The room was small and simply furnished with a single bed to the right, a wardrobe to the left and a desk straight ahead under the window. Ash's rucksack was standing in a corner, opened and with clothes spilling out around it but still mostly packed. Ash himself was sitting with his back to the door, deeply absorbed in shaping a lump of clay on the tiny area of desktop that was not already covered in little sculptures of Hunter. He carried on undeterred with his task, not turning around.

Pike's eyes swept the walls.

Every inch was covered in drawings, stuck up with blue tack. Whole series of Hunter. Some of Blue, Inigo and Casta, a few of Pike, a portrait of Aaron and Sarah sitting on a couch, even one of Eleanor playing the guitar. And then there were the dozen or so of Wendy.

"You know," he addressed his friend's back loudly, "If I didn't know you, I'd think this was majorly creepy."

Ash put the modelling knife down and finally swivelled around to face him.

"Hey," he said barely above a whisper, swallowing Pike with his eyes as if he was an apparition.

"Hey," Pike answered and went over to him to sit on the mattress at the foot of the bed, close enough for their knees to touch. He looked up at Ash. There was so much Pike could have asked, so much he could have said but in the end he settled for tilting his head at the backpack on the floor.

"How come you haven't unpacked yet? It's been weeks."

Ash shrugged.

"My older brother is coming home for Christmas. It's his room, really, so no point in settling in. I'll move into Aiden's room with him or kip on the sofa when the time comes. Aiden's my younger brother."

Pike took one of the finished little clay Clydesdales off the table and examined it more closely.

"Yeah, I know. We've met. — This is great. Are you going to paint them?"

Ash mimicked his action, taking the unfinished little horse and the knife off the table to carry on working on it, leaning heavily into their shared space.

"Can't decide. I like the rough quality they have like this. I think if you paint them, they'll lose a lot of their texture. But if I want to sell them, they probably need to be painted and glazed. People like tacky. Don't know."

Pike looked from the finished product in his palm onto the shape in Ash's hands and smiled.

"Hm. What happened to *your* room?"

"Never had one. Always shared with Aiden before. But I think it's not fair. Aiden's had his own space this entire time and then I turn up again and suddenly…I don't want him to feel like…I don't know…I just don't think it would be fair on him. Don't worry about me. I'll sort out something somewhere once I've found a job. It's hard." He looked up and grinned almost apologetically. "Not many vacancies for fire jugglers in Woolwich."

"But I do," Pike said simply and got to his feet.

"Do what?"

"Worry about you. And I miss you. *We* miss you. All of us. Wendy's acting all big about it but you know, she lights a candle every night, puts it in her window. I'm sure it's for you. She said she was doing it for Strawberry but she's still doing it. We managed to get him back in the end, believe it or not, but there is still a hole. About your height, your width. And *we* have rooms aplenty." He took a step into the middle of the room and spread out his arms, indicating their surroundings. "Look around you, Ash. This is bullshit. This is like the biggest load of bull I've ever seen. You're more than just a fire juggler. You're a really talented artist and a damn fine groom for mostly dead horses and a brilliant babysitter for wayward girls and I bet you'd do a much better job at teaching her to read than I am. Did you know she couldn't read? Fucking tragedy. So yeah, you could get a shitty job in Woolwich and you could get a room in a shared house with people who don't give a fuck about you, or —" He moved back in on Ash, put his hands on the other's shoulders and pinned him down in his gaze, alight, alive, good and proper. "You could fucking well come *home!*"

Chapter 34

That night two things saw Pike through the most painfully boring dinner he had ever had to endure. The first was the amazing girl in the elegant green cocktail dress sitting diagonally opposite him and the other the knowledge that the very next day three of them were going to leave London.

Together.

It had taken all of two seconds for Ash to say yes. They had hugged and shed a tear each then gone to get Eleanor to talk about the details of their departure.

He raised his glass to her now and she excused herself politely from the animated conversation she was having with the 300-year-old president of the Society of Apothecaries to her right to raise hers in return. She strained her neck a little so their eyes could meet across the table above a skyline of ridiculously tall wine glasses and for a moment the rest of the room fell away as they celebrated their triumph silently between them. He watched as her lips touched the glass and she drank before flicking her tongue along the outer edge to gather up a drop of liquid that had escaped onto the wrong side. It wasn't a conscious thing, not designed for flirting but a primeval voice inside of him responded to it loud and clear.

Want, it growled.

He quickly looked away, up and down the table of embalmed personalities and pruned egos. It served him better than the proverbial cold shower in no time.

"You two are very serious, aren't you?" John's voice, low and for once non-judgemental, found his ear. Pike turned to his father who was sitting at the head of the table by his elbow. Like the king and queen presiding over a banquet, Alice had also seated herself at the small end, to John's left and looked a little put out by Eleanor's ability to hold the apothecary's attention. She had clearly placed the man at the corner to sit between herself and the girl, so as to avoid having to talk to her son's girlfriend at length but hadn't anticipated being left without a conversational partner entirely. To fill the void she spoke loudly to other people across the table or gave superfluous orders to the waiters about filling up people's glasses. Pike felt a little sorry for her and wondered briefly why she had arranged to put John, herself and their roughly twenty guests through this. His father was notoriously uncomfortable in gatherings like this. Silent and brooding presence that he was, he didn't exactly qualify as the life and soul of any party, least of all one held in his honour.

Pike realised that he hadn't responded and finally nodded, bracing himself for some nugget of unwelcome advice about sexually transmitted diseases, teenage pregnancy and ruining your life. But it didn't come.

"I'm happy for you, Paytah. Hold on to it as fast as you can and don't let go."

Pike felt a sudden splurge of love hitting him from the side that he couldn't deflect. It had always had a different ring when John spoke his given name, a timbre that send vibrations all through his core and that he liked to banish as quickly as possible. It didn't fit with their relationship as was and there was a strong part in Pike that refused to make it fit, too. Abandonment was abandonment. And that was that.

"How is college coming along?" John changed the subject to even less neutral territory. "Any idea what university you want to go to yet? Or—" John hesitated for a moment then decided to proceed across the treacherous ground in front of them, "what subjects you want to study?"

"Who says I'm going to go to uni at all? Who says I want to start adult life with a debt no mortal can repay in any normal amount of time?"

"Don't be silly. I'm not going to let you get a student loan. I can afford to put my son through university, so I will put my son through university."

"Who says I want to go?"

"You're a Hawthorne."

"Actually, to most people I'm a Pike. Who says, I'm not going to follow in Grandpa's footsteps? I might go on the tools. There is something immensely satisfying about a set of hooves well done. I'd make a good farrier."

"I'm sure you would. And you'd end up just like Dad. With a broken back and a brain that never quite got used to its full capacity. Dad's bright. Really, really bright. But he never got the chance to do anything with his IQ. Utterly wasted. You want to end up like him?"

Pike laughed and got up.

"You know what?" He ran his hands through his hair in exasperation. "I have no idea where you get these airs and graces from. You're not some lord, John Hawthorne. You are the son of a blacksmith and a circus performer. Maybe you should remember that some time. And yes, I'd absolutely love to end up like Grandpa. Minus the dead wife and the strokes but hell yeah. Fancied by the hottest seventy-something in a hundred mile radius? Surrounded by horses and young people with a grandson who loves me and will look after me till the day I die, no matter what? Sounds bloody good to me. See, that's where you are wrong. Utterly, utterly wrong. He did use his brain. He used it with his heart and he's made a damn fine life out of it. Excuse me, I'm going to wash my hands."

"You know, you look good in a suit and tie."

Eleanor was grinning at him from her perch opposite the

cloakroom doors. Looking at her he appreciated the sentiment. She was sitting decoratively on a shelf, built into the wall for the sole purpose of housing a large vase full of oversized dried flowers, dangling her naked legs which ended in green ballerina shoes matching her dress. She looked classy and slightly ethereal, so much not like the girl in unravelling jumpers and mud streaked jodhpurs who happily skipped through life with him yet so totally like the fey creature he'd first laid eyes on so long ago. He went to stand in front of her, bending down until their foreheads touched.

"Was it very bad?"

She reached up to touch his cheek, tracing his scars.

"No. It was honest. They've moved on already. Main's arrived and they're talking about the sauce. We should get back there. I hear it's divine."

He took her hand in his, withdrew a little and kissed her finger tips. It elicited a sharp intake of breath on her part that made him unable to resist her mouth when she offered it. They kissed for a long time, undeterred by other restaurant guests coming up the stairs and passing behind them, some of whom cleared their throats loudly to no avail.

"I love you," he whispered when they finally detangled and suddenly a smile like a super nova radiated from her eyes.

"You know, you've never said that to me before," she whispered back.

He was astonished.

"Really?"

"Really," she stated more loudly then added, "And there is someone else who needs to hear those words from you."

"Who?"

"You know who."

"No way."

"Yes way."

"Why? Why should I?"

"Because he is just like you, only without one of me to kick his butt. And because that's who you are. I've been watching you since I got back from spending time with *my* dad and you know, you keep collecting all these souls to bring home but it looks to me like the one person who you really *need* to collect is the one you refuse. He *loves* you. And you love him, too. You don't want to but you do. It's obvious. I look at the two of you next to one another and I can *see* the bond. All this Hawthorne talk, it's just his attempt at trying to find a connection. If he could make you a doctor he'd finally have a way to talk to you. It's idiotic but I swear that's what he's trying to do. Your mum? Different ball game. Cold fish. No idea why she decided to have a child. Probably thought she had to. I don't know. But John? Give him a chance. Give both of you a chance."

She jumped off the shelf and grabbed his hand.

"Come on, there are three more courses to get through. Let's eat."

Chapter 35

They had survived the rest of the meal in truce and when they got back to the apartment, John tentatively asked his son if he cared to join him for a tea or coffee in the study. Pike was about to refuse but one look at Eleanor's raised eyebrows and a second one at his father's face, serious as ever but also scarily vulnerable underneath, made him change his mind.

Once they had entered John's tiny, dark and chaotic den, the only space with at least some character in this petri-dish of a flat, they positioned themselves across from one another at the desk and sat in silence.

Pike studied his father who seemed deep in thought, elbows on the table, hands folded, staring at them almost as if praying. The idea made Pike laugh out loud and the sound jerked his father back into the room.

John frowned deeply.

"What's funny?"

Pike snorted.

"Nothing. Look, if this is going to be another talk on what I should or shouldn't do with my life, what uni to go to and whatnot, forget it. I've got my own plans and strangely enough I don't even think you'll find my choices that disagreeable. But I'm not discussing it with anyone until after my exams. I might not get the grades I need anyway."

There was a sudden spark in John's eyes.

"So it is something you need good grades for?"

Throw the dog a bone.

"Yes."

He could see curiosity and a smidgen of pride flicker up behind his father's studied gaze until the older man cleared his throat and shook himself forcefully. The fire died abruptly in time with a knock on the door. It didn't open until John had clearly stated that Alice could come in. Pike tensed a little. This was unusual. His mother would not normally wait before entering. She'd knock and walk in. The look his parents exchanged when she set down a tray bearing a tea pot, cups and sundries needled Pike even more. This was bigger than the regular Hawthorne talk by a wide margin. She left the room again silently and he watched his father pour the tea.

"No," John said heavily while staring at the liquid stream from the spout. "Your future wasn't what I was going to speak to you about. I'm sure you'll work it out yourself just fine. Although I do want you to know that the money is there *if* you want to go to university. And —" He sighed deeply and handed Pike a cup. "I want you to realise that I don't care *what* it is you study. A humanities degree still constitutes an education, albeit not a very useful one. I've seen some of your essays over the years, Dad photocopies the best ones for me, and you have a way with words. Not surprising, really." He stopped himself there. "Sorry, that really wasn't how I was going to start and I don't want you to feel barraged. What I wanted to talk to you about is…um, well…Dad rang me a while back and mentioned that you had found an old photograph of me. Of a young woman and me, to be precise."

A lightning bolt hit Pike's core and he sat up straight, pushed his cup away and placed his arms on the desk.

He had brought the picture with him to London with a vague idea of maybe showing it to John over breakfast and casually asking how come he didn't ride anymore by way of broaching the subject.

The fact that his father had decided to bring it up himself and was fumbling for words for the first time ever in Pike's living memory made every nerve in his body stand to attention.

He delved into the inside pocket of his dinner jacket and took out his wallet, from which he fished the picture. It was bent in the middle now and a bit frayed at the top. He doubled it back on itself to smooth it out somewhat then laid it down in front of John.

"This."

His father had shut his eyes.

"Yes."

"You're not looking."

"Yes I am."

"Who is she?"

John's eyelids opened slowly to fix Pike with an intense stare. Pike could hear his heart beat grow overwhelmingly loud in his ear drums.

"She is dead," John replied. "She left the house a week after your birth and never came back."

"That's not what I asked, I..."

"You know who she is," John stated simply. "I'd hazard a guess you knew from the moment you found the picture."

"Tell me anyway," Pike said quietly.

"She was your mother," John answered equally softly. "Her name was Oona. She came to us from Pine Ridge on a scholarship. She was writing a book about your great-great-grandmother and found, well, me."

John smiled.

Pike racked his brain, trying to remember when the last time had been that he'd seen his father smile.

Never, he thought with a shock, *John Hawthorne doesn't smile.*

He was now, though, and it was irritating Pike. There was so much still unanswered, so many jigsaw pieces still out of place. It wasn't bloody well time for smiling yet.

"Okay, so she's my mother, she's dead, great. Everybody is always fucking dead around me. And if they are not dead, they've killed someone. It's ridiculous, absolutely effing ridiculous. — So what about my brother? Is he dead, too?"

"You don't have a brother," John answered calmly. "What are you talking about?"

"There was another boy. Another boy with my eyes. Her eyes? Right? That's where I get them from, isn't it? You can't really see them in the picture but I'm right, aren't I? That's why you find it so bloody hard to look at me."

John opened the top drawer of the desk and took out a picture in a frame. He handed it over to Pike.

The sensation of looking into his mother's face, his *real* mother's face — large, open and friendly, and with his own amber stare reflecting back at him — almost left him nauseous. He trembled before he looked away after barely a second. It was all he could bear for now. He laid it face down on the table then stared at his father.

"There wasn't another child," John said in a soothing tone. "Just you."

Pike scowled.

"But Gladys said there was. She said your grandma came to the ward with a toddler in tow, same eyes as me. But since your grandma died when I was a newborn that can't have been me, right? So who was he then? Go on, tell me about *all* the lies, not just half of them."

"You. I don't know who this Gladys is but it would have been you. And to be clear, *that* wasn't my lie, *that* came from my parents. - You were actually nearly three when my grandma passed away, so you wouldn't remember her but she doted on you, took you absolutely everywhere with her."

"So why lie? What's the point? I don't get it."

"You walked in on a conversation one day. You were still little, I don't know, about five or six? My parents and Karen were talking about Oona but all you heard was a snippet about someone dying just after you were born. I don't actually know the details, I wasn't there. I doubt anyone will remember. But when you asked they told you they'd been talking about my grandma, simply to satisfy your curiosity — " John paused. "But the problem with lies to cover up lies is, at some point all of it becomes the truth for someone. So that became the truth for you. I'm sorry, Paytah, I truly am."

After all he had just learned it surprised Pike that it seemed to be this last bit of information that truly sliced his soul. Then it dawned on him. They hadn't just taken from him a mother he'd never known, they'd taken the memory of a great-grandmother he *had* known. The feel of his little palm nestled in an old leathery hand suddenly came back to him and the ghost of a smell that he'd missed for a long time. He could feel fury like a trapped wild horse thrashing around in his gut but gentled it, directing his thoughts back to the woman in the picture in front of him. He turned it around again to look at her face once more.

"How?" he asked flatly after a while, knowing full well he wouldn't have to explain what kind of 'how' he meant.

"She took her own life."

John sighed deeply as if exhaling a breath he'd held for nearly eighteen years.

There was a long silence during which Pike looked at his father with the different eyes Aaron had prophesised on the night of the storm.

"Shit."

It was the only thing he could think to say as he suddenly saw the man in front of him for the shadow he really was. For a fleeting moment, until he couldn't hack it any longer, he imagined himself in John's shoes and felt deep sorrow for his father.

"Why?"

John shrugged, looking at his hands again, wringing them for answers he clearly didn't have.

"I don't know. She didn't leave a note. Life isn't a novel, Paytah. People don't commit suicide neatly. They just do. And the people left behind need to make the best of it."

Pike could feel his composure slipping, giving way to anger about the budding justification. He dropped his voice.

"No, really, why? I'm not asking for a scientific dissection, I'm asking for your opinion. Surely you have one."

John closed his eyes again and began rhythmically pinching the bridge of his nose between thumb and index finger of his right hand as he spoke, as if milking the sentences from his frontal lobe.

"She was like you. Alive. Intense. But also afraid. Of death. Afraid of death like nobody else I've ever met. She'd laugh about it, used to say the only cure for her fear of dying would ultimately be to die. I didn't understand. I still don't. We die. It's a fact. No point in fretting about it. — And I think when you were born she got lost in her fear. I should have seen it coming. But we had a baby to look after, everything was new and different and I was so happy that I just didn't see it. I just didn't see it coming." He took the fingers away from his face and looked across at Pike, visibly surer of the next part. "You've heard of post natal depression, I assume. When women give birth, their hormones are in freefall for a while and I think with her it hooked right into her fear. I think it overwhelmed her, the idea that she might only get to spend a fraction of eternity with you. I know it doesn't make sense and I'm not sure I'm right. How could I possibly know? It is all based on the conversations we had before and on the last thing she said before she walked right out of the house and kept on walking until she ran out of ground."

Somewhere within what he was hearing, Pike's mouth had dried up and the next sound he made scratched his throat, making his voice come out brittle and hoarse.

"The old quarry," he stated.

John flinched.

"How…"

Pike didn't let him finish.

"Never mind. What did she say?"

John looked up.

"I love him too much."

Pike pushed the chair back and rose to his feet.

Too much.

So many flames in the bonfire of his thoughts.

So many questions he already knew nobody would ever have answers to.

So much loss.

So many *parallels*.

"You should have told me," he said matter-of-factly. "Or let one of the others tell me."

John bowed his head again, nodding slowly in agreement.

"I know. But when?" he asked the table. "When do you burden a child with something like that?"

It was a valid question.

Pike looked down at the crown of his father's head, so acutely aware of the emotional choice he was being asked to make here, as if a floating neon sign had appeared above it. He thought of Eleanor's words, of Hunter and Wendy and Straw and Ash and took a deep breath.

"You're right, you know. I've read plenty of books and life really isn't a novel. Especially not a bloody classic. Get out of the classic you're stuck in, John. There is a whole world out there. Not just work and saving people. You should go and live in it some time."

He made towards the door, stopped in front of it and pressed the snapshot of John and Oona up against the wood. Exhibit A.

"See the guy in this picture?" he asked without turning around. "He sits well on a horse, don't you think? He even looks like he likes it. — Maybe, just maybe, one day he'd like to come riding with his son."

He didn't wait for a reaction but opened the door, stepped through and shut it behind him. Standing in the corridor he looked at the photograph in his hand one last time. He could see it clearly now and wondered whether John had been right, whether he had not actually seen it all along. It was so bloody obvious. He tucked it away and began walking towards the guest room.

Alice intercepted him at the living room door as he passed.

"He has told you?" she asked, no discernible emotion in her eyes.

Pike nodded.

"I'm pleased," she said, touching his arm lightly, a learned gesture devoid of any true meaning. "It must have been dreadful to think one's whole life that one has such a distant mother as I must have appeared to you. If it had been my choice, this farce would have ended a long time ago."

Pike looked at her hand, amazed at how a person could possibly give off absolutely nothing while touching you and shook it off gently.

"You have no idea."

Then he left her to find his sanctuary.

They talked all night.

Hushed voices in a strange place, huddled against each other in a pull out guest bed that dipped in the middle and turned them into peas in a pod, twins in a womb. Their naked bodies slung around each other tightly, he remained in a state of permanent arousal, pressing against her until the early hours of the morning when she suddenly shuffled away a little.

"P?" she whispered.

"Yeah?"

"I think you're ready."

There was no impatience, no teasing in her voice, just a statement of fact.

She was right.

.

Chapter 36

It seldom snowed on the South coast, so when Pike looked out of the Watchtower window on the morning of New Year's Eve and found the twilight world outside smothered in white icing his heart bucked with joy.

Quietly he climbed into his clothes, went over to kiss the girl in his bed and made to leave the room. She murmured, catching his wrist before he could slip away.

"Where are you going?" she asked with eyes still shut.

He sat down on the edge of the bed and traced Eleanor's forehead, cheekbones and nose with his thumb. She made an approving sound and snuggled more deeply into the pillow.

"A ride," he answered.

Her eyes opened a millimetre.

"Come with?" she mumbled sleepily before her eyelids fell shut again.

"Alone."

"Hmmm."

She was drifting off again. He waited a while until her breath had become long and even. Then he left to find his horse.

He had never planned for it to be a pilgrimage, just woken with a feeling, a *need* to do something, to ride and be. But peeling off from the road into the woods now, just as more snowflakes started to settle on Inigo's mane, he suddenly knew where their round would lead.

They crossed the woods at a canter, the path before them dimly illuminated by the rising sun breaking patchily through the branches above their heads. Once back on open ground, they travelled across the fur-coated hills at a more leisurely pace, the stallion picking up his hooves like a gaited horse at first, carefully testing temperature and texture of the cold, crunchy stuff beneath his feet.

It was a long ride over to the estuary and by the time they reached it the sun was fully up in the sky, making the landscape left and right of the dark waters sparkle brightly. As Pike rode the stallion nearer to the water's edge, he couldn't help but inhale the glorious beauty of the land before him. While Inigo started to look around, alert and a little tense in the unfamiliar spot, Pike rested a hand on the animal's shoulder and let his eyes wander up to the old stone bridge.

It had taken the Council nearly five years to mend the gap in the wall properly where Inara's trailer had gone off the road and over into the water. Pike realised with surprise that from here he already couldn't say for sure anymore where it had been.

He turned his attention back to the ever more fidgety animal beneath him. Contemplating the wildly swivelling ears of the fine young stallion who had grown from the orphaned foal of that day he felt untainted pride and gratitude. He patted Inigo's neck, a reward for standing still despite the obvious wish to be moving, and the horse grunted impatiently in response. Pike obliged and turned him around to start the long trek towards their destination.

His heart began drumming long before they reached the top of the quarry but when he looked down into the pit, all blanketed over in peaceful white, there were no echoes. The pull had gone, a fleeting moment in his life, just like the person who'd left it there. Disappointment washed over him and a little relief.

Just then his phone vibrated in his pocket and he slipped off the stallion's back to check the message.

Are you alright? You've been gone hours.

Yes. Home in an hour or so.

Good. Hurry up. There is a man here wants to see you.

Tall, dark and handsome?

Not as handsome as his son.

You have weird taste, lady.

He grinned as he put the phone away and jumped back onto Inigo.

John had come.

Pike was still angry with his father and somewhere deep inside he knew there was a part of him that always would be.

But in the meantime they would ride.

★

Thank You

I skipped this part the last couple of times, mainly because once I started thinking about who I needed to thank the list quickly grew thicker than the novel or novella itself. Cliché though it may be, it is a fact that everyone I have ever felt a connection to has somehow influenced my writing and should be given some credit. That said, there are four people who are not mentioned in the dedication and four ponies I definitely owe a big fat thank you to. So here goes:

Thank you to my mum, Ange, who has supported my writing since the first time I tottered up to her with a silly poem about stars in my little palm, at the age of about 6 ¾ .

Thank you to Steve, who has supported my writing since the first time I tottered up to him with a pint of Scrumpy in my hand, at the age of about 24 ¼ .

Thank you to Angelique for supporting me with my kids and my ponies and making a whole load of things possible without which I wouldn't be able to write.

Thank you to Jane Badger, who through her website has supported all horse book writers, present and past, for some years now and who did the most respectful yet effective job when editing this book.

Last but not least, thank you to Phoenix, Ben, Breeze and Rupert for taking me on as their designated hay dispenser and supporting me through all the doubtful times with their unconditional love and affection.

Made in the USA
Las Vegas, NV
31 August 2022